SHADOW OF A D[...]

There was a coat cupboard under the stairs and she scrambled inside, shutting the door on herself. It was dark in there and safe. The coats, with their warm, soft, denseness surrounded her. Howard's voice was now muffled and distanced, although she heard him remark, 'I can't find her. I'll have to talk to her later.' Then she heard no more and she guessed he had returned to his office.

She pressed back among the coats. She was now free to emerge but, ridiculously, she couldn't bring herself to leave the safety of the darkened cupboard. It was like being a child again, hiding in her mother's wardrobe because something had happened to frighten her; what, she couldn't now remember. All that remained of the memory was the comforting closeness of the confined space and Rose's voice calling and calling her. She hugged her arms about her and wept as she had done on that previous occasion, unaware of the footsteps that were crossing the hall.

Also by June Thomson in Sphere Books:

SOUND EVIDENCE
TO MAKE A KILLING
THE DARK STREAM
A DYING FALL
NOT ONE OF US

Shadow of a Doubt

JUNE THOMSON

SPHERE BOOKS LIMITED

SPHERE BOOKS LTD

Published by the Penguin Group
27 Wrights Lane, London W8 5TZ, England
Viking Penguin Inc., 40 West 23rd Street, New York, New York 10010, USA
Penguin Books Australia Ltd, Ringwood, Victoria, Australia
Penguin Books Canada Ltd, 2801 John Street, Markham, Ontario, Canada L3R 1B4
Penguin Books (NZ) Ltd, 182–190 Wairau Road, Auckland 10, New Zealand

Penguin Books Ltd, Registered Offices: Harmondsworth, Middlesex, England

First published in Great Britain by Constable & Company Ltd 1981
Published by Sphere Books Ltd 1985
Reprinted 1988

Printed and bound in Great Britain by
Cox & Wyman Ltd, Reading

Part One

1

'For God's sake, aren't you ready yet, Claire?'

The sound of her husband's voice came unexpectedly behind her as Claire Jordan leaned towards the triple dressing-table mirror to apply a tentative outline of pale lipstick. Startled, she looked beyond her own reflection to his, standing in the open doorway, so very solid and black and white in his evening clothes. And so many of him, too, for his image was caught not only in the three mirrors that confronted her but was reflected back yet again in profile from the long pier glass that stood at an angle beside the window.

A reflection of a reflection, she thought. A visual double negative; and she was struck once again by the potency of mirrors to reveal the significance, heightened and yet curiously distanced, of quite familiar objects.

She could even view Howard quite dispassionately as he stood in this looking-glass world, placed in the doorway of the dressing-room where he now slept and through which she could just glimpse the setting of his re-assumed bachelor life: the single divan bed with its severe masculine cover, the pile of books and papers on his desk, the functional reading lamp; outward signs of a return to his student days of more than thirty years before.

He had changed, of course, but less than she. Time had been kinder to him. Whereas for her, each year seemed to rob her of a little more substance so that, catching sight of her own reflection, she was surprised to find there was enough of her left to form an adequate image, it had added to his so that he now appeared as this larger-than-life figure with the handsome profile and upright, confident carriage, who was moving

5

forward into the room, glancing at his watch as he did so, impatient at having found her daydreaming in front of the dressing-table.

'I shall only be a moment, Howard,' she replied, her voice too high and anxious. She leaned forward again but it was useless. She couldn't keep her hand steady or focus on her own face in the glass. She gave one quick little dab, pressed her lips together and gathered up the long evening scarf that lay beside her on the stool.

'There, I'm ready!' she cried, with an effort at gaiety and drew the stole hurriedly round her shoulders to demonstrate to him how efficient she could be when she tried. But he was neither looking nor listening.

'I particularly wanted to be early this evening,' he was saying. 'There's something I must discuss with Hannah before we meet the new patients for sherry.'

'Of course, Howard,' she agreed foolishly, as if she had known this all along, although he had not mentioned it to her before. Getting hurriedly to her feet, she turned away from the dressing-table and, as she did so, the end of the stole, which had been lying across its polished surface, caught the powder bowl in its folds and dragged it towards the edge.

'Look what you're doing!' Howard shouted. But it was too late.

She saw the bowl balance and then topple forward on to the carpet, its lid bouncing free while a small cloud of scented powder rose about her feet.

'Oh, I'm so clumsy!' she cried, anticipating his rebuke. It was a habit she had learned in childhood. 'Own up to your mistakes,' her father had always told her. But it hadn't worked even then. There had been no mitigation of his anger and her sense of guilt had only been increased. At least Howard wouldn't send her to her room to learn an appropriate verse from the Bible.

Not that there was one, she thought, to cover this particular contingency; only the one about the spilling of seed on the ground which was hardly apt under the circumstances; and she felt a small bubble of crazy laughter begin to gather somewhere just above her diaphragm so that she had to pull in her stomach muscles in order to control it.

'What a damn mess!' Howard was exclaiming. He had backed away from the flying grains and was slapping at the immaculate legs of his trousers.

Her own shoes were covered with the stuff; so, too, was the hem of her dress; and it wouldn't brush off, either, without leaving pale streaks on the dark blue silk.

'I'm so sorry, Howard,' she said quickly. 'I'll have to change. You go on without me. I'll come later in my car.'

But he had anticipated that as well and was already striding towards the door.

'Then try not to be too long about it,' he told her over his shoulder, in that calm, flat voice which meant he was very angry. 'I don't want everyone kept waiting.'

Everyone, she thought as the door closed behind him. As if the whole world were dependent on her coming. He meant, of course, his world; the staff at the clinic, Hannah Kerr and Janet Ingham in particular who, if they knew the cause, would accept it as just another example of her inadequacy. She could imagine Hannah's shrug of impatience, that quick dismissive movement of her shoulders; Janet's impeccable eyebrows momentarily raised. Eunice Hart, on the other hand, would make some kind, non-committal remark, laying the blame nowhere in particular except on the perversity of things in general with their maddening capacity to create chaos at the most inconvenient times, while nice Donald Midgley, too young and not yet well enough established at the clinic to be partisan in the matter, would only be embarrassed on his own account for not knowing how he was supposed to react.

As for the patients, they were unknown to her apart from their number. There were five new ones this week, who must include someone of importance for the dinner party to be held. But Howard had told her nothing about them. It was a long time since he had discussed any individual case histories with her.

She struggled to unhook the back of her dress and, releasing the zip, stepped out of the folds of silk and crossed the room to the wardrobe, faced with the decision of what to wear instead. The grey chiffon, she supposed, even though she felt like a wraith in it and the neckline exposed too pitifully the hollows in her throat. Salt cellars her mother had called them. As a

7

child, she had thought it a strange description because the salt cellars at home had been such sturdy silver objects. But it would have to be the grey chiffon, worn with the garnet necklace because they went together; like the pearls with the blue silk or the gold locket and chain with the black lace.

I'm not like my sister, Rose, she thought sadly. I haven't the courage to change the established order of things; Rose, who wore three rings on the same hand and had her hair tinted auburn and who had once called Father a bloody old bore to his face.

Oh, the bliss of being Rose for just five minutes! To say, 'Oh, sod it,' to the spilt powder and walk away, leaving it scattered on the carpet; to arrive half an hour late at Howard's dinner party and not feel the need to apologise; to sit with her legs crossed showing her knees; or, best of all, to announce to Hannah Kerr . . . .

But the pity of it was she would never be like Rose. So she would clean up the powder, put on the grey chiffon and the garnets, say to everyone, including Hannah, how sorry she was to keep them waiting, that is if they noticed her at all, because she would take care to slip unobtrusively into the room as she had been trained to do. 'No lady makes herself conspicuous.' Father's words; Mother's example; and Howard's unspoken expectation.

2

Simon Boyd stood by himself near the window, sherry glass in hand, and looked about him, finding it easier to concentrate for the time being on the room rather than the people it contained. It was, he supposed, part of the private wing of Hawton Hall, an area of the clinic which he hadn't been shown when he had been taken earlier that afternoon on a tour of the public apartments. Unlike those, it was a small, intimate drawing-room but furnished all the same in that style of bland good taste and impersonal elegance that one can find in any international hotel and, God knows, he had seen enough of those during his tours as a concert pianist. Beirut, London, Rome, New York, it really made no difference. You could count on finding the same pale, fitted carpets, a similar sheen on fabrics and furniture, the almost obligatory touches of gilt here and there in lamps and mirrors. Even the flowers seemed familiar; daffodils and forsythia because it was late March and real no doubt, but arranged with such florist's skill in their Sèvres bowls that they appeared artificial.

And yet he had seen them growing wild in the woods that surrounded the clinic as Hubert Tate's Daimler had crunched slowly and majestically up the drive under the budding trees.

'Rest,' Hubert had told him in much the same way as one might say 'Sit' to a dog. 'Get strong again.'

And for a time it had seemed possible. Hawton Hall, viewed from the outside, had looked so safe and substantial, so terribly English, that he had been lulled into a sense of security. It was going to be all right after all, despite his reservations about Dr Jordan. At their first meeting in Jordan's consulting rooms in Harley Street, Simon Boyd had not been able to assess exactly what it was about the doctor that aroused this antipathy. He was, after all, as Hubert had pointed out, one of the best psychiatrists in London with a high success rate for treating patients with his condition.

His condition? Well, yes, he supposed exhaustion could be called a condition. So, too, could stage-fright, ridiculous though that phrase sounded, which in no way approximated to the terror that overwhelmed him before each concert. Or the growing resentment that he was being used, bundled like a parcel in and out of planes and dressing-rooms and hotels, subject to Hubert's itinerary and the vociferous demands of audiences that seemed now to feed on the very substance of his soul.

He yearned to go home but that, too, was ridiculous. Home to where? To the flat over the tobacconist's shop in Fulham from which he had come? It was gone anyway. He had made the pilgrimage once, only to find that the whole street had vanished under a council development scheme of high-rise apartment blocks and a multi-storey car park. And certainly not home to the comfortable detached house in Surrey which he had bought for his parents, where they now lived in uneasy retirement and where he dutifully visited them each time he was in England.

Catching sight of Jordan across the room, he doubted very much if he would be capable of supplying those missing roots for, in that private moment when the doctor was unaware of being scrutinised, Simon Boyd recognised those qualities which had given rise to his initial doubts about the man.

Like the room, and indeed the whole clinic, there was a gloss of success and self-confidence about the doctor, an air of professional benevolence and good-grooming which gave the impression that they had been purchased, together with his well-cut clothes and hair and all the material possessions that surrounded him, in some emporium that specialised in made-to-order excellence. Surely he couldn't be as perfect as his handsome, rather heavy features and carefully manicured hands suggested? Simon Boyd found himself observing the doctor closely, on the look-out for the hidden flaw.

At the same time, he was conscious that he, in his turn, was being watched. A sixth sense warned him of another pair of eyes and he turned his head quickly just in time to watch Dr Jordan's woman deputy director turn her gaze away from him with equal alacrity. Dr Kerr – at least, he believed that was her name, the tour of introduction that Jordan had earlier conducted round the room being of necessity brief, no more than a mere exchange of names and a brisk handshake – was now talking to her companion, a businessman and fellow patient, Boyd understood, whose identity did not much interest him. Dr Kerr's, however, did. She was a woman in her early thirties, thin-featured with black hair cut very short, almost like a man's, and coming low on to her forehead to meet two very positive and sarcastic eyebrows. It was a clever, intelligent face; and attractive, too, which was strange for, despite the dark-red evening dress she was wearing and the gold studs in her ears, she gave the impression of sexlessness.

Afraid to be caught a second time watching her, he turned his attention to the other two women in the room although they did not attract him nearly so much as Dr Kerr. One of them, Mrs Ingham, whom Jordan had introduced as his secretary, was of

10

the type he had seen before. Hubert Tate's personal assistant was out of much the same mould, a product of the better-class secretarial college; crisp, neat but much too easily assimilated as if each one of her features had been outlined by a very hard, sharp pencil. Smartly dressed in a long black velvet skirt and a ruffled white lace blouse, a sort of professional mufti for out-of-office hours, her blonde hair drawn back into an elegant roll at the nape of her neck, her face carefully made up, she was much more obviously pretty than Dr Kerr but, to him, much less intriguing. The expression on the heart-shaped face was just a little too charming, the smile a little too ready to be entirely convincing, and the small, sharply-pointed eyeteeth which it revealed gave the whole face a feline look.

The third woman was Mrs Hart, Jordan's housekeeper, who had shown him round the clinic earlier that afternoon and who had struck him then as a comfortable, sympathetic personality, with that brand of efficient yet genuine kindliness that some nurses or primary teachers possess. She had been wearing an overall coat of flowered nylon, substituted now for a dress of flowered silk, as if her off-duty clothes, like Mrs Ingham's, reflected her professional position in the clinic. She was older than the other two, in her early fifties, he guessed, and gave an impression of softness; soft skin, soft greying hair, soft flesh beneath the flowing skirt and gathered bodice but her dark eyes were constantly on the alert, with a hostess's attentiveness, making sure that the sherry decanter and dishes of canapés were being properly circulated.

Seeing the three of them together for the first time in Jordan's company, he was suddenly struck by their relationship to one another and to him. It was as if the women were satellite moons to Jordan's planet, drawn into his orbit and circling round him, dependent on his influence to keep them in motion.

There was a fourth whose existence he had almost forgotten – the young man whom Jordan had introduced as 'my new assistant' and who, like himself, was standing a little apart from the others, wearing a dinner jacket and too large a bow tie that gave an incongruous pussy-cat look to his otherwise chunky, earnest appearance and anxious expression.

It was an anxiety that seemed to be shared, although less

11

obtrusively, by the rest of the company, including the other patients, all male, three of them businessmen or civil servants, the fourth a well-known actor whose face, familiar from the cinema screen, had nevertheless startled Simon Boyd by its unexpected age and sullen expression. There was an air of expectancy about them all as if they were waiting for something to happen. Conversations were dying or were kept alive by an effort of will which put a glaze on smiles and made laughter sound amateurish. He saw Dr Kerr glance towards the door a couple of times. Even Dr Jordan, for all his social aplomb, looked covertly at his watch. They were clearly awaiting the arrival of another guest whose non-appearance was postponing the announcement of dinner.

She came at last, slipping quietly into the room; a small, slightly-built woman, dressed in grey, with hair almost the same colour as her frock so that she seemed at first glance like a figure out of a black and white film. Simon Boyd felt drawn to her at once. Something about her frailty, the thin arms and delicate bone structure of her face, her air of flustered shyness, touched some answering chord in himself. She was, he decided, born to be passed over; much too nice to make herself conspicuous and frightened by the awfulness of arriving last and so dreadfully late.

It was this anxiety that made him warm to her – for hadn't he experienced much the same symptoms himself? – and also, through a process of negative attraction, by the manner in which Jordan greeted her. She had gone straight towards him on entering the room and appeared to be apologising to him. Simon Boyd saw him frown quickly at her before introducing her briefly, almost curtly, to those standing nearby. Mrs Hart meanwhile had brought her a glass of sherry which she was drinking in quick, nervous, little sips. He could see the cords in her throat contract convulsively with each small swallow. And all the time she kept smiling with that bright, fixed stretching of the lips which he knew, too, from experience and he felt his own facial muscles tighten with the same tension. Then her glass was whisked away and Jordan turned to address the room.

12

'If you're ready, ladies and gentlemen, we'll go in to dinner.'

Somehow he managed to invest even this simple announcement with a critical overtone as if implying they had all been kept waiting far too long already.

The double doors at the far end of the room were opened back by a woman in a waitress's bottle-green and white uniform and the guests, tension released, began to talk more freely again as they moved in small groups into the dining-room.

3

Claire Jordan took her place at the foot of the long dining-table and waited while the guests found their seats. At the other end, across the silver and glasses laid out on the white linen, she could see Howard still in conversation with the tall, grim, grey-faced man who she assumed was one of the new patients and whom she was glad hadn't been placed next to her. What on earth would she have found to say to him?

Instead, Eunice Hart, thank God, had put Donald Midgley on her left and, opposite him, on her right, a man she hadn't noticed in the drawing-room during the flustered moments between her arrival and the announcement of dinner. He was, she supposed, in his forties, with one of those thin, dark, mournful faces that she always found appealing, in which all the features, forehead, cheek-bones, nose, seemed to be brought slightly forward above the flatter planes to give an expression of sad, questing eagerness.

She glanced quickly at the little printed card that Eunice had arranged near his plate and read the name Simon Boyd. It was familiar to her for, although she had never been to any of his concerts, she had heard him play several times on the radio. She could speak about that, she supposed. Or would it be better to find a less personal topic of conversation? She was never quite sure how to talk to Howard's patients and usually fell back on a few well-worn subjects – the local church, for example,

13

although as she described it she was conscious she was boring them in much the same way as Father had bored his guests with long dissertations on ecclesiastical architecture.

As it happened, there was no need for her to search about for an opening to the conversation for, as they sat down and Mrs Summers served the first course, he turned to her and asked in a quiet voice.

'You're Dr Jordan's wife?'

'Yes,' she replied.

The question surprised her. It was unusual for any of Howard's patients to take the least interest in her and she supposed it was mere politeness on his part. And yet there was a sincerity about his expression that was disarming.

For his part, Simon Boyd's curiosity was not assumed. He was genuinely intrigued by her and by her relationship with the others in the clinic. She had arrived late, a fact that wasn't itself significant although her unobtrusive entrance and Jordan's ill-concealed impatience had been revealing. So, too, was her position at the foot of the table, for it was quite obvious, at least to him, that she had very little to do with the organisation of the dinner party. It was Jordan who had given the signal for the meal to begin and Mrs Hart, the housekeeper who, from her place half way down the table, was keeping a quiet but efficient eye on how the meal progressed.

What role, therefore, did Jordan's wife play? Hardly the society hostess. She was much too low-key for that. In fact, in that respect, she reminded him of his mother, a recognition that evoked in him all the familiar sad and guilty tenderness. There was about her, too, an actual scent that, for the moment, he couldn't exactly place but which recalled childhood memories; an ordinary, everyday, commonplace aroma which he associated with cooking and domestic chores.

And then he recognised it – the scent of cloves, and he was instantly reminded of Sunday dinners in the small, cramped flat above the shop, his father poised over the joint, eyes intent and serious behind his reading-glasses, as he carved the lamb into thin slices with the bone-handled knife, worn over the years with too much sharpening; and afterwards apple pie and custard, with the same scent released as his mother passed the

14

plate to him, its pattern of green leaves forming a wreath round the edge. How he had hated those Sundays! The long, grey, interminable afternoon hours spent in the sitting-room while his mother knitted and his father dozed or read the *News of the World*. He was forbidden to practise on the piano. 'Let's have at least one day a week of peace,' was how his father put it.

For them, his interest in music had been a mere hobby, something he would grow out of, like stamp-collecting. They had never understood the nature of his obsession and, because of this, he had become distanced from them over the years. Not even their pride in his subsequent success had been enough to bridge the gulf so that now, when he thought of them at all, he saw them as two kindly strangers with whom he had nothing in common.

As for himself, this alienation had left him with a nagging need to prove himself and his talent until he had reached his present state of exhaustion.

' . . . . and such pleasant walks through the countryside,' Mrs Jordan was saying and he returned with a start to the present to find her looking at him with an expression of sweet anxiety as if she were afraid she had been boring him. 'Do you like walking, Mr Boyd?'

He roused himself with an effort, angry that his absorption in his own thoughts might have distressed her.

'Yes, I do, when I can find the time,' he replied with more enthusiasm than he really meant. 'I noticed the gardens of the clinic when I arrived this afternoon. I suppose one could walk through those?'

'Oh, yes, of course. There are some very pretty woodlands as well as the more formal gardens. The grounds are quite large.'

'Over three acres,' Dr Midgley interposed earnestly from the other side of the table as if facts and figures were best left to the men.

'It's a pity you're too early for the roses,' Mrs Jordan continued, a pale flush of pleasure staining her cheeks, not unlike the delicate pink of a wild rose, and he saw in her suddenly the pretty, fragile girl she must once have been.

'But I was in time for the daffodils,' he remarked, knowing she would respond.

'Oh, the daffodils have been *glorious* this year!'

Her enthusiasm robbed the sentence of any false brightness although Simon Boyd saw Clive Ransome, the actor who was seated across the table, glance at her with amusement and he took an immediate dislike to the man on account of it.

'And there's always golf,' Midgley said heavily, as if embarrassed at the turn the conversation was taking.

'I don't play golf,' Simon Boyd replied.

'Pity,' Midgley said and turned his attention back to his plate, unaware of the damage he had done.

Simon Boyd saw her expression falter although she made an effort to keep the subject going.

'There's quite a good local club,' she said. 'The course runs along the north side of the grounds.'

'Do you play?' he asked, trying to retrieve the situation.

'No, I'm afraid I don't. Howard does. But I sometimes walk across the links.'

Midgley glanced up from his plate again and Simon Boyd was prepared to admit that he might have misjudged the young man for he gave Mrs Jordan a look of unexpected gentleness as he remarked, 'You must get Mrs Jordan to show you the local church while you're here, Mr Boyd. She's quite an authority on it.'

The flush had returned to her face, heightened this time by shyness.

'I'm afraid Donald's exaggerating,' she said quickly. 'I only know what I've read in the little booklet you can buy at the door.'

'All the same, I'd like you to show me round,' he replied. 'We must arrange to meet one afternoon.'

Her reply was lost as the plates in front of them were cleared away although her smile indicated her pleasure and, when the second course had been served, she picked up the subject again.

'There are one or two rather nice old houses in the village that you might also care to see,' she was saying.

The conversation moved on to a more general discussion of architecture, assisted from time to time by Donald Midgley in his heavy-handed way and, towards the end of the meal, even

16

Clive Ransome joined in with a long, involved anecdote about a country house he had once visited on location, into which well-known actors' names, Fra, Larry and Mitch, were dropped with seeming casualness.

Simon Boyd sat back, pretending to listen but watching the faces along the table as one by one, they stopped their own conversations and turned towards Ransome, caught by his beautiful voice and his actor's skill at putting over the story, his sullen features animated at having an audience.

Jordan was leaning back with the pleased, slightly proprietorial look of a host whose guest is providing amusement for others, as if he were personally responsible. Next to him, the grey-faced man listened with a judicial air, not quite ready to commit himself, while the faces of the others expressed amusement and interest: Mrs Ingham's lips set in a bright, social smile; Dr Kerr's dark eyebrows raised in quizzical approval; Donald Midgley watching each change in Ransome's expression with grave seriousness as if afraid of missing the point when the time came; and Mrs Jordan, her hands clasped together on the table, listening with the rapt attention of a child being told a bed-time story.

But how pale she was! Boyd noticed her pallor for the first time and the dark stains under her eyes like bruises in the skin. There was, too, a faint trembling of her head as if her neck were too fragile to support its weight.

Watching her, he missed the final line of Ransome's story and was aware only of the ripple of amusement along the table as it ended. There was a slight pause as it died away and then Mrs Hart, with perfect timing, glanced at Dr Jordan who announced, 'Shall we join the others for coffee in the main drawing-room?'

The women, rising first from the table, began to leave the room; Mrs Jordan last, he noticed, fumbling as she went with a long lace stole which, with an inept awkwardness that he recognised as one of his own symptoms of unease, she had difficulty in arranging round her shoulders.

4

He lost contact with her in the main drawing-room, part of the central public block of the house which he had been shown earlier in the day by Mrs Hart, and where the other patients, already installed in the clinic, joined them, all of them men, he noticed; eleven in number, none of whom he had a chance of meeting had he wished to, for Clive Ransome attached himself to him on entering the room.

'Been here before?' Ransome asked as they stood together in front of the fireplace in which a log fire was burning, holding cups of coffee which Mrs Hart had brought round to each guest.

'No,' Boyd replied. He would have preferred to be left alone but Ransome seemed determined to engage him in conversation.

'I came here a couple of years ago,' Ransome continued. His face had lost its animation and had sunk once more into the discontented lines of an ageing, disappointed, once-beautiful young man. 'I suppose it's not too ghastly. Better than those God-awful health farms. I tried one of them once and decided never again. They're all bloody carrot juice and self-discipline. At least here one gets decent food and the occasional glass of sherry. One pays, of course, through the nose.'

'Yes,' Boyd replied. There seemed nothing much else to say, not that Ransome noticed his lack of response.

'Jordan's good, mind you,' Ransome went on. 'I've been consulting him on and off for the past three years. As he pointed out to me, anyone who's at all creative can only give out so much before stress begins to build up. Even the bloody directors don't understand one's problems half the time. They treat you like some kind of talking head that can be switched on and off emotionally like an electric light bulb and then wonder why you kick up a fuss on the set. Take the last film I've been working on. Shot mostly on location in Morocco, of all places. You can't imagine the heat and the dust . . .'

'No,' Boyd said automatically. He had just caught sight of Mrs Jordan across the room talking to the grey man who was looking down at her from his immensely thin height, a look of polite boredom on his face.

'Who's that man standing next to Mrs Jordan?' he broke in to ask, deciding that he would take the first opportunity to rescue her.

Ransome glanced towards them, impatient at being interrupted.

'Oh, him,' he replied, without much interest. 'His name's Sutton. He's someone high up in the Home Office, I believe. Dreadful man. I was talking to him before dinner. He has absolutely no small talk and he actually had the gall to tell me that he thought too much public money was spent on the Arts. Quite frankly there's no one here this time worth meeting,' he added; presumably, Simon Boyd thought wryly, he himself was included in that category. 'They all seem to be businessmen suffering from ulcers or the male menopause. I met Paoletti on my last treatment. Don't tell me you haven't heard of Paoletti!' he exclaimed in disbelief, catching sight of Simon Boyd's expression. 'He's only the most important stage designer working in Europe at the moment. You must have seen his sets for Lakmé at Covent Garden? No? Well, you do surprise me.'

'I've been out of the country a good deal recently,' Simon Boyd replied, stung into self-defence by Ransome's tone of voice.

'Oh, really? Where?'

'The Far East mainly; Japan and Hong Kong and then on to Australia and New Zealand . . .'

'Oh, my God, *Australia*!' Ransome cried. 'I once did a tour there myself years ago. Ibsen of all people. Imagine performing *The Wild Duck* to a lot of sheep-farmers in the outback.'

'Yes,' Simon Boyd said flatly and finished his coffee. He had had enough of Ransome. It was time to rescue Mrs Jordan from the grey man, Sutton, or seek out Mrs Hart or Dr Kerr.

The groups of people in the room were shifting anyway, breaking up and forming new patterns. Midgley was now talking to Sutton, with Janet Ingham making up the trio. He

19

could see the shining coil of her hair under the lamps and Sutton's face, bent down towards her, showing more interest than it had for Mrs Jordan. Of Dr Kerr there was no sign; or of Jordan either, while, as he excused himself from Ransome and crossed the room, Simon Boyd saw Mrs Jordan slip through the door at the far end as quietly as earlier that evening she had made her entrance.

5

Claire Jordan closed the door behind her and stood for a moment leaning against it. The noise and the heat in the room had made her feel momentarily faint. Worse still was the press of personalities; so many separate identities, none of which she had been able to relate to.

The entrance hall was quiet and empty. Ahead of her, the broad staircase ascended to a dim upper landing while, on either side of it, lit only by the wall sconces, two passages led off at right angles, one towards the kitchen and the private east wing, the other towards the offices and the treatment rooms.

She turned to the left, intending to shut herself in the downstairs cloakroom for a few minutes' solitude. No more. Howard would be angry if she absented herself for too long.

Passing the door of his office, she was surprised to find it half open and the murmur of voices coming from inside and she paused in the passageway to see who the occupants were, for the last time she had seen Howard he had been talking to a small, plump man in the drawing-room, whose name she couldn't now remember.

She saw that only the desk lamp was lit, which seemed to give an added intimacy to the scene. Howard was seated behind the desk, leaning back in the padded leather chair, in an attitude that was relaxed and informal, talking to Hannah Kerr who was perched on the corner, her legs crossed, one foot in its red satin shoe swinging free.

Claire Jordan faltered in the doorway. Something about the

20

two of them, grouped together in that way, struck her as particularly close. It was ridiculous, of course. She had seen them in conversation many times before and had experienced this feeling of isolation, as if she were the interloper. But until that moment she had never thought of them paired so exclusively, which was how they suddenly appeared to her. A couple. Herself on the outside, like a passer-by witnessing some small domestic scene through a window, not especially significant in itself but expressing a total relationship.

As she hesitated, Howard glanced up and saw her standing there. Hannah Kerr, also, turned her head and, slipping down from the desk, went to stand beside his chair, as if she, too, were aware of the intimacy of the grouping.

'Claire?' Howard asked and there was nothing she could do except move forward into the room.

'I'm so sorry, Howard,' she apologised although for what she wasn't herself quite sure. 'I didn't realise you were here.'

'I was finalising tomorrow's arrangements with Hannah,' he replied. 'There wasn't time before dinner.'

His voice was pleasant enough and yet the remark reminded her of her own late arrival.

'You hadn't forgotten I'm going to London tomorrow?' he continued.

She had, in fact, remembered although there had been occasions in the past when she had muddled up the days he went to town to see those patients in his consulting rooms who hadn't been admitted to the clinic.

He had turned back to Hannah Kerr.

'I thought I'd take Midgley,' he continued. 'It's about time he had some experience of the Harley Street end of the practice and there's a particular patient I want him to see – Morley's son.'

'The heroin addict?'

'Yes. I might as well make use of Donald's expertise in these cases. He's much more up to date than I am in the new treatments and I promised Morley I'd do my best. In fact, I can't afford to turn him down. He's got a lot of pull in the City and he could be a useful contact.'

'You'll admit him?' Hannah Kerr asked.

'I can't see how I can refuse.'

'It means specialised nursing.'

'I'm well aware of that. I must have a word with Eunice later this evening. She'll have to get a room ready in the east wing, separate from the other patients. I don't want a repetition of the last time we had an addict in for treatment. I'll make quite sure Morley's kept isolated from the main rooms.'

'And get his luggage searched before he settles in,' Hannah Kerr advised. 'Remember those Diconal tablets Gardner had hidden in his dressing-gown pocket? It was a lucky thing Eunice found them.'

Claire Jordan stood listening quietly to this exchange. Neither of the cases meant anything to her and yet, at one time, she would have typed up Howard's notes on them.

He turned to address her over his shoulder.

'By the way, I shan't be in for dinner tomorrow night. I'll dine at the club with Midgley.'

'Very well,' she replied but he wasn't listening. He had resumed his conversation with Hannah Kerr as if she were no longer in the room.

'What do you think of Donald? How's he shaping up in your opinion?'

'Not too badly. Of course, he's still got a lot to learn but you're right in thinking he's good in his own particular field. I thought he did an excellent job with Cunningham.'

Feeling herself dismissed like a mere stranger, Claire Jordan walked quietly to the door where she stopped and looked back again at the scene. Howard was relaxed and expansive once more while, even as she watched, Hannah Kerr resumed her seat on the edge of the desk. They were both of them unaware of her continuing presence; as far as they were concerned, she had ceased to exist. The sick, churning sensation which earlier, when she had knocked over the powder bowl, had gathered like hysteria deep inside her, began to coalesce once more. She felt it fermenting, swooping upwards to overwhelm her so violently that she could feel her head tremble although she was powerless to control it. She could only gasp out loud and the heavy exhalation of breath seemed to release her.

Howard heard it, too, and looked up quickly, frowning.

'I thought you'd gone, Claire,' he said.

'Yes,' she agreed foolishly and then the bubble broke and she stepped forward, aware herself how ridiculous she must appear, with her head shaking like an old woman's and the saliva glistening on her lips. 'Yes, I'm going, Howard. I'm leaving. It's quite obvious I'm in the way.'

'For God's sake, Claire,' he began.

For the first time in their marriage, she found the courage to interrupt him.

'Don't talk to me about God, Howard! I don't believe any more that He has the answers. But perhaps Rose does. Perhaps I should have listened to her.'

She knew he had understood what she meant by the way he started to his feet.

How easy it was to frighten him, she thought. It had never occurred to her before that the higher he rose, the greater became her own power to pull him down.

Beside him, Hannah Kerr looked from one to the other of them, her thin features sharper than ever with amusement and ironic curiosity.

It was the sight of her face rather than Howard's which broke Claire Jordan's resolve. Aghast at what she had done, she turned and ran from the room.

She had meant to turn right outside the office and seek refuge in the ladies' cloakroom, a little further down the corridor. Instead, in her confusion, she turned left and found herself back in the entrance hall, huge and empty and exposed under the lights. Ahead of her stretched the passage leading to the kitchen and she fled along it, hearing Howard's voice behind her, calling her name, 'Claire! Claire!' in a peremptory manner. Suddenly, the desire for concealment overwhelmed her.

There was a coat cupboard under the stairs and she scrambled inside, shutting the door on herself. It was dark in there and safe. The coats, with their warm, soft, denseness surrounded her. Howard's voice was now muffled and distanced, although she heard him remark, 'I can't find her. I'll have to talk to her later.' Then she heard no more and she guessed he had returned to his office.

She pressed back among the coats. She was now free to emerge but, ridiculously, she couldn't bring herself to leave the safety of the darkened cupboard. It was like being a child again, hiding in her mother's wardrobe because something had happened to frighten her; what, she couldn't now remember. All that remained of the memory was the comforting closeness of the confined space and Rose's voice calling and calling her; 'Claire! Claire! Where are you?' And she hugged her arms about her and wept as she had done on that previous occasion, unaware of the footsteps that were crossing the hall.

6

Janet Ingham walked briskly out of the drawing-room, her high heels clicking on the tiled floor, one hand holding up her skirt, the other cradling the bright crescent of her hair.

In the ladies' cloakroom, she examined her face critically in the mirror before she re-powdered it and applied fresh lipstick. She was still young and pretty enough to catch the attention of Howard's middle-aged patients and the thought amused and, at the same time, repelled her. They were so damned obvious, she thought, with their compliments and their admiring glances. Even Sutton, that cold fish, had run his eyes over her like hands.

It was part of her job, of course, to look attractive. Howard had chosen her for that reason; she was placed in the front office for effect, in the same way that a a shop-keeper put his best goods in the window.

While it lasted, she had no real complaints. She was well-paid and the work wasn't difficult. It was only on occasions, such as now, when she looked deep into a mirror, searching for the first signs of decaying youth, that she wondered how long it would last. She had no illusions about Howard. He'd drop her the moment she ceased to be useful to him and there'd be someone else younger and prettier to step into her shoes. God knows, there were plenty of them; attractive, ambitious girls, as skilled in fashion and make-up as they were in shorthand and typing. In the end, it was women like Hannah who finally won out, she thought bitterly, who had learnt to stand on their own without needing the goodwill of men. She sometimes envied Hannah that aloofness.

All the same, she wasn't sure she really wanted to change places with her. It was fun at times to be herself, to know that she could have, if she wanted to, the pick of any of the men who clustered about her and with a smile and a hand placed on an arm could reduce even the most distinguished of them to a ridiculous, quivering mass of desires and appetites.

Stepping back from the mirror, she turned to examine her profile, the firm line of chin and neck, the high thrust of her breasts, smoothing the soft fabric of her skirt over her hips.

Satisfied, she gathered up her handbag and re-crossed the hall just as a door on the far side opened and someone emerged into the corridor.

Absorbed in her own thoughts, Janet Ingham registered the other's presence but made no sign of recognition as, turning aside, she entered the drawing-room and rejoined Howard's patients.

7

Simon Boyd didn't notice her return; he was not particularly looking out for her. A plump man called Reeves, with a damp, glistening brow, had engaged him in conversation about interest rates and how the strong pound was affecting his exports. Boyd half-listened, nodding from time to time. He was feeling deadly tired and wondered how soon he could decently leave and go to bed. Over the top of Reeves' head he saw Jordan and Dr Kerr return together and stand just inside the door for a few moments, Jordan gazing about the room as if searching for someone; possibly his wife, Boyd thought. There was still no sign of Mrs Jordan although it was some time since he had seen her slip away. He would have liked to do the same. The room was hot, the air heavy with the scent of wood smoke from the log fire and the odour of cigars. It was an effort to keep his eyes open, let alone take in what Reeves was saying. The man's voice went on and on, buzzing interminably like a fly trapped under an upturned tumbler and it was with relief that he saw Dr Midgley coming in their direction.

He left them together, withdrawing as soon as Reeves, after a few polite conversational preliminaries, got back to the subject which was evidently uppermost in his mind.

'You see, Midgley,' he was saying, 'until the pound weakens against other currencies we're priced out of the foreign markets.'

As he retreated, he heard Midgley reply apologetically, 'I'm afraid I was never very good at economics.'

Boyd doubted if they noticed his absence; certainly not Reeves who now had an entirely new pupil to instruct in the intricacies of international finance.

'More coffee, Mr Boyd?'

Mrs Hart's voice coming behind him, startled him momentarily.

'No thank you.'

'It's fresh.'

She spoke in the coaxing voice of a nanny urging a child to drink up its lovely hot milk and he felt suddenly exasperated by it. It had been his mother's habit to break in on his thoughts with the same concerned insistence.

'No, thanks,' he repeated more shortly and then, in case he had sounded too abrupt, he added, 'I'd like to slip away if that's allowed.'

'Allowed?' she sounded amused. 'You may please yourself, Mr Boyd. Until tomorrow morning when your treatment begins, you are free to do as you wish.'

'What exactly happens?'

'Tomorrow, you mean? You'll be examined by Dr Kerr as Dr Jordan will be in London for the day. There'll also be a dietitian and a medical practitioner at hand and between them they'll draw up the details according to your individual needs. But Dr Kerr's the best person to advise you.'

She smiled and moved away to offer coffee to the next group of people.

'Insist on the massage.' It was Ransome seeking him out

again. 'The last time I was here I had it every day. It's added on to the bill, of course, but it's worth every penny. By the way, are you a bridge player? Kennedy and Sutton are keen to have a game and we're looking for one more to make up the four.'

He nodded across to where the other two men were waiting and, as Simon Boyd followed his glance, he saw Claire Jordan standing alone by the heated trolley from which the coffee had been served. She looked ill, he thought, and oddly bedraggled, the lace stole looped unevenly round her shoulders while small wisps of hair fell loose across her forehead. No one else seemed aware of her existence. Jordan was nearby, talking to Midgley and a square-shouldered man, but he had his back to her. Mrs Hart was still making the rounds of the room, offering coffee, while he could see only the back of Dr Kerr's sleek dark head in the centre of a group of patients near the window.

'Not this evening,' he said to Ransome. 'Perhaps some other time.'

Without waiting for Ransome's reply, he turned and began making his way towards her, pushing past Mrs Ingham who, with three or four men in attendance, was taking up the centre of the room.

'Are you all right?' he asked, as he reached her side.

Now he was close to her, he could see the vague, dazed expression in her eyes and the deep crease of pain across her forehead. But she made an effort to smile.

'It's nothing, Mr Boyd. I have a headache, that's all.'

'Can I fetch you something? A glass of water and some aspirin?'

He glanced about for Mrs Hart and caught instead Jordan's eye who frowned and came across to them.

'So there you are, Claire,' he said abruptly. 'I've been looking for you.'

'Your wife's not well,' Boyd replied, angered by Jordan's insensitivity. He was reminded of Hubert Tate standing calmly beside him while he vomited just before a concert, saying nothing except, 'Are you ready to go on stage?' when the bout was over.

'What's the matter?' Jordan asked. 'Is it one of your migraines?'

She nodded and added in a whisper, 'It's so hot in here, Howard. I feel rather dizzy.'

'For heavens sake, try not to draw attention to yourself,' Jordan began. He was interrupted by Mrs Hart who joined them unobtrusively, her skirt rustling softly as she approached.

'Is Claire feeling ill?' she asked in a low voice.

'She has a headache,' Jordan explained. All the time he was glancing about, making sure no one else had noticed.

'Oh, I'm so sorry,' Mrs Hart replied. 'Would you rather go home, my dear? You look ghastly.' To Jordan, she added, 'I could take her, Howard. I'm sure she's not in a fit state to drive.'

She seemed to have taken over the situation and Simon Boyd, feeling his presence was no longer needed, withdrew as Jordan said sharply, 'No, I need you here, Eunice. Donald can drive her back. Give me your keys, Claire. Simmonds can return your car in the morning.'

Shortly afterwards, he saw Midgley, whom Mrs Hart had extricated from conversation with Reeves, escort Mrs Jordan from the room and the small group broke up, only Jordan remaining alone by the trolley for a few moments.

Simon Boyd watched him. The man appeared unaware of the people round him, standing sunk in thought, and Simon Boyd was aware that he was seeing a rare glimpse of another persona that was normally hidden from public view. Jordan's features had taken on a heavy, sombre look, the lower lip jutting morosely, the eyebrows still contracted in the frown of impatience with which he had greeted his wife. It was the expression, Boyd decided, of a man who had suddenly come face to face with a bitter and deeply disturbing reality. The next moment, his expression cleared as Sutton joined him and the two men walked away together to talk to Dr Kerr, Jordan's features once again professionally affable.

The way was now free for Simon Boyd to make his own exit and he left the room before Ransome, or any of the other patients, should claim his attention.

The hall was empty, although a murmur of voices came from one of the corridors where presumably Mrs Jordan was collecting her coat, for he heard Midgley say, 'Here, let me help you on with it.'

It would have been a simple enough matter to have gone to her and said something pleasant, wishing her better soon, but he felt too exhausted to make the effort and instead he mounted the stairs to his bedroom which was in the front of the house, overlooking the main entrance. Someone, Mrs Hart or one of the maids, had unpacked his suitcase and his possessions were neatly put away. For once, he didn't mind the bland anonymity of his surroundings. All he was interested in was sleep although sleep did not come very easily without the tablets he had been prescribed. There were two left which he swallowed with a handful of water from the basin in the adjoining bathroom. More would be given him, he assumed, the following morning when his treatment as an in-patient began.

As he was undressing, he was aware of the front door closing downstairs and footsteps crossing the gravel. Then he heard Midgley's voice again, speaking in that tone of over-loud concern that some people adopt towards the elderly or sick.

'Wait a moment, Mrs Jordan. I'll give you a hand.'

Going over to the window, Simon Boyd lifted aside the curtain and looked down. Midgley was hurrying round to the passenger side of a car parked below to assist Mrs Jordan into the front seat. He heard her soft murmur of thanks but couldn't catch the words.

'All set?' Midgley asked, only the top of his head visible as he bent solicitously towards her. Then he closed the door and, getting into the driver's seat, started the engine. The twin rear lights moved off down the drive.

Simon Boyd let the curtain drop back into place. He half-wished now that he had taken the opportunity to speak to her downstairs and to remind her of her promise to show him round the church. But he supposed there would be other occasions when he would meet her. It wasn't until later that he realised it was the last time he was to see her.

8

Donald Midgley drove slowly, the car headlamps lighting up the wide grass verges, scattered with the pale clumps of daffodils which Mrs Jordan had referred to with such embarrassing delight during dinner. She sat beside him silent now, her hands folded over her small black evening bag.

He felt at a loss what to say to her. Although he had been at the clinic only a short time, he had picked up enough to know that some of the members of staff, Hannah Kerr and Janet Ingham in particular, had very little sympathy for her and this knowledge created a barrier which made conversation difficult. In a way, he could understand Hannah Kerr's impatience. She was too brisk and efficient herself to suffer fools gladly and, to be strictly truthful, there was a vague, muddled air about Mrs Jordan, however kind and gentle she might be.

Janet Ingham's hostility took on a less overt form for, although she was never openly unfriendly to Mrs Jordan's face, behind her back she took every opportunity of making small, disparaging remarks about her in his hearing, perhaps because he was new to the clinic.

Take this morning as an example. She had been typing out the place cards for the dinner party when he had entered the general office and she had remarked, as if to herself, 'I'd better not put her next to Sutton. She'll be frightened out of her wits by him.'

The memory of it made him awkward now in Mrs Jordan's presence. He felt he had been disloyal by not openly showing his displeasure.

They were approaching the house, just inside the main gates to the clinic and set back from the drive behind white posts and chains. He turned the car into the entrance.

'Would you like to come in for a nightcap?' Mrs Jordan asked. She was trying to find her front-door key in her bag and he reached round to switch on the interior light for her.

He saw immediately how ill she looked. Her mouth was trembling, one corner jerking up in little spasms as if a small, invisible wire were pulling it upwards; a symptom of the migraine, he assumed. He felt he ought to accept her offer and yet it was so damned embarrassing. He'd had experience of women like her. Lonely, unhappy, neurotic, they tended to confide in anyone who seemed at all sympathetic and he had no intention of playing that role if he could avoid it. It might mean getting too involved. After all, his first loyalty was to Jordan and it could be awkward professionally if he became too closely associated with his wife.

'No, I don't think I will, thanks all the same,' he replied. 'I ought to be getting back.'

His eyes, behind the heavy horn-rimmed glasses he wore for driving, looked uneasy and he avoided her glance.

There was a small silence and then she said gently, 'Thank you for bringing me home, Donald. I'm afraid I've been rather a nuisance.'

'Not at all.' He tried to sound convincing. 'I hope you'll feel better soon.'

She got out of the car and, as he backed and turned, he looked briefly towards her. She had opened the front door and switched on the hall light and was standing on the threshold, while the rest of the house was in darkness. Seeing her there, it struck him suddenly what a small, lonely figure she seemed in that one oblong of brightness.

9

The last patient had gone, either to bed or to the writing-room where Jordan understood, with the omnipresent knowledge of the whereabouts of any particular patient at a given time, Sutton and some of the others were playing bridge. He felt his own responsibility towards them had ended. He could now retire himself, putting aside for the rest of the evening that public face that at times he found wearisome to maintain.

Thank God, he thought, Claire had left early and there had been no scene. For a moment, when she had confronted himself and Hannah, he had been afraid she was going to lose control and blurt out the truth and, once that was out, it could ruin him professionally. He couldn't afford scandal and, if she carried out her threat, he could imagine what some of the popular newspapers would make of it.

He'd have to talk to her, make her see that it would do neither of them any good.

Mrs Summers was clearing the dirty coffee cups from the main drawing-room and he withdrew to the small sitting-room, used by the staff in their free time, where Eunice Hart was already seated, smoking one of the few cigarettes she allowed herself when off duty.

'You look tired, Howard,' she remarked as he entered.

'I am,' he replied. It was an admission he could make to her and few other people.

'Coffee?' she suggested. 'And a brandy?'

He nodded and sat down thankfully in one of the armchairs by the fire. Over the past year it had become almost routine for him to spend half an hour at the end of a particularly long and exhausting day in her company, a brief interlude of relaxation that he had come to value in much the same way as the occasional evenings spent in his London club – a time for the private man. It also gave him the opportunity to discuss with her the domestic details of running the clinic which he rarely had the chance to do during the day.

'I thought this evening went quite well,' she added, bringing him coffee and a glass of brandy before taking her seat opposite him. Her long, flowered silk skirt subsided softly around her feet and the lamp behind her made her hair look darker than usual.

'I suppose so,' he admitted grudgingly. 'Thanks entirely to you, Eunice. Claire, of course, nearly ruined everything.'

He tried to speak lightly, as if her behaviour had caused him nothing more than amused exasperation. All the same, it caused him a pang of guilt to discuss his wife in this way, although there was no one else he could trust. Besides, it wasn't exactly disloyalty. Claire and Eunice were friends. It would

32

have been a different matter to talk of her with Hannah or Janet.

'You mean her leaving early?' Eunice asked. 'Oh, I don't think anyone noticed. She looked most unwell, I thought.'

There was a comfortable assurance about the way she spoke which invited further confidence.

'She'd upset herself for some reason or other. God knows what it was all about.'

It would have been easy enough to explain the reason behind Claire's outburst but he could not bring himself to do it. It was too humiliating.

'She's very highly-strung,' Eunice Hart said. It was the comment she usually made about Claire but tonight he could find no comfort in it.

'I sometimes wonder if she isn't heading for a breakdown. She certainly seems to get more and more neurotic.' He laughed bitterly. 'Ironic, isn't it? I'm responsible for running this clinic and my own wife shows the same symptoms as some of the patients I treat. Get me another brandy, Eunice.'

She rose at once and, taking his glass, carried it over to the table on which stood the decanters.

'Perhaps you ought to prescribe her tranquillisers,' she remarked over her shoulder. 'I know you're against the idea, Howard, but it might help her migraines as well. Of course, I'm no expert on these matters.'

She had put forward the same argument before in their late evening talks and he voiced the same objection that he always did; not the real reason, of course. That, too, he found impossible to put into words.

'I want to avoid it if I can. Once she starts, she may come to rely on them.'

'Poor Claire. I do feel so dreadfully sorry for her.'

As she handed him the glass of brandy, she touched him lightly on the shoulder with her other hand, one of her sympathetic, motherly gestures that seemed so natural. In many ways, she was an inarticulate woman. Certainly, compared to Hannah, she found it difficult to express herself freely and these mute signals were her only way of demonstrating her

33

understanding. He laid his own hand briefly over hers in recognition of her sympathy.

'I sometimes wish ... ' he began and then stopped short. During these *tête-à-tête* conversations, he had never been able to express his final judgement on his marriage – that he wished himself free. He couldn't even remember any longer why he had married her. There had once been a pretty, shy, gentle girl, with an air of sexual inexperience about her that had excited him. And then, of course, she had loved him very much and that kind of adoration had its attractions. Now she was like a millstone round his neck; a threat, too, to his continuing success.

'But we'll leave it there,' he concluded. 'What I wanted to see you about is a new patient I'm thinking of admitting, a young drug addict called Morley. Do you think you could get a room ready for him on this side of the house? I'd prefer to keep him apart from the other patients.'

'There's an empty room near to mine he could have, then I could keep an eye on him myself. I assume you'll engage a male nurse?'

'Yes, of course. I'm hoping to get that fixed up when I'm in London tomorrow, I want Midgley's opinion on Morley first. If he agrees, we'll arrange to have him admitted next week-end.'

'That's no trouble,' she assured him. 'Sutton, by the way, seems to be settling in quite satisfactorily.'

'Good. I was concerned about him. He's the type to make a fuss if the slightest thing goes wrong. Keep him smoothed down, Eunice.'

'I'll do my best.'

'I'm sure you will. You always do. I don't know how I'd manage without you.'

'Well, I have been trained for the job,' she pointed out.

He finished his brandy and rose to his feet.

'I ought to be going home, I suppose,' he added reluctantly. The room, warm with the banked heat from the log fire, subsided now to a mound of hot white ash and glowing fragments of small wood, suddenly seemed very desirable. Home, he realised, was here in the clinic, in the spacious elegance of its high-ceilinged rooms, the generous sweep of

34

lawns and tended flower beds. He had created it and it reflected all those qualities in life which he felt should have been his birthright.

'Yes, I really must go,' he repeated.

All the same, he lingered at the door, taking a last look back at the room.

He had come a long way, he thought, from his own modest, suburban background which he rarely remembered now and never with any regret. It was part of his past which, unlike Claire, he had managed to put aside, like a shabby, outworn coat; something to be discarded as no longer useful to him.

He recalled only the struggle which had got him to his present position; the long hours of work and study by which he had dragged himself step by step to the top, an achievement which he had no intention of abandoning.

10

After Howard left, Eunice Hart remained seated by the fire for quite a long time, watching it slowly sink in upon itself, the white ash shifting and subsiding as the heat went out of it, the bright wood dwindling as it blackened and died.

It seemed to her that, in the same way, Howard was losing vigour and energy. Like the fire, he, too, seemed to be collapsing inward, turning cold and ashy as the strength flowed out of him.

It saddened and alarmed her. What would happen to them all if Howard failed? Not just herself, but the others also; Janet, Donald Midgley, even Hannah Kerr? It seemed to her that, without his direction, the clinic, the little world they shared, would lose its momentum and balance, like one of those spinning tops which by degrees topples slowly sideways as its force is spent.

She was too old, she felt, to begin again. Since her husband's death twenty years before she had moved from one living-in job to another: housekeeper to a family in Norfolk; nurse-companion to an elderly spinster; deputy matron in a succession of private schools; with each move improving her professional status and qualifications little by little until, finally, she had obtained the post at the clinic, the best paid as well as the most rewarding. She could not bear to think of it ending.

Although she was rarely affected by the moods of others, Howard's low spirits seemed to evoke in her a melancholy reverie and, as she sat by the dying fire, the past was very close and she mourned it with a sense of loss and self-pity that she seldom allowed herself to indulge in: Charley's tragic death of cancer at thirty; the months of nursing him before he died in her arms; the break-up of their comfortable little home in Petts Wood; watching the dealer's men carrying the furniture out to the van: the light oak bedroom suite, the hall-stand, the grandmother clock that Charley had been so proud of – her home, Charley's home, collected together with such hope and love in those few, brief, happy years of marriage.

She had wept then as she hadn't been able to weep at Charley's funeral; the tears, which had been held back for so long, suddenly bursting free, she remembered, as she had sat on the bottom step of the stairs, holding on to the banisters with both hands, doubled over with the agony of grief.

The waste of it all! So much invested in a future that had ended so abruptly! The children that had never been conceived! The years of loving companionship of which she had been cheated!

I must not give way, she told herself, shivering and drawing her chair closer to the hearth. It was like coming to the edge of a cliff and looking down to the rocks and the surging water below; too great a temptation to allow oneself to be sucked down; to abandon the struggle. How silly, she thought, when I have so much to be thankful for: my strength; my health; the trust of people like Howard.

And wasn't it also ridiculous, just because Howard himself was feeling tired and dispirited, to assume the worst?

All the same, as she rose stiffly from her chair and made her customary round of the building, checking that the doors were locked and lights switched off before going to bed, she could not shake off the feeling that she had looked into an abyss and things would never be quite the same again.

Part Two

1

At a quarter past eight the following morning, Donald Midgley drove back to the Jordans' house, parking his Renault modestly alongside the doctor's Rolls Royce which was already standing in front of the garage doors. He had mixed feelings about the day to be spent with Jordan in his consulting rooms. On the one hand, it was a feather in his cap that the head of the clinic should consider his opinion worth having although the prospect of dinner afterwards at Jordan's London club caused him some alarm.

He knocked at the front door and Jordan opened it, remarking as he let him into the hall, 'Exactly on time, I see, Donald. I like that quality.'

It was a good beginning to the day, Midgley felt, and he asked, carefully constructing his sentences as he always did in Jordan's presence and choosing the right tone of subordinate concern, 'How is Mrs Jordan this morning? I do hope she's feeling better.'

'A little. I was extremely grateful to you for bringing her home last night.'

It was the kind of remark that didn't require an answer except for the slight inclination of the head that Midgley had seen Jordan himself make in acknowledgement of gratitude or praise.

'Coffee before you go?' Jordan continued. 'Or shall we make a start? The traffic could be heavy and the first appointment's at half past ten.'

'I've had breakfast,' Midgley replied which was obviously the answer Jordan was looking for.

'Good. We'll get off at once, then. I'll just say good-bye to Claire.'

He crossed the hall and, opening a door on the left, went inside leaving it ajar so that Donald Midgley was uncomfortably aware of overhearing the conversation that followed. He caught a glimpse, too, of Mrs Jordan, standing at the window, dressed in what appeared to be a long housecoat and one of those gauzy caps which some women wear over their hair at night. It was an intimate scene that he felt he had no business to witness and he turned aside to study a painting that hung above the telephone table.

'How do you feel now?' he heard Jordan ask her.

Her voice was too low-pitched for him to catch the words.

'I wish you'd stayed in bed a little longer,' Jordan continued. 'There was really no need for you to get up.'

Again, there was a low murmur as she replied.

'You do what you think best.' Jordan's voice again. 'The fresh air will probably be good for you but don't over-exert yourself, Claire. If you feel any worse, ring Eunice or Hannah at the clinic. I shan't be back myself until about eleven o'clock.'

'Very well, Howard.'

This time Mrs Jordan's voice was clearly audible, as if she had turned to face Jordan. Midgley then heard the door close and, judging it safe, moved away from his study of the picture as Jordan came towards him, pulling on a pair of driving-gloves and frowning as he did so.

'Mrs Jordan's better?' he asked, as if he had heard nothing of the conversation.

'So she says,' Jordan replied. His voice which had been unaccustomedly gentle when he spoke to her took on an exasperated edge now that she was out of earshot. 'I wish something could be done about those damned migraines of hers. I'm sure they're psychosomatic. You've done some research into the subject, Donald. Perhaps you could prescribe a treatment for her.'

'I could certainly try one of the new drugs,' Donald Midgley replied, a little alarmed at the thought of treating Jordan's wife. 'It might be her diet, of course. Certain foods, chocolate for example, can cause them.'

'In her case, I'm sure it's tension. She finds it very difficult to relax. Ridiculous, really, when you think that most of the patients I treat, and on the whole successfully, are suffering from stress in some form or other and yet I can do nothing for my own wife.'

As he spoke, he was collecting up his briefcase and a copy of *The Times* which were lying on the hall chair before opening the door. Midgley followed him outside.

On the step, however, Jordan paused.

'Damn!' he said. 'I've left some letters on my desk that need posting. You go on, Donald. The car's unlocked.'

Climbing into the leather and rosewood comfort of Jordan's Rolls Royce, Midgley pondered the question of success. If cars were considered a symbol of it, Jordan had certainly arrived. For his own part, it would be a boat, a four-berth cabin cruiser with an 80 h.p. inboard diesel engine and a sun-deck. But all the same, as he sank into the padded luxury of the passenger seat, he had to admit that a Rolls wasn't a bad symbol of achievement.

A few seconds later, Jordan emerged from the house, holding some letters in his hand and, apologising to Midgley for the delay, started the engine and turned the car towards the gates.

2

A few hours later, Simon Boyd let himself out of the clinic by the front door and set off down the drive, glad of the chance to be alone. It had been an exhausting morning although it had involved him in nothing more strenuous than the kind of questioning and examination that he supposed was routine for a new patient. First Janet Ingham, crisply tailored in navy blue and white, had filled in the details on his personal record, rattling off his answers on the typewriter, her eyes fixed on the middle distance as if her swiftly moving fingers were quite dissociated from the rest of her body.

From her he had been passed on to two specialists, one a dietitian, the other a medical practitioner, who had weighed him, tested his reflexes and blood pressure, listened to his heart and asked more questions.

Wearing one of the clinic's dark-red towelling dressing-gowns, he had then progressed to Dr Kerr's consulting room where the results of all these examinations were already waiting on her desk in the form of a dark grey manilla folder. By that time he no longer cared. He had reached that stage of suspended personality in which he had ceased to regard himself as an individual, merely as a case history. Besides, there was an asexual and astringent quality about Dr Kerr that made the interview seem curiously distanced. He might have been discussing an acquaintance whom they both knew and whose clinical symptoms were a matter of mutual professional interest.

'Physically, you're perfectly fit,' Dr Kerr had told him briskly. 'A little underweight but that can soon be rectified by diet. Your blood pressure's up, but not too high. Stress, of course.'

'Of course,' he agreed wryly. 'And the treatment?'

He trusted her more than Jordan. She would be quite straightforward with him, he felt.

'Drug therapy would relieve the symptoms,' she replied.

'And the alternative?'

'You could be helped to understand and control them for yourself. It's a longer process and involves a certain amount of self discipline.'

He felt she was offering him a challenge.

'How long?' he asked. There was always Hubert's itinerary to consider.

'That depends on you. Several weeks, possibly. But I can't guarantee either the length of time it will take or its success.'

'I'll take it,' he had replied, as if the offer were a cut-price Christmas turkey. 'Shall I be on your list of patients?'

'If you wish, Mr Boyd. We'll begin the treatment then tomorrow morning at ten o'clock.'

And that had been all. She had written his name on her appointment list and he had gone away to get dressed, feeling that the decision, so coolly and unemotionally made, had nevertheless marked an important stage in his life.

This realisation seemed to increase his awareness so that, coming down the clinic steps, he was conscious for the first time in years of the details of his surroundings. Normally they were blurred over by tension and anxiety, his regard being turned only partially outwards, while the greater part of his attention remained fixed on the constant surge and shift of the inner grey tide that at times seemed to engulf him.

Now he saw that it was one of those clear, fragile March days when the sky was as clear as a crystal bell and every bud and blade of grass seemed encased in the same glassy light. Even the small stones of the gravel winked and glittered individually as he walked across them. It was as if the retina of his eye was set wide open so that he was able to absorb in one glance the stones, the grass, the trees whose great, bare, intricate structures laced the sky.

He was reminded suddenly of Mrs Jordan. Perhaps it was the image that evoked her. Her eyes had displayed a childlike openness when she had spoken of the daffodils as if she, too, had absorbed them with the same totality of vision. He remembered too, with a faint stirring of guilt, caused as much by his mother as by her, that he had avoided her last night and he decided on the spur of the moment to call on her and ask her to accompany him on a walk through the clinic grounds.

The house was modest enough from the front; a long, low structure of old brick, perhaps the original home farmhouse that had served the estate. But the front door of panelled teak was new and in keeping with Jordan's style, in its heavy, handsome solidity. He knocked and waited and, receiving no reply, walked round to the back.

The modern two-storey addition at the rear of the building startled him with its total inappropriateness. It jutted out like the upper deck of a liner, in a bold thrust of concrete and plate glass above which the irregular roof line of old tiles looked ridiculously dwarfed and cockeyed.

There was no garden either, which also surprised him, remembering Mrs Jordan's obvious interest in flowers; only a paved terrace, set with urns, and a semi-circular lawn, backed by shrubs which merged into the surrounding woods.

Stepping on to the flag stones, he approached the long windows that formed the entire back wall of a drawing-room which he could see was furnished with huge leather chairs and pieces of contemporary bronze sculpture; Jordan's choice, surely. He could not imagine Mrs Jordan feeling at ease in such a setting.

The room was empty; more than empty, he felt. There was a static, self-conscious look about it that suggested it was seldom used.

It was clear Mrs Jordan was not at home and he turned away, only half-sorry. He had no particular desire for her company and it would be pleasanter to walk alone; something he rarely had the opportunity to do and certainly not this aimless, unhurried ramble through the trees.

After about a quarter of an hour's walk, he reached the edge of the wood where he paused. A low iron fence marked the boundary of the clinic's grounds and beyond it he could see, on the left, the neat green grass and carefully crafted landscape of the golf course of which Mrs Jordan had spoken at dinner the previous evening. Two figures, tiny at that distance, were marching towards him along a fairway to where a little toy flag fluttered on a green.

To his right stretched open farmland, the regular ridges of the ploughland softened by the new green shoots of winter wheat, glossy in the thin, bright sunshine. Rooks were feeding along the furrows, walking with the clumsy, lurching gait of men with no arms and, as he climbed the fence and began walking along the uncultivated edge, they took to the air, complaining loudly at his intrusion, their heavy black wings beating laboriously upward.

It was gone eleven o'clock that evening before Jordan's car drew up in front of the house, its huge headlights raking the façade which was in darkness.

'You'll come in for a whisky, of course,' Jordan said. It was a statement rather than an invitation which Donald Midgley did not like to refuse although it seemed likely, from the absence of lights in the windows, that Mrs Jordan had already gone to bed.

Even the hall was unlit, a fact that Jordan commented on as he unlocked the front door.

'That's odd,' he remarked. 'Claire usually leaves the downstairs light on when I'm home late. Look, Donald, you go on through to the drawing-room. It's the last door on the right. Pour a couple of whiskies and I'll join you in a moment. I'll just make sure first that she's all right and then I'd like to discuss Morley's case with you.'

He put down his briefcase and mounted the stairs, unbuttoning his overcoat as he went, leaving Donald Midgley to enter the drawing-room alone and fumble inside the door for the unfamiliar light switch.

The lamps, large bronze bases with drum-shaped shades of watered cream silk, flowered twice; once inside the room and again in the dark expanse of glass at the far end across which the curtains had not yet been drawn, so that the room seemed curiously incomplete as if one entire wall was missing and there were no barrier between the safe interior world of armchairs and rugs and the more menacing external world, only partly perceived, of shadows and the dark, tangled outlines of trees. Above them a full moon hung, partly obscured by long streamers of cloud, so that at first Midgley was confused and took it to be some strange lamp burning with the others inside the room itself.

It was this momentary distraction of vision that caused him

to react so slowly when Jordan entered, still wearing his overcoat.

'Is Claire here?' he asked abruptly.

'Claire?' Midley repeated. For a moment he couldn't associate the name with Jordan's wife, not that Jordan seemed aware of it.

'She isn't in her bedroom,' he continued. 'In fact, her bed's not been slept in. And she's nowhere else in the house. I've checked all the other rooms.'

'Perhaps she's gone out for the evening,' Midgley suggested.

'But she never does; not at night and never alone. Besides, she would have left a note,' Jordan retorted. He sounded annoyed rather than worried. 'Look here, Donald, check the garage for me, will you? See if her car's there or not. Simmonds should have brought it back this morning. Meanwhile, I'll phone the clinic. It's possible she felt worse during the day and rang Eunice or Hannah who drove over and picked her up. All the same, one of them might have thought to leave a message on the hall table.'

He turned and walked out of the room, Midgley following him into the hall where he could see all the downstairs doors were open, the lights burning inside the rooms, as if Jordan, in his impatience to find his wife, hadn't bothered to close them after him. There was a dining-room, Midgley noticed, in the front of the house, while a kitchen, brightly lit by a fluorescent tube, opened off a short passage alongside the staircase. The room, where Jordan had said good-bye to his wife that morning and which Midgley had briefly glimpsed, appeared to be a small sitting-room or breakfast-room with a sash window overlooking the terrace.

Jordan was already picking up the phone as Midgley let himself out of the front door. A paved path led to the garage, the door of which swung easily upwards, and there was enough moonlight for him to see that Mrs Jordan's Mini was parked inside, occupying about a quarter of the space.

Feeling a little foolish, he checked the interior of the car but it was empty and he returned to the house where Jordan re-admitted him.

'Well?' Jordan asked, the moment he stepped inside.

'Her car's still there,' Midgley replied, not sure if this were good news or bad, for it was obvious from Jordan's expression that he had drawn a blank at the clinic.

'Then where the hell can she be?' Jordan demanded. There was a different quality about his anger now and Midgley realised that underneath the exasperation he was genuinely concerned about his wife.

'Could she be at a friend's house?' he suggested.

'She knows very few people locally,' Jordan replied. 'Besides she'd've taken the car. I don't mind admitting, Donald, I'm getting worried. It's nearly half past eleven. It's so unusual for her to go out in the evening, unless it's with me. She's not at the clinic. At least, Hannah hasn't seen her. She's going to check with Eunice and, if she knows nothing, they'll look round the main rooms. Could you do something for me?'

'Of course,' Midgley replied promptly.

'Wait here in case Claire phones. I'll drive down to the village. She could be at Janet's although it doesn't seem very likely. Failing that, I'll call on Mrs Leighton. She's Claire's charwoman and she was here this morning, doing the cleaning. She may know something. Help yourself to that whisky while I'm gone.'

He left before Donald Midgley had time to reply and, a few minutes later, the sound of the car's engine was heard starting up, its headlights shining briefly across the hall window, as it headed down the drive towards the gates.

When it was gone, Donald Midgley made for the kitchen which seemed a preferable place in which to wait than the empty drawing-room with its disconcerting view of the darkened garden. Tea, too, seemed a better option than whisky and, with the practical confidence of a man long used to coping with unfamiliar kitchens in furnished flats and hospital halls of residence, he began to open cupboards and find what was necessary. He even produced a tray on which he set three cups for, despite Jordan's obvious concern, he had no doubt that Mrs Jordan would return quite soon.

A knock at the front door ten minutes later seemed to justify this optimism and he went to open it, expecting to find her on the doorstep, breathless and apologetic at having caused so much fuss. It wasn't until he saw Hannah Kerr standing there instead that he realised Mrs Jordan would have let herself in with her own key.

'Any news of her yet?' Hannah Kerr asked briskly, stepping inside. There was an impatient air about her that seemed intensified by the glitter of raindrops on her dark hair and the shoulders of a loose red jacket she was wearing over black trousers.

'It's raining,' he said inconsequentially.

He could see it slanting down in the light from the hall.

'Just started. Well? Has she turned up?'

'No, she hasn't.'

He closed the door.

'I'm making tea. Would you like some?'

'I'd love some. I was just going to bed when Howard phoned. Where is he by the way?'

'He's gone down to the village to call on Janet Ingham and Mrs Leighton, Mrs Jordan's char. He's hoping one of them will know where she's gone. He seemed rather worried about her.'

While they were talking, they had moved into the kitchen where Donald Midgley poured tea and handed her a cup. She had propped herself up against the sink and he was reminded of other occasions when, as a houseman, he and another doctor would gather in a ward kitchen in the early hours of the morning for tea and a cigarette. Some of that camaraderie seemed to colour this occasion and, for once, he forgot that he didn't much care for her as a person.

'You know what Claire's like,' she replied, shrugging. 'A creature of routine and habit. I can understand he'd be a bit alarmed not to find her at home. She collapsed once so he's probably afraid the same thing might have happened.'

'Collapsed?'

'Well, passed out.' She sounded scornful. 'She'd gone for a walk over the golf links and was taken ill. The club secretary had to bring her home in his car. I suppose Howard's concerned she might have had another fainting fit.'

'But it's dark and it's started to rain!'

He was touched himself for the first time with real anxiety.

'Exactly.'

'But what can we do?'

'Nothing much for the moment except wait for Howard.'

He returned just after midnight, alone, and looking tired and dishevelled, his grey hair, usually so immaculate, wet with rain and his shoes and the bottoms of his trousers spattered with mud.

'Is she back?' he asked almost as soon as he was inside the front door and then, when he could see they were alone, 'Has she phoned?'

'No, not yet,' Hannah Kerr replied, sounding deliberately brisk. 'What did you find out in the village?'

'Nothing. Janet hasn't seen her all day and what's more worrying, Claire was gone before Mrs Leighton arrived. She found the back door locked and had to let herself in with her key. There was no sign of Claire and no note to say where she'd gone or what time she'd be back.'

'What time was this?'

'Half past ten. She left about twelve. I had to get the woman out of bed. Afterwards I drove round to all the places where Claire might have called, the vicarage, that woman who runs the craft shop . . .'

'You need a whisky,' Hannah Kerr interrupted. She led the way into the drawing-room, the two men following, Jordan still talking as if he had reached that point of exhaustion when it is impossible to keep silent.

'After that, I simply drove about for a time. She could have gone for a walk. I remembered she'd said something this morning about feeling better if she got out into the fresh air. But how the hell do you find someone at this time of night? I tried the golf club but it was locked and all the lights were out. I even walked part of the way across the course and then gave up. It was impossible to see a damned thing.'

'Drink this,' Hannah Kerr told him. While he had been speaking, she had poured whiskies for all of them. 'And take that wet coat off.'

Her tone was harsh and he obeyed automatically, slinging the coat down over the back of one of the chairs before taking the glass she held out to him. The room was already beginning to look dishevelled, a rug kicked awry, their wet footmarks

48

smeared across the parquet flooring, Hannah's bag and cigarette packet dumped down on the drinks cabinet alongside a piece of abstract sculpture.

'What do we do now?' Jordan continued. The question was oddly appealing. 'Ring the police?'

'Not yet,' Hannah Kerr replied. 'It's too soon for that.' She glanced at her watch and Midgley, repeating the action, verified the time; it was a quarter to one. 'Give her until half past and then we'll start phoning the hospitals.'

'And meanwhile?' Jordan asked. 'I can't just sit here and do nothing.'

'There must be other places we can check. Has she any friends or relatives she might have gone to?'

The question was greeted with silence on Jordan's part. For a moment, he sat immobile, hunched over as if cold. Then he straightened up and looked directly at her.

'Are you suggesting that my wife might have left me?' he asked.

She coloured up briefly; the first time Midgley had ever seen her at a loss. But she recovered quickly and made a small, dismissive movement of her shoulders.

'I'm implying nothing, Howard. I'm simply suggesting that before you start calling in the police or even contacting the hospitals, it would be sensible to check first on anywhere else she might have gone.'

Her voice was reasonable, without emotion, and yet Midgley was aware of a contest of wills taking place between them. It was Jordan who dropped his gaze first.

'There's a sister in London,' he replied, 'but it's unlikely Claire's gone there.'

'I still think we ought to try,' Hannah Kerr replied.

'Would you like me to phone her?' Donald Midgley put in eagerly. He wasn't quite sure himself why he made the offer. It was partly to show a willingness to help; partly a need to escape from the room.

'Would you, Donald?' Jordan seemed grateful for the offer. 'You'll find her in the address book under Vincent.'

'Of course,' he agreed and, putting down his glass, left the room, wondering how the hell he was going to break the news to Mrs Jordan's sister.

The telephone rang for several moments before anyone answered it and then a woman's voice demanded abruptly, 'Yes, what is it?'

It was a hard voice, not at all what he would have associated with Mrs Jordan, and obviously angry at being woken up at that time of night.

'Mrs Vincent?' he asked, making his own voice sound apologetic and conciliatory.

'Yes.'

'My name's Donald Midgley. I'm Dr Jordan's assistant. We wondered if Mrs Jordan could possibly be there with you.'

'Claire? No, she isn't. Why do you want to know?'

'Well, you see,' he began awkwardly, 'Mrs Jordan's gone out and hasn't yet returned. We thought she might have visited you and missed the last train home.'

'She'd've phoned, surely?' Mrs Vincent demanded with devastating logic.

'Yes, but you see, Dr Jordan's been out . . .'

'That doesn't matter. She could have rung the clinic and left a message. Was there one?'

'I'm afraid not,' he was forced to admit.

'And she isn't home yet?'

'No.'

'She certainly isn't here with me. Look, young man. What's happening? Has Claire left him?'

It was the same possibility that Hannah Kerr had implied, only this time stated more bluntly.

'Oh, no, there's no question of that,' he said hurriedly.

'Isn't there?' Her tone expressed disbelief and an odd triumph. 'Where is she then?'

'I'm sorry, there isn't time to go into detail,' he replied, ducking the question. 'We're trying to contact any friends she might have called on . . .'

'Now, listen. Before you ring off, I want one thing made quite clear. Howard's to keep in touch with me. Is that understood? I want him to ring me the moment there's any news.'

'Of course,' he agreed and replaced the receiver before she

could press him any further. It had been a disastrous conversation, he felt, which wasn't made any better by Jordan demanding, as soon as he re-entered the drawing-room, 'Was she there?'

'No, I'm afraid she wasn't,' he replied.

'I didn't think she'd be.'

It was said with a cold disdain that clearly expressed his dislike for his sister-in-law and then Jordan stood up and began putting on his overcoat with a new, determined air, as if he had reached a decision.

'I want you to come back with me to the clinic, Donald,' he said. 'We'll ring the hospitals from there. There are more phones and I'll get Janet in to help. Hannah will stay on here in case Claire comes back or there's a message. It's better to have a woman on hand in case she's been taken ill. First, though, I want you to get in touch with Simmonds, the gardener. You know where he lives in the village? Drive him back to the clinic and help him look over the outbuildings. It's too dark to search the grounds but we'll make a start on those as soon as it's light.'

4

For Midgley it was the beginning of a bizarre night that was to grow more extraordinary as the hours passed. Together with Simmonds, a tall, slow-moving man of few words, he went over the outbuildings of the clinic, some of which he had never been inside before. The moon had disappeared behind clouds and the darkness was almost total except for the narrow cones of light shed by their torches that lit up the interiors of greenhouses, sheds and old stables, turned now into garages, surprising them, Midgley felt, in some secret, withdrawn existence of their own that he had not been aware of until that moment. Plants suddenly appeared in the brief illumination, suspended in a world of vegetable existence, secret and mysterious, whose ritual life would be resumed as soon as they went away. A whitewashed wall, showing the softened contours of the underlying bricks, appeared and vanished, along with the fine-spun cobwebs which hung like purses in the corners. At one point, Simmonds propped his torch against a pile of seed-boxes in an outhouse and rolled himself a cigarette, only his hands, with their huge, blunt fingers, visible, between which the little oblong of tissue paper appeared as fragile as a moth's wing.

But nowhere was there any sign of Mrs Jordan.

At four o'clock they returned to the clinic to find lights burning in the downstairs offices and Janet Ingham, dressed as if it were a normal working day, sitting at her desk and speaking into the telephone while Jordan stood beside her, still wearing his overcoat and muddy shoes, looking old and fatigued.

Eunice Hart was up, too, serving coffee and sandwiches in the kitchen; not fully dressed like Janet Ingham but wearing a long dressing-gown of blue quilted nylon, a comfortable, motherly figure with her hair loose, as if she had not had time to arrange it properly.

It was strange to be sitting in the kitchen at that early hour of the morning, the uncurtained windows still dark while the bright, white lights shone down on the shelves of saucepans and the glittering surfaces of enamel and stainless steel. Because of the seriousness of the occasion, voices were kept low and yet Midgley was aware of the undercurrent of suppressed excitement that any emergency generates, as if all of them were, in some inexplicable manner, pleased to have been jolted out of the routine of normal, everyday living.

At first light, Simmonds was despatched in the clinic's mini-bus to collect from the village anyone willing to help in the search, including the under-gardeners, the handyman, and Steve, the part-time assistant who helped out in the sauna.

It had stopped raining when they set out on the search although the air still retained a watery atmosphere and the sun rose behind the vapour, turning it to a diffused gold. They had been divided up into two groups, Midgley delegated to Simmonds' party which was to comb the woods to the north of the clinic and, as they walked, he could hear the men's voices, several yards on either side of him, carrying clearly through the trees, their feet shuffling through the litter of last year's dead leaves and bracken while the woods rang with the early morning song of the birds, very sweet and piercing in the bright, chilly air.

That, also, seemed dissociated from normal experience, a reaction that Midgley realised was brought on largely by fatigue which, like certain drugs, has the effect of distancing sensation.

It was partly this fatigue which caused him to mishandle the encounter with Sutton when, the search completed, the men returned to the clinic. Mrs Jordan had still not been found and, while the men tramped round to the back of the house where breakfast was being prepared for them, Midgley entered by the front door and was crossing the hall when Sutton, wearing a dressing-gown and slippers, came down the stairs.

'What the hell's going on?' he demanded. 'There's been nothing but car doors slamming and telephones ringing half the night. I'd like an explanation.'

'It's Mrs Jordan,' Midgley explained, alarmed by Sutton's cold fury. 'She's missing and we've been out looking for her.'

'Missing since when?'

'Since yesterday.'

'Has she been found yet?'

'I'm afraid not.'

As he spoke, he was aware that Simon Boyd had emerged from his room at the head of the landing and was leaning down over the banisters listening to the exchange. His face, in the pale early morning light, looked drained of all life and colour, the nose and chin jutting forward, like the profile of some great, mournful bird of prey.

'What's going to happen now?' he called down to them. 'Are you contacting the police?'

'I'm not sure,' Midgley replied helplessly. He felt he was taking too much on himself.

'Where's Jordan?' Sutton asked abruptly, ignoring the interruption.

'In his office, I think,' Midgley replied. He could hardly withhold this piece of information although he was considerably frightened when Sutton pushed past him and, striding ahead, threw open the door of Jordan's consulting room without any ceremony. Midgley, who had trailed miserably after him, hoping for an opportunity to explain his own part in this unfortunate episode, was able to witness the scene that followed.

Jordan, who had been seated behind his desk, with Janet Ingham beside him, rose to his feet as Sutton entered.

'Have you rung the police?' Sutton asked in a hectoring tone.

'No, I haven't yet,' Jordan began.

'I assume you intend doing so?'

Jordan held out his hands in a gesture that was expressive of his own uncertainty.

'There appears to be no alternative,' he said simply. 'My wife has still not been found.'

'Then give me the phone,' Sutton snapped and as Janet Ingham, looking affronted and alarmed, pushed the receiver towards him, he added as he began dialling, 'I have no intention of letting some bone-headed country copper take over the case.' Then, as the call was connected, 'Give me the Chief Constable. I don't give a damn if he is still in bed. Get him up. Tell him this is Sutton of the Home Office and I want to speak to him immediately.'

Part Three

1

'I still think it's a bit thick,' Boyce repeated for the third time. They were in the car, on their way to Hawton, the detective sergeant at the wheel. 'I mean, it's the sort of case the local CID would normally handle, not headquarters and certainly not someone with your rank.'

It was the third time, too, that he had referred to Finch's recent promotion to Detective Chief Inspector. The reason was certainly not envy; Boyce was too generous-spirited for that. But it was possible that he was trying to get used to the more exalted position while at the same time feeling slightly aggrieved that so far it had netted them nothing more spectacular than a Missing Persons case.

It rankled with Finch, too, but for other reasons. He suspected that Superintendent Davies, in asking him to take over the investigation, hadn't been entirely honest with him.

'I'd like you to be in charge,' he had said. 'It needs tactful handling. I gather there's a few important toes that could be stepped on if it's bungled.'

A mere sop to his ego, Finch had thought at the time, to make up for any resentment he might feel about the request.

The Superintendent had looked ill at ease, too; a sure sign that he was hiding something. And Finch thought he knew what it was. Someone had put pressure on Davies who, while disliking it, hadn't been in a position to refuse; and that meant someone with authority and rank. Davies wasn't the type to be easily persuaded into any action he didn't want to take.

As if aware of Finch's thoughts, Boyce added darkly, 'If you ask me, someone's been pulling strings.'

'Perhaps,' Finch agreed. 'God knows who though.'

'The chap who runs the place, do you reckon? Whatsisname, Jordan, whose wife's disappeared?'

It didn't seem likely to Finch unless Jordan had influence in fairly exalted police circles. In his opinion, it was more probably one of his patients. Davies' comment about important toes certainly suggested it.

'I don't know, Tom,' he replied non-committally. 'But one thing's certain. Someone with clout in the right places is going to be watching us from the wings and I don't much care for the idea.'

'There's no question it might be murder? It could be the reason why we've been called in on the case.'

'According to Davies it was a straightforward Missing Persons inquiry that had to be handled discreetly.'

'He could be holding out on you.'

'I don't think so.'

As far as he could judge, it was a fair conclusion. Davies might have shuffled off the exact reason why Finch had been given the case but he doubted if the Superintendent's deception went further than that.

'Only I was thinking,' Boyce continued, still occupied with the same idea, 'that given it's some kind of funny farm . . .'

'For God's sake, Tom,' Finch interrupted impatiently, 'get that notion out of your head for a start. It's a clinic not a mental hospital. The patients, if that's the right word for them, are all highly respectable businessmen or civil servants, in for a few weeks' rest. They're not round the bend by any stretch of the imagination.'

'Rest!' Boyce exclaimed disgustedly, determined to have the last word. 'They want to do our job for a few weeks. Then they'd really be in need of a holiday.'

'And Jordan's wife went missing from home, not the clinic,' Finch continued, ignoring Boyce's interpolation. 'So there may be no connection at all although that's something we'll have to look into when we get there.'

'Which won't be long now,' Boyce put in as they passed a signboard with Hawton on it.

It was a large, well-kept village, a few miles north of Chelmsford, where the flat fields of east Essex lifted a little into a gentler, tree-rich landscape; its centre dominated by the church alongside which ran a row of gabled brick houses, all of the same design, with white-painted windows and porches in the Gothic style which gave their otherwise modest exteriors an ornate air. They were, Finch guessed, the cottages built originally to house the estate workers when the Hall was in private hands.

Facing them and set back from the road behind wide grass verges were a pair of massive stone pillars supporting tall wrought-iron gates and a noticeboard announcing in black letters on white: 'Hawton Hall Clinic. Strictly Private.' The gates were closed but as the car approached them, it depressed two rubber-covered plates set in the road and they swung silently open, a piece of simple mechanism which seemed to please Boyce for he remarked, 'Clever, that!'

The drive ran between woodland and shrubbery which finally opened out into lawns and formal rose-beds, facing which was the plain, almost severe, façade of Hawton Hall, with its three-storeyed central block of balanced sash windows and two smaller wings with mansard roofs, slightly recessed from the main section.

They parked the car and walked up the steps to the front entrance, the heavy outer door of which had been set open, revealing a pair of inner glass doors through which they could see a large, square hall with a tessellated floor of coloured tiles and an ornate brass chandelier hanging from the ceiling.

'Posh!' commented Boyce in a low voice as the Inspector rang the bell, and Finch thought irritably that he hoped to God Boyce wasn't going to complicate matters further by becoming overawed by his surroundings. It was bad enough having some unidentified observer watching them from the wings.

A young woman crossed the hall; tall, blonde, dressed in a navy blue suit and a white blouse; attractive, certainly to Boyce, who gave Finch an appreciative nudge with his elbow as they watched her approach, but too made up for his own liking and much too self-possessed.

'Detective Inspector Finch?' she asked.

'Detective *Chief* Inspector,' he replied, with quiet emphasis.

Now that he'd got the promotion, he didn't see why it shouldn't be recognised. But she appeared not to hear.

'If you'll come this way,' she said, 'I'll tell Dr Jordan you've arrived.'

She preceded them across the hall, her trim little buttocks moving up and down briskly under the straight-cut linen skirt, and showed them into what Finch assumed was a general office.

'If you'll wait, Dr Jordan's in conference with his deputy director at the moment,' she told them and, going over to the desk, she murmured softly into the intercom.

Finch wandered as if casually over to the window and appeared to be interested in the view of carefully tended lawns sloping gently down to the surrounding woodlands where the spiky outlines of the trees were already hazing over with the faint green of new leaves. At the same time, he kept an ear cocked towards a door on his left which he thought probably communicated with Jordan's private office but it was too heavy and close-fitting for him to hear any conversation that might be going on in the room beyond.

2

'The police have arrived,' Jordan announced, switching off the receiver and turning to Hannah Kerr who, like Finch, was standing at the window. 'Before I ask Janet to show them in, I'd like to make sure that we're both agreed on the line we ought to take.'

'Yes, of course,' she replied a little impatiently although she could understand his concern. 'We've been over it, Howard. As far as possible, we keep them away from the clinic and the patients, certainly from Sutton. But I honestly can't see any problem arising there. Sutton's not going to push himself forward. Quite frankly, I think he over-reacted in phoning the Chief Constable in the first place but at least we're assured of getting someone who'll handle the case discreetly which is what

Sutton wanted. A man in his position with a penchant for teenage girls needs all the discretion he can get. He was damned lucky the parents of the last one decided after all not to make a fuss.'

She spoke more critically than she intended, partly out of tiredness, partly to jolt Howard into a more positive frame of mind, although, thank God, he looked as if he had a better grip on himself. He had, at least, shaved and changed out of his dishevelled clothes. There had been a time during the night when, finding him sitting alone in the medical room, she had thought he might be on the verge of breaking down. She had forced him to take some tranquillisers but the sight of his haggard face had roused in her a quite unfamiliar sensation of pitying contempt.

Even now he appeared to be only half-listening to her.

'We can't afford a scandal,' he was saying. 'And it's not just Sutton. There are the other patients to consider as well. The reputation of the whole place could be ruined by the wrong sort of publicity.'

'But I don't see they need be questioned at all. Claire disappeared from the house, not the clinic.'

'All the same, people talk.'

'What people?' she asked sharply. His remark struck her as irrational, as if he were trying to express some obscure obsession of his own.

'Staff. Servants.'

'But for God's sake, what about?'

'I don't know.' He sounded harassed. 'But they might pass on all sorts of ridiculous rumours.'

There was very little real substance to him, she thought wryly. Of course, he was charming and she supposed someone in his position needed that personal charisma; it was this quality, after all, which brought in the patients but she had serious doubts about his ability as a therapist. It was probably one of the reasons why he had opted out of the National Health Service: the going had been too tough. Certainly, he always passed on to her the more difficult cases, making the excuse that administrative duties didn't allow him the time. She didn't much mind, preferring the challenge.

The same basic weakness affected all his relationships, even his marriage. He should have separated from Claire years before. Instead of which, he had hung on, keeping up the pretence for God knows what reason; probably out of sheer pride. He hated failure of any sort; it struck at his ego.

Well, judging by the little scene that had occured in his office yesterday evening, it seemed highly likely that Claire had left him. Hannah Kerr had not completely understood what Claire had meant but the implication had been clear enough. She had been jealous, seeing Howard and herself together, ridiculous though the idea might be. It was, however, a typical neurotic's reaction and, as such, was hardly worth considering except with pity and contempt. Certainly, she had no desire to gossip about it to the police or anyone else. In fact, the whole situation had got quite out of proportion. Within a few days, Claire would come home, Howard would take her back, using her defection as another weapon in his armoury against her, and she, like a fool, would submit, because, for their own different reasons, they needed one another. Hannah Kerr had seen plenty of marriages based on the same sado-masochistic principle and they seemed, in their own strange way, to be successful. And so it would go on.

If Sutton hadn't panicked and thrown his weight about, the local police would have handled the case and the whole affair would have blown over with the minimum of fuss.

'I can't see the need for the police to question any members of staff, except possibly Mrs Leighton,' she pointed out. 'Look, Howard, shouldn't you let them make a start on the inquiry? It's nearly eleven o'clock and we ourselves have got patients to interview. You won't need me to stay, will you?'

He seemed to rouse himself.

'Of course not, Hannah,' he said more positively. 'I shall obviously be delayed for a time but I'll start my own interviews as soon as I can.'

'The folders are on your desk,' she replied as she walked towards the door.

'And thank you,' he added, rising to his feet. 'For everything. I'm sorry it's been such a difficult time for all of us.'

An odd way of expressing it, she thought but she supposed

there were few suitable words for covering that particular contingency.

As she closed the door, he had already resumed his seat and was pressing down the switch on the intercom that connected with the outer office.

3

'You can go in now,' Janet Ingham said. 'Dr Jordan's ready to see you.'

She indicated the communicating door but made no attempt to open it for them or show them into the further room, an omission which put them, Finch felt, at a disadvantage, for they arrived unannounced with the small, added complication of closing the door behind them, a task he left to Boyce.

It gave him, however, a few seconds in which to survey the room which was large and well furnished, more in the style of a study than an office or consulting room. There was no leather-covered couch which he had expected from films he had seen about psychiatrists, only a large, mahogany, knee-hole desk, with its back to the window, from behind which, as they entered and Boyce fumbled with the door handle, Dr Jordan was getting to his feet, holding out a hand but not, Finch thought, expecting it to be shaken. It was intended more as a general gesture of welcome and he saw, as he padded forward over the pale green carpet that yielded softly under his feet, that the extended arm was now waving them towards a pair of low-backed armchairs, covered in the same leaf-patterned brocade as the elaborately swagged curtains, that had been drawn up facing the desk.

The gesture, slightly larger than life as if intended for a more numerous gathering than just the two of them, seemed to typify the doctor. He was not a very tall man and yet he gave the impression of presence. It was concentrated in his head and shoulders which seemed slightly out of proportion to the rest of his body; particularly the face which, with its frame of thick grey hair, carefully cut, Finch suspected, to make the most of it, seemed all features. Nothing about any of them had been skimped in the making. The eyebrows were well-defined, the mouth and eyes full for a man, the nose and chin strongly modelled while the hands, resting now together on the top of the desk, showed the same generosity of form. There was an immaculate quality, too, about his grey suit and silk shirt with its sharply pointed collar-ends that made Finch aware, as he sat down and jerked at the knees of his own baggy trousers, how shabby and badly-ironed he must appear in contrast. He was particularly conscious of his shoes, well-worn suede, shiny on the toe-caps and with deep creases cut into the uppers, and he glanced surreptitiously at Jordan's as they rested side by side on the green carpet under the desk, as black and gleaming as if they had just been french-polished. It was small consolation to know that Boyce's appearance wasn't much of an improvement on his own. The sergeant was wearing what Finch called his bookie's suit, in chocolate brown with an over-loud red check, and a green satin tie which in strong sunlight appeared almost fluorescent.

'Detective Chief Inspector Finch?' Jordan asked as if uncertain which of the ill-assorted pair in front of him was actually in charge of the case and Finch made a small inclination of his head, acknowledging the responsibility.

'And my assistant, Detective Sergeant Boyce,' he added.

Boyce shifted his backside on the chair but had the sense to say nothing.

'I don't know how much you've been told,' Jordan began, turning his attention back to Finch.

'Only what Superintendent Davies has told me, which wasn't much,' Finch replied. It was time, he felt, to make his own presence felt. If he wasn't careful, Jordan would take over the interview. 'I understand your wife has been missing since yesterday morning but I'm not even sure what time she was last seen.'

'At approximately quarter past eight,' Jordan said. 'And by me. One of my assistants, Donald Midgley, can verify the time if it's necessary. He was in the house when I said goodbye to Claire before setting off for London.'

'Did she say she might go out later that day?'

'Not specifically. She hadn't been well the previous evening, which would be Sunday, I think.' For a moment, Jordan sounded nonplussed as if the events of the past two days had caused him to lose track of time. 'Yes, Sunday. She was suffering from a migraine and went to bed early. But she insisted on getting up yesterday morning. We had breakfast together and then I left shortly afterwards. When I said goodbye to her, she mentioned she might feel better if she got out in the fresh air but I assumed she meant a little gardening or a walk to the village and back. I left with Midgley and about an hour and a half later, Mrs Leighton, the charlady, arrived and found the house locked and my wife already gone, which was unusual. Claire was always there to let her in. I've already spoken to the woman, by the way, and asked her to wait at the house in case you might want to question her.'

'I assume you've already made some inquiries of your own?' Finch asked.

'Of course, Inspector. I arrived home about quarter past eleven to find the house in darkness and no sign of my wife. I was naturally alarmed. Claire very rarely went out alone in the evenings and besides, her car was still in the garage. Midgley went to look.'

'So Dr Midgley was still with you?'

'Yes. We'd spent the day together in London at my consulting rooms and I asked him in for a night-cap. There was a case history I wanted to discuss with him as well. When I realised my wife wasn't in bed, I searched the house and then went to the village to make inquiries. But no one had seen her. It had started raining by then and I was becoming seriously alarmed. From there, I drove on to the golf club...'

'Why the golf club?'

'Because my wife often walked across the course. I even tried walking part of the way across it myself but gave up. It was too dark to see anything. I might add that the course has since been exhaustively searched by the club groundsmen and my own staff, as well as the clinic grounds, the house itself and the outbuildings. I even asked the vicar to look inside the church. Claire often went there. We've rung the hospitals, the local police stations, any friends or relatives she might have visited but everywhere we've drawn a blank.'

'And so you decided to get in touch with us?' Finch asked in his blandest tone. The business with Davies still rankled and he was determined to find out just how far Jordan had been involved in the string-pulling that had undoubtedly gone on. He saw his answer in the doctor's momentary confusion from which he quickly recovered but not before Finch noticed the gleaming shoes shift their position under the desk. It was an old interviewing technique of his. Never mind their hands or faces. Most intelligent witnesses with something to hide will have those under control but few people are as aware of themselves below the knee and any tension will often express itself in some small involuntary movement of the feet.

'Yes. It was decided this morning when no trace of my wife was found that the police should be called in,' Jordan replied.

It was a nice use of the impersonal construction, Finch thought, and one which confirmed his suspicion: it wasn't Jordan who had caused pressure to be put on Davies but someone else; a patient, no doubt, whose identity Jordan preferred to keep concealed.

'What form will your own inquiries take, Inspector?' Jordan asked, taking the initiative back into his own hands.

'You seem to have already started quite a few lines of investigation yourself which we'll continue,' Finch replied. 'I'd like a description of your wife, of course, and a recent photograph if you have one.'

'I have one here.' Jordan opened the top drawer of his desk and produced a shiny print which he handed over to the Inspector. 'It's a group one, I'm afraid, taken last Christmas. My wife disliked being photographed so I have none of her on her own. She's standing on the far left.'

It had been taken, Finch guessed, by a professional photographer at some official function, for the people in it were grouped tightly together as if to get as many of them as possible into the picture. There were eight in all, taken against a background of patterned draperies, the women in evening dresses, the men in dinner jackets, all except Jordan who, in white tie and tails, was in the centre, dominating the group. The woman on the far left was standing a little apart from the others, smiling timidly as if bidden to do so and clutching a small handbag in front of her with both hands. It was a pleasant face that had, despite the harsh light of the flash bulb which made details stand out very clear and hard, a soft, almost blurred look about the features. The forehead was high with a childlike curve and width to it, the chin small, so that the total effect was of an inverted triangle that had been gently sketched in.

'She's fifty-two,' Jordan was saying. 'About five feet four in height. Grey hair. Grey eyes. No distinguishing features.'

He might have been reading the details from the front page of her passport, Finch thought as he wrote them down in his notebook.

'And the clothes she was wearing when she disappeared?' he asked.

'I can't be absolutely positive on that,' Jordan replied, looking a little embarrassed. 'When I said goodbye to Claire she was still wearing a dressing-gown. I've checked since and I'm quite sure her mackintosh is missing and a brown tweed skirt. What else she had on, in the way of a jumper or blouse, I have no idea. I'm not that knowledgeable about the extent of my wife's wardrobe, Inspector.'

Many men would find themselves in the same position but would not be quite so defensive about it, Finch thought. It was as if Jordan disliked having to admit to any failure on his part.

Out loud he said, 'I'd also like a list of her friends and relatives, including those you've already checked.'

'My secretary, Mrs Ingham, has already typed one out for you at my request,' Jordan replied. 'You may collect it from her in the general office on your way out.'

He had placed his hands on the desk top in readiness to rise, clearly considering the interview over.

'There are a couple more questions,' Finch said, remaining firmly seated. 'Have you any reason for suspecting your wife might have committed suicide?'

Jordan subsided into his chair, his face expressing displeasure.

'Certainly not, Inspector.'

'Or that she might have left you?'

Jordan answered so quickly that Finch did not have time to soften the inquiry with any additional remark.

'That is also impossible.'

'So there was no quarrel or disagreement between you?'

'When I said goodbye to Claire yesterday morning, we parted on perfectly amicable terms,' Jordan replied stiffly.

He had risen completely this time and there was little Finch could do except catch Boyce's eye before getting to his own feet. But he was determined not to be dismissed in quite so magisterial a manner.

'If I need to contact you again . . . ' he began.

'I'm interviewing patients this morning but my secretary can always arrange another meeting. Perhaps you would be good enough to get in touch with her first.'

And that seemed to be that. Jordan was making another of his large gestures, indicating the door and, as they left the room, he had already seated himself again at the desk and was opening one of the folders that lay on the top of it, as if he had dismissed them from his mind as well.

They entered the outer office where Mrs Ingham, Jordan's secretary, was speaking into the telephone and they were able to catch the tail end of the conversation.

'I'm sorry, Mrs Vincent,' she was saying, 'but as I've already explained to you earlier this morning, Dr Jordan is too busy to speak to you. No, there's still no news, I'm afraid.' She glanced up as Boyce and Finch came in and, acknowledging their presence with a brief nod of her head while the telephone quacked angrily, she continued, 'The police are here at this moment. I assure you I'll get in touch with you the moment there is any new information.'

She replaced the receiver briskly as if glad to terminate the conversation and turned to Finch.

'Yes?' she asked.

'Dr Jordan said you have a list of the people Mrs Jordan might have visited,' he replied.

There was no need for her to search her desk. It was lying on the top, neatly typed out. All she had to do was hand it over to him. Efficient, Finch thought, but it didn't cause him to feel any warmer towards her as a woman, even though she smiled at him.

'Thank you,' he said briskly, matching her efficiency with his own and then, with Boyce in tow, he turned away.

4

'What did you make of that?' he asked the sergeant a few minutes later as they walked down the steps of the clinic.

'The interview with Jordan, you mean?' Boyce's thoughts seemed to be elsewhere; on Jordan's secretary, Finch suspected. 'An odd bloke, I thought. We used to have a saying about people like him. "He's got all his goods in the shop window." Clever, of course. He'd have to be, wouldn't he, to run a place like this? But not much warmth. I know if my wife had gone missing, I wouldn't be quite so calm about it.'

'To be fair to the man, he may have already got over the worst of the shock,' Finch pointed out. 'After all, we didn't see him last night. And he'd be trained to keep his own feelings under control. But I know what you mean. Nothing he says or does seems quite spontaneous. You feel even the smile he gives you has been worked out on a percentage basis.'

'So what do we do now?' Boyce asked gloomily. 'There's not much to go on, is there? She went missing between a quarter past eight and half past ten yesterday morning, according to Jordan. She could be anywhere by now; shacked up with a lover in Paris or passing herself off as a Colonel's widow in Bournemouth.'

'Jordan seemed to think it unlikely. He went very cool when I suggested she might have left him.'

'And he didn't take too kindly either to the idea she might have committed suicide.'

'Which doesn't necessarily rule out the possibility she's dead.'

'You think it likely?' Boyce asked.

'I don't know. But assuming she left the house of her own free will some time before the cleaning woman arrived, we've got no

67

evidence exactly where she went. She was on foot; at least she didn't take her own car, but even so in an hour, even half an hour, she could have covered a good distance and that's a hell of a lot of countryside to search. What happened after that is pure speculation but let's run over the possibilities. She could have had an accident and be lying somewhere injured, or dead. Or she could have died from natural causes; a sudden heart attack, say. In both cases she'll be found sooner or later. The third possibility is that she's lost her memory and is wandering about somewhere not knowing who she is or where she's from; more dramatic but it's been known to happen. Then there's abduction; again less likely. She's a middle-aged woman, not the sort that a passing motorist with psychopathic tendencies is likely to take a fancy to but it can't be ruled out. As for deliberate kidnapping, we've no evidence for that unless Jordan's holding out on us which doesn't seem very likely. Finally there's murder, by someone she met while she was out, and it could be for no stronger motive than the money in her handbag. In that case, she could still be found, lying somewhere under the bushes although if she's been buried, even in a shallow grave, it could be months before the body's discovered, if ever.'

They had reached the car and stood talking beside it. Suddenly Finch was aware of being watched. A gardener, hoeing slowly between the rose bushes in one of the formal flower beds, had moved to the other side so that he was now facing them, although he was too far away to hear what they were saying. They were being observed also from the house. A tall, thin, upright figure, dressed in a dark suit, was standing at one of the large windows in the central block, looking down on them with an air of disdainful curiosity like a city businessman watching workmen dig a hole in the road.

'Take the car, Tom,' Finch said, coming quickly to a decision. 'Drive round the village for ten minutes. I'll meet you outside Jordan's house. I'll walk there; I need to stretch my legs, get a breath of fresh air.'

It wasn't the only reason. He wanted to be alone to absorb the feel of the place and sniff up the atmosphere which wouldn't be possible with Boyce present, discussing the case.

The sergeant seemed to accept the excuse, for he got into the car and made off towards the main gates, leaving Finch to follow on foot.

5

For a short distance he kept to the main drive but as soon as he was out of sight of the house, he turned off among the trees, walking with apparent aimlessness, his hands deep in his pockets, his shoulders hunched against the wind which, despite the bright, clear sunshine, had a chill edge to it.

The wood, if that was the right name for it, was one of those mixtures of part natural, part man-made landscapes which surround many large country houses, the indigenous trees like oak and ash being interplanted with more ornamental species. In places, the ground between them was left open to form grassy glades in which primroses, celandines and the fragile white wood anemones were growing. Bluebells, not yet in flower, formed close patches of green leaves, so dense that he was forced to trample across them, hearing the stems crush juicily under his feet.

Elsewhere, the wood thickened into undergrowth, with the same variety of wild and cultivated bushes, blackthorn giving way to rhododendrons, between which narrow paths twisted this way and that. Occasionally Finch stopped in front of one of the more massive evergreens and parted the branches to peer underneath. Jordan had been quite adamant that the clinic grounds had been thoroughly searched but, even so, it would be very easy to miss a body that had been concealed under one of them.

A body. It was, of course, too early in the case to make such an assumption. As he himself had explained to Boyce, there were many other possibilities that would have to be investigated. And yet, without quite knowing why, he was convinced that the face he had seen in the photograph was that of a dead woman. Perhaps it was the blurred image that gave him this impression; or some quality about the bright, thin sunlight that was falling between the trees that made him think of death; ridiculous and irrational though it seemed. Spring was, after all, a symbol of life and new beginnings.

He had been walking in the general direction of the Jordans' house and, hearing a car approach, he cut back towards the drive just as Boyce turned in through the gates and drew up outside.

6

They approached the house together, up a broad, flagged path to an imposing front door where Finch banged on the knocker. It was answered by a short, plump, middle-aged woman, dressed in a blue nylon overall, who said with common-sensical brevity, 'I suppose you're the police. Dr Jordan said you'd be coming,' before showing them into the hall. 'No news of Mrs Jordan?' she continued as they stepped inside.

'I'm afraid not,' Finch replied.

Her pleasant features showed immediate concern.

'But she's been gone now for hours and it's not like her . . .'

'Isn't it?' Finch asked comfortably. 'That's something I'd like to discuss with you, Mrs Leighton; her habits, her routine, where she was likely to go. You probably know her better than most people.'

It was a bit of harmless flattery that she seemed to respond to for she smiled at them both before opening a door that led off the hall into a small sitting-room.

'Dr Jordan said I was to make coffee for you when you came. Would you like it now? Or would you rather look over the house first? It's up to you. Answer any questions they ask you, he said, and let them see round the place.'

'I think coffee first,' Finch replied and Boyce nodded in agreement.

'I'll fetch it then,' Mrs Leighton replied. 'Make yourselves at home.'

The room was bright and pleasantly furnished; a woman's room, Finch decided, looking round at the cream chintz patterned with sprigs of yellow flowers and the high, old-fashioned mantelpiece which was crowded with the kind of knick-knacks that women collect: small objects in ivory, glass and silver; a crystal rose in a miniature vase, a box only a few inches square inlaid with mother-of-pearl.

It seemed to be intended also for general use, for there was a gate-legged table under the window while an easy chair stood beside the fireplace. A rosewood bureau, too fragile to suit most men, occupied one of the chimney alcoves.

'We always have our coffee in here, me and Mrs Jordan,' Mrs Leighton said, entering with a tray which she put down on the table. 'It's her sitting-room really, although she and the doctor would have their breakfast in here together. I don't think she ever used the big drawing-room except when they had guests.'

'So she'd usually be at home when you came?' Finch asked, accepting a cup of coffee and helping himself from the sugar bowl which she had passed to him.

'Always. I've never known her not to be unless she'd gone to London for the day and then she'd always tell me the day before. Not that she went all that often and it was usually to visit her sister, Mrs Vincent.'

The name seemed familiar to Finch and then he remembered where he had heard it. Jordan's secretary, Mrs Ingham, had been speaking on the telephone to a Mrs Vincent when they had emerged from the doctor's consulting room. It had been clear, too, from the overheard conversation that Jordan had not wanted to speak to his sister-in-law. Finch wondered why.

'Were they close as sisters?' he asked, feeling his way carefully.

'Not very,' Mrs Leighton replied. 'They kept in touch, mind you. Like I said, Mrs Jordan would go up to London to see her three or four times a year but I've never known Mrs Vincent come down here.'

'When was the last time Mrs Jordan went to see her?' Finch asked.

'About a month ago, I think. I remember her telling me she

71

and Rose had met for lunch. Why? Has Mrs Jordan gone to her sister's?' Mrs Leighton asked quickly.

'No. Dr Jordan's checked and I gather she isn't there. Nor at any of her friends'.'

'She hadn't many,' Mrs Leighton admitted. 'No one really close, I mean. There's a few in the village that she sees from time to time, Mrs Woodham, the vicar's wife, for instance. They go shopping together in Lemchurch from time to time but that's all. I think she looks forward to me coming every morning. It's a bit of company for her.'

'Can you tell me a little about your routine here?' Finch asked.

'There's not much to tell. I always arrive at half past ten and make a start on the cleaning; then we'd have coffee together in here, because there's nowhere to sit down in the kitchen; after that I get a bit more done and generally leave about twelve for the clinic. I help out there until four o'clock. I'm only part-time, you see. I've got my own family, my husband and three sons, to see after.'

It sounded more like a full-time job to Finch, although he didn't say so. Instead, he asked, 'And Mrs Jordan? What would she do?'

'While I was here? Well, she'd perhaps arrange the flowers or clean the silver. She liked sewing, too; embroidery, dressmaking, things like that. Sometimes she'd do a bit of gardening although one of the groundsmen from the clinic was sent down once a week to cut the grass.'

It seemed a limited life to Finch. All the work in the place appeared to be done by others and yet Mrs Jordan had contrived to fill her time somehow. He wondered how bored she had been.

'And the afternoons?' he asked.

'I wasn't here to see,' Mrs Leighton replied. 'But she's spoken about taking the car into Lemchurch to change her library books or to do some shopping. Then there was the church flowers; she's on the rota for doing those. She liked walking, too, I do know that. She'd tell me the next day. "It was lovely over the golf course," she'd say. Or, "Have you seen the primroses out in the woods?" Not that I have time to look.'

'Do you know anywhere else she might walk to?'

Mrs Leighton looked doubtful.

'She never went far; she tires easily. But there's one or two nice places round here she could go to, Hangar Hill for instance. Or Barton Mill on the river. Come to think of it, she did mention once seeing a kingfisher and you get those by water, don't you?'

As he asked the next question, Finch noticed Boyce was making a discreet note of the place names.

'I'd like to move on now, Mrs Leighton, to the last time you saw Mrs Jordan, which would be Friday. How did she seem?'

'Much the same as usual. Nothing out of the ordinary.'

'Not depressed?'

'No. Quiet, but then she always is. She's never been one to chat about herself.'

'What did you talk about?'

Mrs Leighton shrugged.

'Nothing special. The normal things; the garden; something she'd seen on T.V. the previous evening; my family. She always asks after them. That was about all.'

It all sounded very innocuous.

'And yesterday?'

'I arrived at the usual time and found the back door locked and bolted, so I had to let myself in at the front. There was no sign of Mrs Jordan anywhere and no note to say where she'd gone. I thought it a bit odd but as it looked like she'd left in a hurry, I didn't pay all that much attention.'

'What gave you that impression?' Finch asked, trying not to look too eager.

'Small things, really. With anybody else I wouldn't have thought anything of it but I've been coming here for five years now so I know Mrs Jordan's routine. For a start, the breakfast things were still in here on the table. Usually she takes them through to the kitchen and leaves them on the draining-board for me. Then there was her nightdress and dressing-gown lying across the bed. She's never done that before. They're usually put away.'

'Anything else?' Finch asked.

'I can't think of anything.'

'What about clothes?' Finch asked, moving on to a new line of inquiry. 'Dr Jordan wasn't sure what she was wearing when she left the house. When he last saw her she was still in her dressing-gown but he thinks her mackintosh has gone and a tweed skirt. He's not certain what else is missing.'

'I could look upstairs,' Mrs Leighton offered. 'Not that I know exactly all she owns. I can tell you one thing, though – she wasn't wearing her walking shoes; not the comfortable ones, that is.'

It was a small point that could be useful and Finch looked interested.

'How do you know that?' he asked.

'Because I saw them yesterday morning when I got the vacuum cleaner out. I can show you if you like.'

They followed her into the hall where she opened a cupboard under the stairs.

'That's where she keeps her mac; you can see it's gone from the peg. And through here,' she continued, leading the way into the kitchen, 'is where she always leaves her shoes.'

She opened a door at the far end of the narrow kitchen, full of functional-looking units, to reveal a walk-in storage space used to house the larger items of household equipment, like the ironing-board and a step-ladder. Just inside, standing neatly side by side on a piece of folded newspaper, were a pair of women's brogue shoes, a little shabby but still good enough for country walks.

'She always puts them in here,' Mrs Leighton explained. 'It saves her bringing any mud through the house if it's wet underfoot.'

'What shoes would she be likely to wear if not those?' Finch asked.

'She's got other flat-heeled ones she puts on if she goes into Lemchurch in the car. She can't drive in high heels. I could go and see what's been taken from her wardrobe if you like.'

'Yes, if you wouldn't mind,' Finch replied. 'And while you're there, you might check if any other clothes are missing. And a suitcase.'

Mrs Leighton seemed about to say something and then

changed her mind. Instead, she nodded briefly to Finch and left the kitchen.

7

As soon as she had gone, Finch turned to Boyce.

'I'll follow her upstairs,' he said. 'I have the feeling she clammed up on us suddenly and I want to find out why. While I'm talking to her, Tom, have a look round down here, especially that small bureau in the breakfast room. It looks as if it belongs to Mrs Jordan. Meanwhile, I'll try to keep Mrs Leighton for as long as possible to give you time for the search.'

'Right,' Boyce agreed and they walked back to the hall, the sergeant entering the breakfast-room while Finch mounted the stairs.

They ascended on to a long landing, containing several doors, one of which was ajar and, as Finch pushed it open, he found himself in a large bedroom, furnished in much the same style as Jordan's office, with elaborate draperies and expensive-looking furniture; burr walnut this time, highly polished and fitted with gilt handles. Mrs Leighton was on the far side of the room, searching through a fitted wardrobe which occupied almost the entire wall, the free space being taken up by another door. Finch strolled casually over to it and opened it. Beyond was another bedroom, much smaller and quite different in style, with a single divan bed, a chest of drawers and a modern desk standing under the window, a revolving office chair in front of it and a set of adjustable shelves on the wall to the right, full of files and folders. On the desk itself was a portable typewriter, an anglepoise lamp and a small tape recorder with several cassettes piled up beside it. The top one was labelled 'Friday March 22nd', a few days before Mrs Jordan's disappearance.

He moved away, stopping to turn back the cover on the bed. On the pillow, neatly folded, were a pair of men's dark blue silk pyjamas. Replacing the cover and smoothing it down, he returned to the main bedroom where Mrs Leighton was going systematically through the hanging clothes, pushing each one aside as she checked it.

There was a change in her attitude, Finch noticed. The air of pleasant co-operation had gone and her face had a closed look about it.

'Can you tell me what's missing?' he asked.

'A tweed skirt,' she replied, 'and a pair of flat brown suede shoes. I think there's a green woollen blouse gone, too, but I can't be sure.'

'Anything else?'

'No, I don't think so. Her best coat's still here, and suits and dresses that I've seen her wearing.'

'What about luggage?'

Mrs Leighton pressed her lips together as if expressing disapproval and pointed to the top shelf where a set of matching suitcases was lined up.

'It's all there, as far as I know from the last time I gave the wardrobe a good cleaning out.'

'So it doesn't look as if Mrs Jordan has left her husband, does it?' Finch asked pleasantly. He saw the colour rise in her cheeks and she avoided his eyes, looking down at the carpet, her hands clasped together in front of her in the attitude of a respectful servant. She had probably been in service at some time in her life, Finch decided, where she had learnt this self-effacing stance which wasn't natural to her.

'How long have they been sleeping in separate rooms?' he continued and when she hesitated, he added more sharply, 'Come on, Mrs Leighton. You must know. You make the beds.'

'About a year,' she admitted in a low voice.

'So they weren't on good terms?'

'I didn't say that,' she retorted. 'The way Mrs Jordan put it to me, the doctor had a lot of work to do in the evening. That's why he moved into the dressing-room. He didn't want to disturb her.'

'But they weren't happy?'

'I don't know about *him*,' she replied, with an odd emphasis on the last word. 'And Mrs Jordan never said anything directly to me about her marriage but yes, I got the impression she wasn't very happy. He was often out in the evenings or away on business. She seemed lonely, as if she didn't know what to do with her time.'

'Did you ever hear her mention any men by name while you were here?'

'No, and if you're suggesting she might have run off with someone, I won't believe it,' Mrs Leighton said with an unexpected touch of spirit. 'She wasn't the sort.'

That remained to be seen, Finch thought. Out loud, he asked, 'Did she receive any phone calls while you were here?'

'Only from people like the vicar's wife.'

'Or letters?'

'They came before I got here,' Mrs Leighton replied. She had grown more distressed as the interview continued and now, with a little burst of emotion, she added, 'I can't tell you much because I don't know. I like her and I feel sorry for her. But she never confided in me. Mrs Hart, the housekeeper at the clinic, may be able to tell you more. She and Mrs Jordan were friendly. Or her sister. You ask them!'

Finch had already decided that Mrs Vincent would be worth a visit and, from what Mrs Leighton had just said, Mrs Hart, too. 'Can I go now?' Mrs Leighton was asking. 'I've got my work to finish. I haven't made a start yet on the kitchen.'

'Yes, of course,' Finch said in a kindly voice.

At the door, she turned, her eyes very bright.

'You'll find her?' she asked.

'I hope so,' Finch replied.

8

He waited until she had gone downstairs before searching the rest of the upper floor, which didn't take long. There was one other bedroom, with its own adjoining bathroom, for guests, he assumed; both empty of any personal possessions. Next to it was a smaller room which seemed to be used partly for sewing, partly as a store, for a dressmaker's dummy stood next to a table on which was an electric sewing machine while trunks and boxes containing back copies of medical magazines were piled up in one corner.

Coming out on to the landing, he paused to listen for a moment. Judging by the noises downstairs, Mrs Leighton was cleaning the kitchen and, satisfied, he returned to the main bedroom where he began a hurried search of the cupboards and drawers which contained nothing more interesting than clothes.

Jordan's own room wasn't of much more use to him either. The desk was locked and the files were too numerous to examine in detail although the few he opened at random seemed to contain only reports on patients or papers relating to the clinic.

He turned back to the desk. The top cassette which he had noticed when he had first entered the room seemed worth a try and, carefully closing the intervening door, he slipped it into the tape recorder and switched it on. But that, too, was a disappointment for it contained nothing of a personal nature, only Jordan's voice dictating letters and a few telephone calls made to the clinic which presumably Mrs Ingham had recorded for Jordan to play back later. Her own comments were interspersed among them, informing Jordan of any action she had taken concerning them.

The tape came to an end and Finch, having run it back again, replaced it on top of the pile. It seemed likely that the other cassettes contained the same kind of material, hardly useful to the present inquiry.

That left only one more room to examine, the Jordan's own bathroom next door, and there wasn't much there either although Finch poked about in the cabinet for several minutes before finally closing the door with a thoughtful look on his face.

He returned to the landing and was about to descend the stairs when his attention was caught by the sight of a man whom he could see through the window facing him. He was approaching the cottage from the direction of the clinic, walking hesitantly, his face turned towards the house, but when he reached the garage he paused and then, with a sudden change of mind, made off towards the woods, averting his gaze and breaking into a rapid stride.

Finch was too far inside the house for the man to have seen him. Indeed his own view was limited by the distance but he had the clear impression of a slight figure, dark-haired and thin-faced with narrow shoulders under a light grey overcoat, before the man disappeared round the corner of the house.

The brief scene had been interesting, he thought, as he continued on down the stairs. Whoever it was, and it was likely to be someone from the clinic, either a patient or a member of the staff, he had clearly intended calling at the house and then had had second thoughts. Why? Had the sight of the police car parked outside frightened him away? But whatever the reason, Finch was determined that, on his next visit to Hawton Hall, he would make it his business to discover the identity of the man.

9

Boyce was still in the breakfast room when he entered, turning over the bottom drawer of the bureau.

'I've been through the rest of the house,' he said, 'and found nothing that's useful to us. And there's not a lot here either, mostly receipts, her account book and some business letters. In fact, the only personal item is this.'

He handed over a small, blue, leather-bound diary to the Inspector who flicked over the pages quickly. Most of them were blank but here and there an entry had been made in a tiny, pointed handwriting. Many appeared at regular intervals; 'Church-flwrs' was one and seemed to refer to Mrs Jordan's turn on the rota to decorate the church. A fortnightly visit to the hairdresser's was also noted down. Apart from occasional guests to dinner and, from time to time, a meeting for coffee with a Mrs W., whom Finch took to be the vicar's wife, Mrs Woodham, of whom Mrs Leighton had spoken, Mrs Jordan's time seemed to be largely empty of appointments.

There was, however, one page, dated a month previously, where an entry was more detailed and Finch read it carefully. 'Lunch R. 1.15 Hrrds,' it said. And below it, 'Appts. Dent. 11.30. M.R. 3.00'.

Holding the diary in one hand, he took from his pocket the typewritten list that Mrs Ingham had given him. R., he decided, could possibly refer to Mrs Rose Vincent, Mrs Jordan's sister, and the date, too, suggested this was correct. Mrs Leighton had mentioned that Mrs Jordan had gone to London to visit her about a month before and they had met for lunch.

The entry could now be deciphered up to a point. Mrs Jordan had lunched with her sister, presumably at Harrods, judging by the abbreviation, having first had what appeared to be a dental appointment. She had then gone on to keep another appointment with someone with the initials M.R.

He consulted the list again. There was no one whose name began with those letters and, turning to Boyce, he said,

'See if you can find an address book anywhere, Tom. There may be one on the table by the telephone.'

The sergeant returned shortly with a red-bound book which he gave to the Inspector who turned to the section marked R. But there was no one there either with those initials.

'Found something?' Boyce asked, looking over his shoulder.

'No, and that's the point. Mrs Jordan went to London about a month ago, to see her sister. Judging by the entry in her diary she also had two other appointments on the same day, one with her dentist, another in the afternoon with someone she refers to as M.R. And yet the name's not written down in the address book or on the list that Jordan's secretary gave me, and I find that strange. It suggests she wanted to keep it a secret but why I don't know.' While he was speaking, he was turning over more pages. 'Look here, her hairdresser's listed and her dentist; a chiropodist in Lemchurch; her optician. So why not M.R.?'

'Perhaps Jordan will know,' Boyce suggested.

'It's possible but I'm inclined not to ask him at this stage. There are one or two other points I'd like cleared up before I see Jordan again, mainly concerning his marriage. He and his wife

80

were sleeping apart and, according to Mrs Leighton, Mrs Jordan wasn't very happy.'

'Which might suggest she's left him,' Boyce pointed out.

'I don't think so. She appears to have taken no clothes, except the ones she was wearing, and there's no luggage missing either. And I'm equally not convinced that she went out for a walk. The shoes she normally wore are still here. There's something else that's puzzling me, too. According to Jordan, his wife had a migraine on Sunday and went to bed early and yet when I looked in the bathroom cabinet, there was nothing in the way of pain-killers, not even aspirin.'

'Perhaps she disliked taking tablets. Some women do.'

'It could be,' Finch agreed, 'and that's something else Jordan may be able to verify. But first I want to chat with someone about their relationship and Mrs Jordan's sister seems the best person to ask. I'll ring her now and try to make an appointment for this afternoon.'

He used the telephone in the hall, keeping his voice low so as not to be overheard by Mrs Leighton. The call was taken by Mrs Vincent herself who seemed eager to see him.

'Of course,' she said when he suggested the meeting. 'I'll be at home all afternoon. You know the address?'

'Yes,' Finch replied.

'And there's still no news of my sister?'

'I'm afraid not.'

For a moment, he thought she would try to keep him in conversation but all she said was, 'We'll discuss it when I see you,' before ringing off.

'That's fixed up then,' Finch explained, returning to the breakfast-room. 'While I'm in London, Tom, could you deal with this end of the investigation? Go down Mrs Ingham's list and chat with all Mrs Jordan's local contacts. Get them gossiping about her if you can but play down the inquiry as much as possible. As far as the people in the village are concerned we're a couple of coppers on a routine Missing Persons case. I don't want it generally known at this stage that we're from headquarters. When you've done that, get McCallum to do a blow-up of Mrs Jordan's face and run off some copies.' He handed over the photograph that Jordan had given him. 'I'd like them as soon as possible. We may need them to hand out at bus and train stations, together with a description of the clothes she was wearing.'

'Right,' Boyce said. 'What about the people at the clinic? Do you want me to start interviewing any of them?'

'No. I'll deal with that end of it myself,' Finch replied. 'I want to get a look at them. There was a man hanging about outside a little while ago. You didn't happen to catch a glimpse of him, did you? Medium height, thin, wearing a light-coloured coat? He seemed to be making for the house and then he cleared off into the woods.'

'I didn't see anyone,' Boyce replied. 'You reckon it was someone from the clinic?'

'Could be. He came from that direction. Anyway, I'd like to check for myself. But I think it can be safely left until tomorrow.'

It was a decision that later he was bitterly to regret.

Part Four

1

Langham House where Rose Vincent lived was a large block of mansion flats in St. John's Wood, built in the '30s of white stone and set back from the road behind carefully maintained lawns and shrubberies. Approaching it, with its curved glass and balconies, Finch was reminded of the setting of an old, pre-war Fred Astaire and Ginger Rogers' movie, although the iron lanterns on brick plinths on either side of the entrance gates were pure English stately home; MGM tempered by NW8.

A gilt lift bore him upward to the third floor where he emerged into a wide, close-carpeted corridor, lit only by wall-lamps, the atmosphere of which seemed oddly dense as if the air had already been breathed many times before, and quite silent except for the subdued pneumatic gasp of the lift doors closing as it was called to another floor.

He was not sure what he expected Rose Vincent to look like. A little dated perhaps, to fit in with the style of the building. Certainly not the smart, contemporary, rather hard-faced woman who answered the door.

She was dressed in close-fitting black velvet trousers and a loose top of finely-pleated bright pink silk which swayed round her at every movement, and was hung about with gold chains and bracelets which added their own tinkling chime to the rustle of silk. Her hair, auburn-tinted, Finch suspected, for surely that rich red gloss could not possibly be natural, was as expensive-looking as her clothes and jewellery. There was something foreign and exotic in her appearance although Finch could see a likeness to her sister. She had similar small features and a narrow chin although none of Claire Jordan's softness and diffidence. Rose Vincent was totally self-assured.

'Chief Inspector Finch?' she asked in the harsh voice he had heard over the telephone and showed him into a sitting-room which reflected the same sumptuous and over-decorated taste that she applied to her own person, so that for a moment Finch's attention was distracted by the sheer volume of objects that surrounded him. It was obvious that Rose Vincent liked to display her wealth in the tangible forms of Impressionist paintings, modern glass and antique silver and, not only to have her possessions about her, but to emphasise their presence in the room so that, although the spring sunshine was pouring in through the huge, curved windows, the lights over the paintings and display cabinets were switched on, their artificial brightness making the sunlight seem mean and pallid.

'Sit down,' she told him brusquely and, as Finch perched himself modestly on a small, fat sofa covered with slippery pale blue satin, she added, 'I assume there's still no news?'

'I'm afraid not,' Finch admitted. 'I was hoping you might know something of Mrs Jordan's whereabouts.'

'You think I might be hiding her?' Rose Vincent asked with a directness that he found refreshing although a little intimidating. She was not the type to suffer fools gladly. 'Well, you're wrong although, if she had come to me, I'd've gladly taken her in. But I have absolutely no idea where she might have gone.'

'How often did you see her?'

'Three or four times a year, that's all. We were never very close, even as children, although I'm very fond of Claire. We're two entirely different people and, after she married Howard, we seemed to have even less in common.'

'I wanted to ask about her marriage,' Finch said boldly. It seemed better to treat her with the same directness with which she approached him. 'Could it be a reason for her disappearance?'

'You think she might have run away from Howard?' Rose Vincent seemed amused at the possibility. 'It would serve him right if she had. She could have done but I don't think it's likely.'

'Why not?'

'Because she loved him. And because she's intensely loyal.'

'But she wasn't happy?' Finch offered tentatively.

'No, I don't think she was. She rarely spoke directly about her marriage, at least not for years, but I could read between the lines. Before they moved out of London, I used to visit them occasionally and it didn't take more than half an eye to see what was going on. Howard's an intellectual bully. He needs someone to put down. In that way, he rises; at least in his own estimation. Other men might use a dog for the same reason. "Sit," they say, or "Heel". And the poor bastard obeys immediately. It gives them some sort of kick to know that they're the masters. Howard uses Claire for just the same purpose. She is his creature.'

'And she accepts it?' Finch asked. Having seen Howard Jordan for himself, he did not doubt that there was some truth in her statement although how far her personal dislike of Jordan coloured her judgement it was difficult to say.

'Of course. She has to. The marriage wouldn't have lasted this long if she'd objected. Besides, it was what she was used to. Our parents' marriage was very similar. My father was a country rector, a good-looking man with too high an opinion of his own rightness. Listening to him in church on a Sunday, you'd've thought that God himself was a bit of an amateur who needed a little timely advice on occasions. I used to call him "Our Father".' She smiled wryly at the memory. 'Claire is very like my mother in temperament. She, too, was a quiet, self-effacing woman who saw herself as secondary in the relationship. It was probably why Claire married Howard. She needs a man like father in order to play the only role she knew, that of the squaw.'

'And you?' he asked curiously.

She laughed abruptly.

'Me? Oh, I got out of it as soon as I could. There's nothing masochistic about me. I married a bookmaker's runner in the days before betting was legal and got cut off without the proverbial shilling. But it was a good marriage; much better than my parents'. I think that's what annoyed my father most. I should have been punished by being poor and unhappy. Instead of which, Wally and I flourished like the green bay tree.' She raised a ringed hand to indicate the richness of her surroundings. 'It obviously angered him because he referred to it in his will, Our Father's voice coming from beyond the grave with the same note of self-righteousness and condemnation I'd heard as a child. "To my eldest daughter, Rose, I leave my forgiveness for the sin of ingratitude, knowing she is more in need of it than any other bequest I could make".'

'So your sister inherited?' Finch asked, wondering if this could be a factor in Claire Jordan's disappearance. With money of her own she could, as Boyce had suggested, have made a new life for herself somewhere else.

'Yes. It wasn't a huge sum, ten thousand pounds, but enough to set Howard up in private practice. He'd been working in a London hospital before then which was where he met Claire. She was the almoner's secretary and when they married neither of them had much money. But Howard's always been ambitious, due probably to his own background.' Finch cocked an inquisitive eyebrow and she continued, speaking in terse, rapid sentences, 'Only child of a widowed mother who thought the sun shone out of the seat of his trousers; intelligent; fought his way into medical school on scholarships; tough as they come under the charm and determined to make it to the top. The National Health Service wasn't going to satisfy him for long. Claire's money came at just the right time. He was able to put up his own plate and start milking a few fat private patients. Of course, it was a struggle to begin with. Claire used to act as his secretary and receptionist until the practice really got off the ground. He needed her then. He doesn't need her now and that's largely the trouble. He's made her feel useless.'

'Yes,' Finch agreed. He could imagine the situation quite clearly. From what he had learned from Mrs Leighton and from his perusal of Claire Jordan's diary, her life was empty of almost anything of value except for arranging the church flowers, hairdresser's appointments, the occasional trip to London.

'In my opinion, it was deliberate,' Rose Vincent continued. 'I think Howard resented the fact that at the beginning his success had been dependent on Claire's money. It took away his self-esteem. And so he punished her. Not obviously. Howard's too clever for that. But I can guess what form it took from what I know of my parents' marriage – the small criticisms that, over the years, eat away at a woman's confidence; the increasing neglect because *his* time is much too valuable to be wasted on something as trivial as an evening at home. It takes a very strong-minded and self-confident woman not to be affected by that treatment and Claire isn't the sort to stand up for herself. Over the years I've watched her become more and more hesitant and apologetic. And, God forgive me, I've been angry with her myself for letting it happen!'

'You last saw her at the end of February, I believe?' Finch asked. 'She made a note in her diary which could refer to a meeting she had with you.'

'Yes, that's right. She'd come to London for a dental appointment. She still preferred to go to the Harley Street dentist who'd always treated her when they lived in London. I met her for lunch at Harrods.'

'How did she seem?'

'Much as usual.'

'She said nothing to suggest she was more unhappy than normal or that she was thinking of doing anything out of the ordinary?'

'Like leaving Howard? Or were you thinking of suicide, Inspector?' Rose Vincent asked sharply.

'It's a possibility that I must bear in mind.'

'It's quite out of the question. Don't forget Claire's a rector's daughter. She has a highly developed sense of sin. She would never commit the crime of killing herself.'

She seemed as adamant as Jordan had been at the same suggestion.

'Besides,' Rose Vincent continued, 'she's lived with the same situation for years. In many ways it was self-chosen. Why should she suddenly decide to put an end to it?'

Finch could think of any number of reasons but he said nothing except, 'So you noticed nothing unusual in her behaviour when you saw her in February?'

Rose Vincent leaned forward to take a cigarette from a green onyx box that was lying on the low table in front of her and lit it with a matching lighter before settling back against the cushions. Finch was aware that she was watching him closely through the smoke; a hard, level scrutiny which told him that

Rose Vincent had used those few seconds to decide not to confide in him.

'Nothing that could possibly explain her disappearance and that's the truth,' she replied.

It might well be, Finch thought. After all, she had every reason for wishing her sister to be found. But she was holding something back, a realisation that made him ask the next question more sharply.

'Do the initials M.R. mean anything to you?'

She looked genuinely puzzled.

'No. I don't think I know anyone that they'd fit. Why?'

'Because your sister seems to have had an appointment with someone she refers to in her diary as M.R. after she had lunched with you at Harrods.'

'Really? Well, she is a dark horse.' To his surprise, Rose Vincent seemed amused and even gratified by this piece of information. 'Whoever could she have been meeting? She said nothing about it to me. In fact, when we parted after lunch, she gave me the impression that she was going straight to Liverpool Street Station to catch a train home, although, now I come to think about it, there was something odd about the way she behaved.'

'How exactly?'

'We came out of Harrods together and I offered to share a taxi with her part of the way. I'd some shopping to do in the West End and the taxi could have dropped me off in Regent Street before taking her on. She became quite flustered when I suggested it and insisted on going alone. I assumed at the time that she was anxious about missing her train and preferred to go directly to the station. I could tell she was upset, though. She dropped her gloves as she was getting into the taxi and the driver had to wait while she picked them up. Nervousness always makes Claire clumsy.'

'Did you happen to hear what address she gave the driver?'

'Unfortunately, no. By that time, I'd called my own cab and hers was driving off.'

It might be possible to trace it, Finch thought. It was an inquiry their liaison officer at the Yard could follow up.

'Do you think whoever she was going to meet, this M.R.,

could have anything to do with Claire's disappearance?' Rose Vincent was asking.

'I'm not sure,' Finch confessed. 'We haven't been able to trace the person yet although I must admit that I find it a little strange that she kept the meeting so secret.'

'You think she might have had a lover?'

There was such a note of irony in her voice that Finch was prompted to remark, 'You seem to find it unlikely.'

'Highly. Claire's the last person on earth to be unfaithful to her husband. Like Caesar's wife, she's above suspicion and not just because Howard wouldn't have tolerated infidelity but because Claire would have found it unthinkable.'

'And what about Caesar himself?' Finch asked.

'He's had affairs; one or two when they were living in London that I knew of or at least had my suspicions about. All very discreet, of course. A man in his position can't afford to play the field too openly. I don't know what he gets up to these days. Since they moved to the clinic, I haven't seen him. He could have reformed although I very much doubt it. He's the type who needs admiration and, quite frankly, I can't imagine Claire ever satisfied him sexually.'

Again, she gave him the hard, direct glance which told him that, despite her apparent frankness, she wasn't being entirely honest with him.

'They've been sleeping apart,' Finch admitted, hoping that this disclosure might prompt her to further confession but she merely replied in her brusque voice,

'It doesn't surprise me in the least.'

Finch waited but she said nothing more and, after a moment, he continued with the routine questioning.

'Do you know of any friends she might be staying with?'

'No, none that I can think of. Claire had few people she was close to. I'm sorry I can't help you but if she should turn up here, I'll let you know straight away.'

As she showed him to the door, she added unexpectedly, 'Not that I think she will. In my opinion something's happened to her and you won't have to look far to find who's to blame – my charming brother-in-law, Howard. You check on him, Chief

Inspector. Find out what he was doing when Claire went missing.'

The implication was only too clear although, as he thanked her and left, it seemed to him unlikely that her theory could be correct. If Midgley supported Jordan's statement, it would appear he had a convincing alibi for the time of his wife's disappearance.

2

'Any news?' Donald Midgley asked, entering the private drawing-room where the others, Eunice Hart, Hannah Kerr and Janet Ingham, were already seated. It was six o'clock, off-duty time, and the relief and exhaustion was apparent in all their faces after a day's work on top of the previous night's exertions.

'Of Claire Jordan you mean?' Hannah Kerr asked with a lazy indifference. She was lying back in one of the armchairs, her legs stretched out in front of her, a cigarette that she seemed too tired to raise to her lips dribbling smoke between her fingers. Opposite her, across the fireplace, Janet Ingham sat crouched in her chair. She looked ill, Donald Midgley thought, her usually pretty features blurred and indistinct, the shining hair slipping loose from its immaculate coil.

Eunice Hart rose heavily to her feet and crossed the room to close the folding doors of the adjoining staff dining-room where one of the kitchen helpers was laying the table. Her profile was tight-lipped and disapproving. Midgley was surprised to see her there at all. Eunice rarely joined them for a pre-dinner sherry and he assumed that she, too, must be feeling the effects of the loss of sleep.

He saw Hannah Kerr watching her with a sardonic expression and when Eunice resumed her seat, she asked in a deliberately taunting voice, 'Not in front of the servants, Eunice? But surely it's too late now? I've heard them myself, gossiping about Claire. It's quite made their day.'

Eunice Hart flushed angrily and, embarrassed at having raised the topic in the first place, Midgley went over to the side table where the sherry decanter was standing to pour himself a drink. He knew Hannah in this mood and he didn't like it.

It was, surprisingly, Janet Ingham who responded, her voice taut and shrill.

'For God's sake, Hannah, don't stir things up. It's bad enough as it is. All of us have been up half the night and I've had Claire's sister on the phone most of the morning, demanding to know what's happening. And now the police are here, they're bound to start questioning everybody.'

'Not here in the clinic, if Howard has his way,' Hannah Kerr replied. She sat up and looked more alert as if pleased at having provoked a response in somebody. 'He's taking the line that as she disappeared from home, none of the patients are to be interviewed.'

'But what about us?' Janet Ingham demanded. There was a note of near hysteria in her voice.

Midgley stood drinking his sherry at the side table, keeping aloof from the three women. For the first time since his arrival he was able to observe them objectively, without feeling disadvantaged by the fact that they had been longer in the place than he had. He had always thought of them before as a group, working together, himself the outsider and newcomer. Now he was aware of the frictions and jealousies that divided them. Jordan's absence, too, made the situation worse. He had gone to London unexpectedly that afternoon and, without his presence, the petty professional squabbles were beginning to surface, exacerbated by exhaustion and the tension caused by Mrs Jordan's disappearance.

'Oh, I expect they'll question us sooner or later,' Hannah Kerr drawled. She seemed to take a cool, malicious pleasure in the remark. 'They'll want to know when we saw Claire last and what our relationship with her was like. If that's what's worrying you, Janet, I can see your problem.'

'I was never openly rude to her,' Janet Ingham retorted defiantly.

Hannah Kerr smiled at her.

'As I was at times? No, I don't think you were. On the other hand, you always managed to make her feel *de trop*. I don't think she liked you very much.'

'The same could equally be said about you!'

'I agree. But the difference between us, my dear Janet, is that I don't mind admitting it while you so obviously do. Eunice, on the other hand, was always totally blameless. What's it like, Eunice, to have such a crystal-clear conscience? Do tell us.'

Eunice Hart looked flustered at the direct question.

'Me? I felt sorry for her at times. She was a thoroughly nice woman, I thought.'

'*Nice*!' Hannah Kerr exclaimed. 'For God's sake, Eunice, is that all you can find to say about her! Yes, she was *nice*. She was also an exasperatingly weak woman; a fool who should have asserted herself more often. But I assume it's too late now for any of us to make amends, including Howard.'

There was a whiff of heresy about the last remark which added to Midgley's discomfort and he placed his sherry glass down on the table, preparatory to adding some comment of his own which would take some of the bitterness out of the situation, when Janet Ingham forestalled him by bursting unexpectedly into tears.

'Oh, God, Hannah!' she cried. 'You don't really think she's dead?'

It was Eunice Hart who stepped forward.

'That's quite enough,' she said sharply, in a tone of authority. 'We don't know yet what's happened to Claire. She could be safe and well somewhere. It's my belief she's lost her memory.'

She crossed the room to stand solicitously beside Janet's chair.

'You look quite worn out. Would you like me to get you a tranquilliser from the medical room?'

Janet Ingham looked up and smiled wanly.

'No thanks, Eunice. I think I'll go home.'

'Aren't you staying to dinner?'

'Not tonight. I feel too tired.'

'Have an early night,' Eunice advised her. 'And try not to upset yourself too much.'

'I'll try. You'll phone me at home as soon as there's any news?'

'Of course.'

Janet gathered up her bag and went to the door, bidding goodnight to each of them by name but deliberately omitting Hannah Kerr who watched her leave, a small, ironic smile on her face.

'So she is as soft underneath as the sweet surface would have us believe,' she remarked. 'I thought it was just a pose.'

Eunice Hart turned on her.

'I think you behaved quite disgracefully, Hannah.'

'Why? Because I told her the truth? But we'll all have to face it sooner or later, including Howard. Claire's dead. I can see, though, what must be worrying Janet: just how far she may be the cause.'

'How do you mean?' Eunice Hart asked sharply.

'Oh, surely you know about the rather special relationship between Janet and Howard? My dear, don't look so shocked. I thought you were broadminded enough to shrug off the occasional act of adultery.'

'I'm certainly not staying to listen to this kind of discussion,' Eunice Hart said with heavy disapproval. 'And I sincerely hope, for Howard's sake, that you don't pass on any of this slanderous and malicious gossip to the police. It's the kind of rumour that could ruin him professionally.'

'Don't worry. I have no intention of washing anyone's dirty linen in public,' Hannah Kerr assured her. 'It's Howard's decision whether or not he owns up to his extra-marital activities. Don't let me drive you away,' she added, as Eunice Hart rose to her feet.

'No one is driving me away. I have dinner to supervise. I assume all of you will want to eat this evening.'

The door had barely closed on her before Hannah Kerr burst out laughing.

'Poor old Eunice! She does take herself so seriously. Without her we'd all come tumbling down.'

'Is it true about Howard and Janet?' Donald Midgley asked. He had remained silent during the exchange between the three women, his presence forgotten, listening with a mixture of bewilderment, embarrassment but mainly curiosity. It was impossible for him not to refer to the subject.

'Lovers, you mean? Why not come straight out with the word? You're not afraid of it, are you, Donald? Or does it embarrass you to think someone as esteemed as our director should have a bit on the side? I believe that's the expression. Certainly Howard's not past it; not by a long chalk. And Janet's available. I can't see what could be more natural. I must say they've been discreet about it. I'd never have guessed if I hadn't seen them together in Lemchurch one evening about a month ago – the night he was supposed to be staying in Cambridge for a conference.'

'And you aren't going to tell the police?' Midgley asked. This aspect of it worried him.

'No, why should I?' she asked with an abrupt change of mood. 'I'm not Howard's keeper and neither are you, Donald. If you want my advice, I'd keep quiet about it. It's Howard's moral responsibility not ours. It'll be interesting, though, to see what he does about it; a small clinical experiment of our own. My bet is he'll do nothing. If anyone owns up, it'll be Janet and she'll only admit to it when Claire's body is found. Now, be a dear boy and pour me another sherry. I'm too exhausted to get up.'

'So you really believe Claire's dead?' Donald Midgley asked as he carried the glass over to her.

She looked him directly in the face and he saw that her amusement had died. Her eyes were now hard and black.

'Yes, I do.'

'But I thought you believed she'd run away. When we were at the house you said . . .'

'I know. I've changed my mind since then. I've had time to think it over. Knowing Claire, I doubt if she'd have the courage to act so positively. Or if she had, she'd've been in touch with Howard before now. And I certainly don't think she's lost her memory, as Eunice believes. That's mere wishful thinking. No, I'm convinced now that she's gone somewhere quiet and killed herself. It's quite in keeping with what I know of her. She wouldn't want to cause Howard the distress of finding her or bring any scandal on the clinic. She'll be found, of course, eventually.'

'But why should she want to do it?'

'On the last straw principle perhaps.'

Her tone was light and ironic but her eyes remained bleak.

'What last straw? I don't understand.'

'How persistent you are, Donald!'

'I'm sorry,' he said stiffly. 'I simply don't follow your reasoning.'

'There isn't any. I'm working almost entirely on intuition which ought to tell you how bloody exhausted I feel. Let me put it another way. Supposing something happened at the clinic on Sunday night to distress her? Something quite trivial and unimportant which she misinterpreted. After all, she was a neurotic woman; there's no knowing what stupid conclusions she may have jumped to.'

'But what happened?'

The conversation bewildered him. It was obvious that Hannah Kerr was referring to some specific incident of which she had personal knowledge and yet, as far as he knew, nothing had occurred either at dinner or afterwards which could have caused Mrs Jordan to take her own life, although he remembered her silence in the car on the way home and he wished with guilty hindsight that he had accepted her invitation to a night-cap.

'I've told you,' Hannah Kerr replied, impatient at his obtuseness. 'Nothing of any consequence actually happened but it could have tipped the balance.'

'Does Howard know about it?'

She gave him an odd, lop-sided smile.

'I doubt if he thought it important. For a psychiatrist, Howard can be suprisingly unperceptive at times.'

'I still don't understand,' he began, risking her anger in his determination to find out the truth. But there was no time for her to reply. The door was flung open and Mrs Simmonds burst in unceremoniously.

'For God's sake, come quickly,' she cried. 'Someone's attacked Mrs Hart!'

3

They ran after her along the corridor that led to the kitchen where they found Eunice Hart seated at the large preparation table that took up the centre of the room, a wet tea-towel held to her forehead. In the few seconds it took him to follow Hannah Kerr through the doorway, Donald Midgley took in the details of the scene: the shocked expression on the face of Mrs Brooks who was standing nearby, too dazed to offer any assistance, and Eunice Hart herself, the front of her blue nylon overall coat covered with mud and torn open at the neck, revealing two long scratches across her throat along which the blood had gathered in bright beads, her hair flopping loose across her forehead. Behind them, Mrs Simmonds, almost incoherent with distress was trying to give an account of what had happened.

'We were in the pantry, preparing the vegetables, so we didn't see him. And then we heard this screaming . . .'

Hannah Kerr took charge with that quiet, firm efficiency which Midgley had grudgingly to admire. With a few brief orders she despatched Mrs Simmonds to make tea, Mrs Brooks to fetch hot water and himself to the medical room to collect up disinfectant, cotton-wool and antiseptic dressings. By the time he returned to the kitchen, he found the table had been spread with a clean towel on which a bowl of hot water was standing while Eunice Hart, divested of her mud-stained overall, was wearing her quilted housecoat, the sleeves of which had been folded back to reveal deep scratches on her arms.

'Superficial,' Hannah Kerr announced in a brisk voice intended to take any lingering drama out of the situation. 'Luckily for you. I think you'll survive.'

'I think so too,' Eunice Hart agreed with a shaky laugh. Her eyes were still big with shock but she was obviously making an effort not to appear too affected by the experience in front of Hannah Kerr.

'Do you want to tell us what happened? Or would you rather wait until after I've cleaned you up?' Hannah Kerr asked.

'I think I'm over the worst of it now,' Eunice Hart replied and, as Hannah Kerr began bathing the cuts and scratches, she continued, 'I was in here on my own, by the sink. I'd just started to prepare the salad for the patients on diets when I saw a figure at the end of the yard. At first I thought it was Simmonds and then I realised it couldn't be him. This was a much slighter built man; not nearly so broad-shouldered. There was something odd about him, too. He was standing half in the shadow of the wall as if he didn't want to be seen. Well, you remember the trouble we had last year with vegetables being stolen from the garden?' The question was addressed to the two women who had taken her place at the sink and were washing lettuces and piling up the wet leaves to drain in huge mesh baskets. They nodded in agreement. 'So I thought I'd go out and see what he was doing. I went into the yard but by that time he'd disappeared behind the boiler-house. I walked as far as the corner but it was too dark to see properly. The next thing I knew . . . ' For the first time she faltered and began trembling and Hannah Kerr, who had been placing medicated dressings over her arms, paused and pressed one of her own hands over Eunice Hart's as they lay tightly clasped together on top of the towel covering the table.

Donald Midgley had never before seen her make such a gesture towards anybody and he was oddly moved by its obvious gentleness and sympathy.

'Do you want to go on?' she asked.

Eunice Hart nodded, the movement shaking free two large tears which had been gathering under her eyelids. They rolled down her cheeks with the slow, coursing glide of raindrops down a window-pane.

'I'm all right, really. Just a little confused. You see, I'm not sure what happened next. I think he must have been hiding because I can't remember seeing anyone. I just felt someone grab me and then I was dragged down . . . I know I screamed out . . .'

'I think you ought to go to bed,' Hannah Kerr interrupted. 'Mrs Simmonds, will you take her upstairs and give her a cup of sweet tea? And when she's settled,' she added in a low voice, turning to Donald Midgley, 'perhaps you'd give her something to make her sleep?'

'Yes, of course,' he agreed.

As soon as Eunice Hart had left the room, accompanied by the other women, she continued, 'I'll phone the police. I think they ought to be informed. And I'll get Simmonds to make a search of the grounds although I imagine the man's cleared off by now.'

'It's all so extraordinary!' Donald Midgley exclaimed. It was only now, after the initial excitement and need for action had passed, that he was able to view the events of the past ten minutes objectively. Aware of the apparent inconsequentiality of the remark, he added hastily, 'I mean, Claire Jordan disappearing and now Eunice being attacked.' A new thought suddenly struck him. 'Do you think they could be connected?'

'I have no idea,' Hannah Kerr replied. She sounded indifferent but he saw that, in fact, she was exhausted. Her whole face had sharpened as if physical tiredness had dissolved the flesh round the cheekbones and chin, exposing the angular structure of the bones beneath. Her eyes, too, had sunk and seemed to glitter in the strong overhead lights from two dark pits. 'One thing's certain, though. This time the clinic's going to be involved. It's brought the inquiry right on to our own doorstep. Howard isn't going to like that. I'd better try to get in touch with him after I've phoned the police.'

'He's gone to see Morley, hasn't he, about admitting his son?' Midgley asked. He knew this information only at second hand, passed on by Janet Ingham.

'So he says.'

The remark was said with such an unexpected, sarcastic emphasis that he didn't know how to respond although, in the event, there was no need for him to find anything to say, for Hannah Kerr, perhaps through tiredness, perhaps through a need to express her exasperation, added without any prompting, 'God knows why he bothered. He could just as easily have phoned. Instead of which he has to go rushing up to London. In my opinion, he's running away.'

'My God!' Midgley said.

Catching sight of his shocked expression, she laughed with genuine amusement.

'For heaven's sake, Donald, I don't mean he's literally done a bunk! Howard's not that much of a fool. I mean he's bowed out of the situation for a few hours; taken French leave.'

'Well, you can hardly blame him,' Donald Midgley replied. Her laughter seemed to relax the tension between them and he felt suddenly warmer towards her as a woman. It also gave him the courage to express his own opinion freely, something he always hesitated to do in her presence. 'He's had a hell of a lot to cope with.'

'And he hasn't proved quite equal to the task,' Hannah Kerr replied flatly.

It was a harsh judgement and, as she said it, his former antipathy for her returned and with it his own diffidence. At that moment, the women could be heard returning from upstairs and Hannah Kerr moved towards the door, remarking, 'I'll make those phone calls and get Simmonds to start the search.'

She went out, leaving Donald Midgley with the uneasy feeling that he had just witnessed a shifting in the old patterns of allegiances and loyalties and that he himself would never again be able to view Jordan with quite the same unquestioning admiration.

Part Five

1

The message reached Finch not long after he returned from London. After the interview with Rose Vincent, he had gone on to the Yard to discuss with Sergeant Bentley, their liaison officer, the possibility of tracing the taxi driver who had picked up Claire Jordan outside Harrods. Bentley wasn't too optimistic but there was a chance, he had said, especially if the cabbie regularly worked the Kensington area. The incident with the gloves might help to jog his memory; a photograph, too, would help of course. Finch promised to send some copies as soon as McCullum had finished his enlargements from the group photograph.

They were ready on his desk when he returned to the office and were better than he had hoped. McCullum had done some skilful touching up without spoiling the essential qualities of the features so that Mrs Jordan's face now smiled up at him with that sweet, shy expression and slightly ducked chin in better focus than in the original.

'We'll get those off to Bentley together with a description straight away,' he told Boyce who was hanging about in the office, looking bored and long-suffering, waiting for his return. 'If we can trace the driver, he may be able to give us a line on who this M.R. is. How did you get on this afternoon?'

'Not too bad,' Boyce admitted grudgingly. 'I was able to see all the people on the list; not that any of them had much that was new to tell me, except to confirm what we'd already guessed – that Mrs Jordan wasn't very happy. I got the most out of Mrs Woodham, the vicar's wife. Those diary entries, by the way, refer to coffee mornings they had together in Lemchurch. She very much doubted if Mrs Jordan had left her husband.'

'That was Mrs Vincent's opinion, too,' Finch put in.

'Which doesn't necessarily mean she hasn't done a bunk.'

'No, but it makes it less likely.'

'For what it's worth, Mrs Woodham believed, without any prompting from me, that she could have lost her memory and suggested we might make a search round her old home in Kent. She seemed to think she might have wandered back there. Evidently, she often talked about her childhood.'

'Interesting,' Finch mused, 'and perhaps worth a try. I had a more dramatic explanation from her sister. She was quite sure Jordan had killed her.'

'Is it possible?' Boyce asked incredulously.

'Not if Jordan's assistant, Midgley, confirms the statement that Jordan made this morning – that Midgley was present when he said goodbye to his wife. It's something I must check first thing tomorrow morning.'

In the event, the interview was to take place much sooner than Finch had anticipated for, at that moment, the telephone rang. Finch picked up the receiver and listened in silence apart from the one remark made at the end. 'Right! We'll be over immediately.'

As he put the phone down, he was already getting to his feet and buttoning up his overcoat which he hadn't yet bothered to take off.

'That was Dr Kerr,' he explained. 'Someone's just attacked Mrs Hart, the housekeeper at the clinic. Come on, Tom. We'll pick up Kyle and Marsh on the way out. And bring those photographs with you. We'll get them despatched to Bentley at the same time.'

2

They left in two cars, Finch and Boyce in one, the two detective constables in the other. It was already dark and there was no moon or stars. The sky which had been clear all day had clouded over towards evening and dusk had fallen quickly. It had begun to rain again, too; not the steady downpour of the previous night but a thin drizzle so that from time to time Boyce had to switch on the wipers to clean the windscreen.

'So what's happened?' Boyce asked. In the scramble to get away, there hadn't been time to ask for any details.

'I can't tell you much more,' Finch replied. 'Dr Kerr simply said that Mrs Hart had been attacked in the clinic grounds at about quarter to seven by a man whom she seemed to assume was an intruder. Mrs Hart was evidently dragged to the ground but I don't know how bad it is or whether she has any injuries. She screamed and the man ran off. Dr Kerr said she was going to get Simmonds, the head gardener, to make a search but I doubt if he'll find anybody. If it was an intruder, the man's not likely to be hanging about, waiting to be picked up.'

'Do you think there could be a connection with Mrs Jordan's disappearance?' Boyce asked, posing the same question as Midgley.

'It's possible,' Finch agreed, 'and if there is a link, it opens up new possibilities that we haven't even considered before – that someone has a personal grudge against the clinic and is taking it out on individuals connected with the place.'

'So Mrs Jordan's disappearance could be murder, after all,' Boyce pointed out. 'In which case, she must have left the house some time after Jordan drove away and before Mrs Leighton arrived, intending, as Jordan suggested, to get a breath of fresh air. She then met up with this man, whoever he is, who attacked her.'

'As a theory, it could work,' Finch agreed. 'In fact, it's quite plausible.'

Too plausible, he added silently to himself. 'But it doesn't quite fit the evidence we have. According to Mrs Leighton, Mrs Jordan left in a hurry, without bothering to clear the breakfast things or tidy away her dressing-gown and nightdress. Admittedly, she might have intended to be out for only a short time and would have put them away on her return. That might also explain the absence of any note to Mrs Leighton as well. But that's not the way I read her, Tom. I know her type. She'd've cleared up first before going out. Besides, it doesn't explain two other bits of evidence that are important. In the first place, she didn't put on her walking shoes...'

'Perhaps she didn't see the need for them,' Boyce objected. 'It was dry underfoot on Monday morning. It didn't start raining until later that night. She may have thought, as she didn't intend going very far, that it wasn't worth changing out of the shoes she was already wearing.'

'I take your point,' Finch said with reluctant agreement. 'But that still leaves one more major drawback to the theory. The nearest place for a brief stroll would be the clinic woods where, if you're right, someone attacked and killed her; presumably the same man who set on Mrs Hart this evening. But, if that's the case, where's the body? Admittedly, we haven't searched the woods ourselves but Jordan's staff have and, according to him, the search was thorough so, unless she's very carefully hidden, the odds are someone should have found her.'

He broke off, unable to explain to Boyce his lack of conviction in the basic theory. It was too neat, too pat. All his instincts warned him against so easy an assumption.

Boyce, who seemed unaware of the reason for the Chief Inspector's hesitation, took the opportunity to expand the idea.

'Oh, she'll be found,' he said with easy assurance. 'She must be there somewhere. Like you said, they couldn't have searched carefully enough. He'd be taking a hell of a risk, though, wouldn't he? I mean, the man who attacked her. It was daylight; there could have been other people about who'd notice a stranger in the grounds. Unless, of course,' and Boyce paused to give his next remark its full significance, 'he was someone who had every right to be there.'

'If you're back to the old argument that it must have been one of the patients ... ' Finch began.

'Not necessarily. But you must admit some of them may be a bit bonkers; perhaps even potentially violent. We don't know either what sort of treatment they're being given. Some of these modern drugs can have funny side effects. Come to that, Jordan could even be treating addicts for all we know. It doesn't take much to push one of them over the edge. Like you said, it could be someone with a grudge against the clinic. Or against women.

If we count Mrs Jordan's disappearance as possible murder, then both victims are women.'

Put like that, the argument sounded more reasonable. And if Boyce was right, Finch thought, the investigation was going to take time and a hell of a lot of delicate probing through professionally-guarded medical case histories that Jordan wasn't going to take very kindly to; nor presumably the anonymous person who had had them called in on the inquiry in the first place.

'If the grudge theory is correct, it could just as plausibly be a member of the staff,' he pointed out. 'I don't know how many Jordan employs but it must be quite a few. Or even someone from the village who objects to the clinic being there at all although that seems less likely. It's been open for about five years, I gather. It's a bit late for protests unless something's happened recently to stir up old hatreds.'

'Like what?' Boyce asked. He didn't sound very convinced.

'Rights of way. Land boundaries. I've known two men come to blows about a disputed footpath.'

Boyce didn't reply but his silence suggested that he considered such country matters too trivial to be worth serious discussion. Finch knew better. His own village upbringing had taught him the depth of animosity that can be aroused by small, seemingly harmless events, and the length of time that old grudges can smoulder on beneath an apparently peaceful surface.

They entered the village of Hawton at that moment and their headlights lit up the flint churchyard wall and the Gothic cottages that faced it. It all looked so quiet and tidy; one of those pretty, prosperous, well-kept villages, photographs of which appear on the illustrated calendars and which overseas visitors are led to believe are typical of England; never the industrial slums or the featureless, lowest-common-denominator designs of some new towns.

Boyce slowed down, flashing his indicator light in good time to warn Kyle and Marsh in the following car of the right hand turn. The tall gates of Hawton Hall opened silently and a little eerily in the darkness as if some huge, unseen hand had swung them back. A row of white posts and chains was briefly visible, indicating the presence of the Jordans' house although the house itself was set too far back for the headlamps to illuminate it in detail apart from a passing glitter as they caught the windows.

At the same time, on their left, something else was caught momentarily in the light: a figure of a man standing on the edge of the drive, thin-shouldered, a little stooped, a paper-white face turned towards them above the collar of a light-coloured raincoat. For a moment he stood there, as mesmerised as a rabbit by their headlights. The next, he had turned and plunged into the trees.

3

'Stop!' Finch shouted and, as Boyce braked violently, the Chief Inspector had flung open the passenger door and set off in pursuit.

The man had the advantage of a few seconds' start but, by his blundering flight, Finch guessed he was still blinded by the car's lights. He ran awkwardly, too, as if unused to the woods at night, bent almost double in an effort to avoid the low branches of the hazel scrub that formed this part of the clinic grounds. Finch had no such hesitation. With one arm held in front of his face, he crashed after him through the undergrowth. Behind him, he could hear the confused shouts of Boyce and the two detective constables who had joined him and their noisy progress as they, too, took up the chase.

Ahead of him, the bushes thinned. By the slight lifting of the darkness, Finch guessed that they were approaching one of the open spaces, set with larger trees, where he might easily lose his quarry. He had only to dodge between the trunks, his footsteps deadened by the grass, and he could make a get-away. But, as the thought crossed the Chief Inspector's mind, a bird, disturbed by their clumsy flight, flew up almost at the man's feet and, with an angry cry and clatter of wings, took off into the darkness.

It was a lucky chance. Finch saw him stop, fling up his arms and, in that abrupt, involuntary movement, could experience himself some of the terror the man must have felt as that whirring object exploded into life directly in front of him. He recovered but not soon enough. By the time he reached the edge of the glade, Finch was only a few paces behind him and, with a dexterity that he hadn't had to use since his rugger-playing days at school, he flung himself forward.

They crashed together on to the ground, Finch scrambling for a grip, the man oddly contorted, his arms wrapped about his body, his knees drawn up close to his chest so that it was difficult to get a hold on him. At the same time, he was gasping out something that, in the flurry of action, Finch didn't quite take in.

'My hands! For God's sake, don't hurt my hands,' he repeated.

He was lying quite passively now, on his side, still curled up in the foetal position he had assumed which, as the other three men approached, was apparent in the light of the torches they had brought with them. His hands, Finch noticed, as he got panting to his own feet, were tucked into his armpits.

'Up!' Boyce ordered, brandishing his own torch like a gun and, in the triple beam, they watched in silence as the man slowly uncurled himself and stood in front of them, his hands still tucked out of sight.

'Take him back to the car,' Finch ordered. 'I'll interview him there.'

He followed behind as, with the man in the centre, escorted by Boyce and Marsh, Kyle going ahead to light the way, the strange little group made its way back to the drive. Finch took his time, brushing the leaf-mould off his coat and his trouser legs, as he tried to regain his breath. He hadn't realised he was quite so out of condition. A couple of hundred yards' run and a not very difficult tackle had considerably winded him. Too much desk work, he thought sourly. And advancing years.

By the time he reached the car, Boyce had already installed the man in the back seat and was standing guard over him while Kyle and Marsh had retired to their own vehicle to wait. Finch approached them first and, having despatched them to the clinic to start preliminary inquiries into the attack on Mrs Hart, he got into the back seat next to the man, gesturing to Boyce to take his place in the front. Stretching up, he turned on the interior light.

He had only seen the man's face illuminated briefly in the car's headlamps and the torches which had intensified with theatrical exaggeration the peaks and hollows of the features. Now they were revealed less dramatically in the subdued steady glow. It was an interesting, bony face, showing strong intelligence and still retaining a lot of dark, youthful charm although the man must have been in his forties; frightened, too, and tense, Finch thought, noticing the little nervous jerk of his lips as he sat down beside him. And so he bloody well ought to be.

He nodded to Boyce who, understanding the signal, got out his notebook and turned ostentatiously to a clean page.

'Right!' said Finch briskly and, folding the skirt of his raincoat over his knees, settled down to enjoy the interview. It was a long time since he had questioned a suspect in the back of a car. More usually it was a routine process carried out in one of the interviewing rooms at headquarters; bleak, anonymous places which, despite the stark regulation furniture and bare painted walls, somehow managed to exude an atmosphere of human misery and despair. Here, at least, the scent of new leaves and the subdued night noises of the surrounding woods were drifting in through the open window.

'Name?' Finch snapped out in his official voice.

'Simon Boyd,' the man replied. His voice was low and hesitant.

'Address and occupation?'

'I'm a patient at the clinic. And that's all I'm prepared to tell you at this moment,' Simon Boyd stated with an unexpected show of spirit. 'I was merely going for a walk. There's no law against that.'

'Of course not,' Finch agreed equably. 'Except most people out for a stroll don't take to their heels when they see a police car. But it's entirely up to you, Mr Boyd. We can either chat here or we can drive you to the police station where you may be asked to make an official statement.'

'About Mrs Jordan's disappearance? But that's ridiculous! I only met her once, at dinner on Sunday evening at the clinic.'

He glanced from one face to the other in appeal and seemed unaware of the significance of the silence that greeted this remark.

It was broken by Finch who repeated, 'On Sunday evening at the clinic?'

It was indeed an interesting piece of information and he wondered why Jordan hadn't made it clear at his interview that such an occasion had taken place at which his wife had been present.

'Well, now,' he continued in his normal conversational voice, at the same time gesturing to Boyce who quietly put away his notebook, 'I'd like to hear about that.'

'But nothing happened!' Simon Boyd protested. 'I sat next to her at dinner; we talked a little; I thought she was a shy, charming woman. I didn't speak to her again until the very end of the evening, when she was taken ill and just before Dr Midgley drove her home.'

'What was the matter with her?' Finch asked.

'A headache I believe, although . . .'

As he hesitated, Finch pressed the question.

'You weren't convinced?'

'Oh, I'm sure she had a headache. But I had the impression that something had happened while she was out of the room to upset her.'

'Have you any idea what it could be?'

'No, I haven't. But either Dr Jordan or Dr Kerr may be able to tell you. They were also absent from the drawing-room at the same time.'

'How long was Mrs Jordan absent?'

'I'm not sure. Ten minutes or a quarter of an hour at most.'

'And the others?'

'A little longer. I believe they left before she did. At least, I noticed they weren't there when I went across to speak to Mrs Jordan. Before I reached her, she left. All three came back at roughly the same time.'

'And no one else left?'

'I didn't particularly notice. There were about twenty people in the room altogether. I wasn't interested in watching what they were doing. Look here, what is this all about?'

'But you were interested in Mrs Jordan?' Finch persisted, ignoring Simon Boyd's question.

'Well, yes, in a way. I felt sorry for her. She looked ill at ease, I thought.'

'And sufficiently interested to walk down to her house this morning? It was you, wasn't it, Mr Boyd? You started to approach the house and then turned off into the woods. What was the purpose of your visit?'

'I'd heard she'd disappeared and I was concerned about her. I hoped she might have returned.'

'But you didn't, in fact, call at the house?'

'No, I saw a car parked outside the house and it seemed inappropriate.'

The word sounded oddly lame.

'And this evening?'

'I walked down here for much the same reason. I wanted some fresh air and I thought I'd come as far as the house on the off-chance I might see her.'

'What time did you set out?'

'I'm not sure. About ten minutes ago, I think. I came straight down the drive. It was too dark to walk through the woods.'

All three glanced at their watches. The time was seven twenty-three.

'Did you see anyone?' Finch asked.

'No, not a soul.'

'And what were you doing at approximately a quarter to seven this evening?'

'I don't see the relevance,' Simon Boyd began. He seemed genuinely bewildered by the question.

'Just answer if you please, sir,' Finch said.

'Very well. I was in my bedroom reading.'

So he has no alibi for the time Mrs Hart was attacked, Finch thought.

'By the way,' he added, out loud, 'what is your occupation, Mr Boyd? You omitted telling me when I first asked you.'

'I'm a concert pianist. And now, if you've quite finished, may I be allowed to leave?'

'Of course,' Finch replied blandly. 'We're on our way to the clinic ourselves. We'll give you a lift if you like.'

'I'd prefer to walk,' Simon Boyd said stiffly and, getting out of the car, began to walk rapidly away up the drive, his thin-shouldered figure held for a few moments in the headlamps before it finally disappeared into the darkness.

'So that's why he wanted to protect his hands,' Finch commented in a musing voice. 'I believe I've heard the name, too. Wasn't he one of the soloists at last year's Proms?'

'Never listen myself,' Boyce replied dismissively. 'I can't take all that heavy stuff although I don't mind a good military band. What do you make of him? Do you reckon he's the bloke we're looking for?'

'I don't know, Tom. We'll need to find out a lot more about him. I admit, though, it looks suspicious. He was hanging about the Jordans' house this morning and then he turns up again after Mrs Hart's attacked. There's something else, too, we must follow up: the dinner party on Sunday evening where he met Mrs Jordan. It's curious Jordan himself didn't mention it. He led us to believe his wife was taken ill at home and I wonder why. It also gives us a direct link with the clinic and that'll need looking into. Boyd seemed to think something happened to distress Mrs Jordan while she was out of the room. I'd be interested to find out what it was. If she's been murdered, it could give someone a motive for killing her.'

'And the attack on Mrs Hart?' Boyce asked.

'That's something we've still to find out about. Come on, Tom. We'd better get up there. We've spent long enough questioning Boyd. It's about time we started interviewing a few of the others.'

4

As soon as he was out of reach of the car's lights, Simon Boyd slowed down his pace. The encounter with the police had shaken him badly and he could no longer control the trembling which he had managed to repress during his cross-examination. He was worried, too, about his hands. There was no external sign of injury; he had examined them carefully when he had first got into the car. But they felt stiff and, as he walked, he continually flexed the fingers, trying to get them to move naturally.

Meanwhile, his mind seemed to be working with the same rapid rhythm, as if his thoughts were keeping time with the nervous, muscular contractions.

What the hell was going on? He had no idea but it was obvious that the inquiry was more serious than a straightforward investigation into Mrs Jordan's disappearance. The police would hardly have given chase like that unless they were suspicious of something more. Of course, he'd been stupid to bolt like that. It had been one of those moments of irrational panic such as he felt before a concert. He felt, too, that his explanation for his visit to Mrs Jordan's house hadn't sounded at all convincing. It was a kind of fastidiousness that made him reluctant to explain his feelings to strangers; and besides, they weren't clear even to himself. He was aware that his concern was mixed up with guilt towards his own parents, particularly his mother, but he now began to wonder if, in fact, there wasn't a subconscious desire on his part that they might disappear, relieving him of at least one of his burdens. Dr Kerr would possibly understand. He felt he might be able to voice these emotions to her. But not yet. At the interview he had had with her that morning, he had merely spoken of his professional anxieties, not his personal ones. There would be time for those when he was convinced that he could trust her absolutely.

On the question of confession, he realised that he hadn't been entirely honest with the police either. He had said nothing about the first occasion he had walked down to the house yesterday afternoon, the day, in fact, as he had found out later, that she had disappeared. And he knew perfectly well why he had refrained from mentioning it. It would look too suspicious.

At that moment, he heard the car approaching him from behind and he stepped on to the grass verge to allow it to pass, standing quite still as the headlamps flashed over him. It seemed to him that the momentary focusing of brightness summed up the police inquiry that was to follow. They hadn't finished yet;

111

indeed, he suspected that they had only just begun and part of that investigation was going to be turned on him, submitting him to a cross-examination that could be as searching as those two probing shafts of light.

5

The inquiry began badly. In the first place, as Finch discovered as soon as he entered the clinic, Dr Jordan was not there.

'He left for London earlier this afternoon,' Dr Kerr informed him. She seemed quietly triumphant at passing on this piece of information; why, Finch couldn't imagine.

He and Boyce had been shown into her office, more plainly furnished than Jordan's; the walls painted a pale blue, the furniture, including her desk, simple in design. She had seated herself behind it, coolly professional in a doctor's white coat, and was observing them steadily from under a severe fringe of black hair. A formidable woman, Finch decided; completely self-assured and not the type to be easily rattled. There was an air of ironic amusement about her which, oddly enough, he rather liked. After Jordan's bland, professional charm, he found her refreshingly astringent.

'I'd like his address,' Finch replied. It seemed a reasonable enough request but she demurred.

'Is it necessary?'

'I think so. Dr Jordan will have to be informed of what has happened.'

'Very well.'

She wrote it down on a piece of paper and handed it over to him.

'It's the address of his Harley Street practice. He has a small flat over the consulting rooms where I believe he intended staying for the night.'

'Have you tried contacting him?' Finch asked.

For the first time, she showed signs of emotion but it was impatience rather than uncertainty.

112

'I've tried ringing his number several times but there's no reply. He could be at his club.'

Finch handed the paper over to Boyce, saying as he did so, 'Find Kyle. Tell him to drive up to London and wait outside this address until Dr Jordan returns. He's to phone me as soon as he's home.'

Boyce left the room and Finch turned back to Dr Kerr.

'I'd like, of course, to talk to Mrs Hart.'

'Quite out of the question,' she said promptly. 'She's still in shock. I can't allow her to be questioned yet. Besides, Dr Midgley's tranquillised her on my instructions. I doubt whether she's in a condition to make a statement. You may be able to see her later. In the meanwhile, if you wish, I can give you a brief account of what appears to have happened.'

It was a damned nuisance that he couldn't speak to Mrs Hart, but at least he'd get some idea from Dr Kerr who, he guessed, would be factual and unemotional.

'Please do.'

'The attack took place at a few minutes before quarter to seven. Mrs Hart had gone into the kitchen to supervise the final preparations for dinner, both the patients' and the staff's, when she saw a man acting suspiciously at the end of the yard. Last year we had a number of thefts from the vegetable garden so, thinking it might be the man responsible, she went out to investigate. By that time, he'd disappeared behind the outbuildings. She went to look and I gather he suddenly attacked her, grabbing her from behind and pulling her to the ground, at which point she screamed and the man ran off. She gave a description of him; not a very detailed one, I'm afraid. It was dark and she only caught a glimpse of him. He was a slim built man, wearing a light-coloured coat.'

A description which would fit Simon Boyd, Finch thought, remembering the glimpse he had caught of him in the head-lamps.

'By the way,' Dr Kerr continued, 'Simmonds has since searched that part of the grounds and has found nobody, not unexpectedly. Mrs Hart managed to get back to the house and Simmonds' wife, who's Mrs Hart's deputy, raised the alarm.'

'Any injuries?' Finch asked.

'Scratches across her throat and arms but in my opinion they were caused by brambles. There's a patch of rough ground at the far end of the yard where some blackberry bushes are growing. She could have fallen into those.'

'Were there any witnesses?'

'No, it appears not.'

'What about the other kitchen staff? Didn't they see anything?'

'Mrs Simmonds and Mrs Brooks were in the pantry, preparing vegetables. There's a window but it's frosted glass so they saw nothing. The other two women were laying tables ready for dinner, one in the patients' dining-room, the other in the staff's. The only possible person who might have seen anything is Mrs Ingham. She left about ten minutes before the attack took place and she'd have to collect her car from the stable-yard which runs parallel to the service area where the attack took place. It's possible she might have seen someone going round to the back of the house as she drove away. I've tried ringing her, too, but she hasn't answered. She may have gone to bed or prefers not to speak to anyone. She said she was feeling very tired when she left.'

'I'll try contacting her myself later,' Finch replied. 'Meanwhile, Dr Kerr, I'd like a list of all the staff employed here.'

'Mrs Ingham will have to supply you with that, Chief Inspector. I have no idea of their names apart from a few. Some, like Simmonds and his wife, are full-time. Most are part-time workers, women from the village who are brought in each day by mini-bus. A number of professional people, such as the physiotherapist, the masseur and the osteopath come only on certain days and are paid a fee for their services.'

'How many live in?'

'Not many. Simmonds and his wife have a flat over the kitchen. As to the rest of the full-time staff, Mrs Hart also has a bed-sitting room in the east wing; Dr Midgley and myself have rooms on the other side of the building. Mrs Ingham has her own house in the village.'

'And the patients?'

'If you're asking me for a list of names, I'm afraid I can't supply that without Dr Jordan's permission.' Again, she seemed

114

quietly triumphant at denying his request. 'All I can tell you is that there are sixteen in number and they all have rooms either in the main block or in the west wing. I might point out that, as far as I know, none of them are aware of the attack on Mrs Hart. It took place at the back of the house, out of earshot of the main rooms. And I'd prefer they weren't informed of it at this stage. Whether or not Dr Jordan chooses to tell them on his return is up to him. I don't myself see the necessity.'

Don't you? Finch thought grimly, remembering the suspicious encounter with Simon Boyd. But that could be left until later. At the moment, he was more concerned with clearing up a few more general issues.

'If that's all,' Dr Kerr was saying, clearly considering her part in the inquiry was over.

'Not quite,' Finch replied. 'I'd like to go back to last Sunday evening.'

'Yes?' she said and looked surprised.

'The evening when I believe a dinner-party was held here in the clinic?'

'That's correct. I don't see the point, Chief Inspector. What possible relevance could it have to tonight's events?'

Finch ignored the question.

'I understand that Mrs Jordan was taken ill at the dinner-party?'

'To be precise, it was afterwards, while coffee was being served in the main drawing-room. But I still fail to see the relevance unless,' and her voice sharpened, 'you're implying that Mrs Jordan's disappearance and the attack on Mrs Hart are in some way connected. It seems a quite outlandish suggestion.'

'Is it?' Finch countered. He had got her measure. With Dr Kerr, attack was probably the best line of defence and would in the long run gain her respect and co-operation. She would despise anyone she bullied. 'I'm not so sure of that myself and it's a line of inquiry I intend following up. I understand that Mrs Jordan, who had left the room, was distressed when she returned and had to be taken home by Dr Midgley. You and Dr Jordan were also absent at roughly the same time. I wondered if you had any idea of what had happened to upset her.'

115

There was a silence in which they faced each other across the desk and Finch was gratified to see that it was she who first glanced away. She looked down at her hands, her expression oddly softened.

'I may be able to supply you with that information,' she said quietly, 'although, of course, I don't know exactly what went on in Claire's mind. She found Dr Jordan and myself in his office. We were merely discussing the following day's arrangements which there hadn't been time for before dinner. I'm afraid we were both a little curt with her; not intentionally but I think Claire may have taken it badly.'

For the first time during the interview she appeared at a loss and, Finch suspected, was not being entirely honest either with herself or with him. She knew damn well why Mrs Jordan had been distressed. The use of the word 'merely' had given that away and raised the whole question of the exact relationship between Jordan and his deputy director. Were they lovers? From what Rose Vincent had told him, Jordan had had affairs with other women in the past but had been discreet. It sounded out of character for him to risk a liaison so close to home. But whether they were lovers or not, the sight of them together had evidently caused Mrs Jordan distress. So had their treatment of her. Dr Kerr had also used the word 'unintentionally' and that, too, had a defensive ring about it and he very much doubted if this decisive woman ever did anything without knowing exactly what she was about.

As far as Jordan was concerned, he seemed to have set out deliberately to diminish his wife and it was suddenly clear to him the exact form it had taken. All her roles had been given to others: the domestic to Mrs Hart, the secretarial to Janet Ingham, the confidential aspect of his professional life to Dr Kerr. He would no doubt argue in his own defence, and not without reason, that as he became more successful, she was no longer adequate to fulfil those roles. He needed properly trained people to assist him. But it could not have made it any easier for Mrs Jordan to face the women who had usurped her functions and he could understand that the relationships between them might be strained; except for Mrs Hart who, from what Mrs

116

Leighton had told him, appeared to have formed some friendship with her employer's wife.

As for the sexual role, someone must be supplying Jordan's needs in that area of his life, too. He had, after all, been sleeping apart from his wife for over a year. But that was delicate ground and, until he knew far more about the background to the case, he wasn't prepared to blunder in just yet.

It was time, he decided, to close the interview with Dr Kerr. Others might tell him what she would obviously never admit to and he silently cursed the fact that he couldn't yet interview Mrs Hart who, as Claire Jordan's ally, might be prepared to talk.

'I'd like to speak to Dr Midgley now, if that's convenient,' he said, getting to his feet.

'Of course. I'll show you to his office and get someone to fetch him,' Dr Kerr replied and, as she showed him to the door, he saw that he had made the right decision. He had lost her. Her expression was quite stony and those two very positive eyebrows were drawn together in a dismissive frown.

6

It was quite obvious, just by looking at his office, that Dr Midgley occupied a much less important position in the clinic than Dr Jordan or Dr Kerr. It was a modest room, both in size and furnishings, and cluttered up with Midgley's personal possessions; a squash racket stood in a corner and a photograph of a girl in nurse's uniform occupied the top of a grey-painted filing cabinet.

Midgley had gone out, at Finch's request, to see if Mrs Hart was fit enough to be interviewed while Boyce had been despatched to find Marsh and send him down to the village to collect Mrs Ingham and bring her back for questioning, a telephone call to her house having been unanswered. Kyle had already left for London.

Finch sat alone, mulling over the inquiry which so far hadn't produced anything much in the way of evidence either of Mrs Jordan's disappearance or the attack on Mrs Hart.

He had unearthed a possible motive, tenuous though it might be, for Mrs Jordan to leave home: her distress over a possible affair between her husband and Dr Kerr or, at least, her suspicious of one, but all the indications were that, in fact, she hadn't walked out. There was no luggage missing and she appeared to have taken no clothes with her apart from the ones she was wearing.

As for Mrs Hart, he had a brief, second-hand account only from Dr Kerr and no clue as to the identity of her attacker, except that the description could fit Simon Boyd; and a good many other people, too.

In Jordan's absence he couldn't begin to inquire into Boyd's background, nor any of the other patients' come to that; nor, until Janet Ingham returned, even find out exactly how many were on the staff.

And that was merely scratching the surface. If he was right and both cases were linked, it could mean interviewing the entire adult population of the village, not to mention past employees and former patients.

'Blast!' Finch said out loud.

Boyce returned at this moment to find the Chief Inspector sitting moodily in front of Midgley's desk, his shoulders hunched.

'Marsh has left for the village,' Boyce announced. 'And while I was at it, I've had a word with the two women who were helping in the kitchen. Dr Kerr was quite right. They were in the pantry when the attack took place and so saw nothing. The first they knew of it was Mrs Hart screaming and then staggering in, covered with mud, and her arms bleeding. One of them, by the way, is bringing us tea.'

'Thank God for that,' Finch replied. It was a very small bright spot on an otherwise totally gloomy horizon.

Tea arrived almost at once with Midgley following close on the heels of the woman who brought it. He declined Finch's offer to share it but carried his own chair from behind the desk to join them so that the interview took on the slightly incongruous air

118

of a tea-party, although Midgley's worried expression robbed the occasion of any relaxed informality.

'Mrs Hart is better,' he informed them earnestly, 'but still rather doped. I'd prefer if you would wait for at least another hour before questioning her.'

'Of course,' Finch agreed. It was a damned nuisance but there wasn't much else he could do under the circumstances.

'And I'm afraid I can't tell you much about what happened this evening,' Midgley continued rapidly with the air of a man anxious to clear himself of any suspicion. 'I was with Dr Kerr in the staff sitting-room when the attack happened. The first I knew of it was when Mrs Simmonds came in to tell us.'

'I see,' Finch replied gravely. It was extraordinary how this young man, who couldn't be more than in his early thirties, managed to inject into the situation a serious, elderly tone which was catching. 'But you may be able to help us with the other inquiry – Mrs Jordan's disappearance.'

'Of course. In any way I can.'

'I'd like to go back to the events of Sunday evening, the day before Mrs Jordan went missing. I believe you were also present at the dinner-party which was held that night, Dr Midgley?'

'Yes, as a matter of fact I sat next to her at dinner.'

'And afterwards, when coffee was being served, I believe Mrs Jordan was distressed about something?'

'I don't know anything about that. As far as I know, she had a migraine. Dr Jordan asked me to drive her home in my car which I did. Simmonds was to return hers in the morning.'

'On the way home, did she say anything?'

'No. She hardly spoke except to thank me.' He looked ill at ease. The memory of that silent drive still caused him guilty feelings and he tried to voice them. 'She asked me in for a night-cap but I was anxious to get back. Perhaps I should have gone into the house with her and made sure she was all right.'

Finch let it pass. Midgley's conscience was no concern of his although he felt a pang of compassion for Mrs Jordan, going home alone into an empty house.

'I understand the following morning you returned to the house? What time was this?'

'About quarter past eight. It had been arranged that I was to spend the day with Dr Jordan in London.'

'And you were present when Dr Jordan said goodbye to his wife?' Finch asked, deliberately choosing the words that Jordan himself had used.

'Well, not exactly present. Mrs Jordan was in the breakfast-room when Dr Jordan went in to tell her we were leaving.'

'But you saw her?'

'Oh, yes.' Midgley was quite positive. 'She was standing by the window. I heard her speak to him, too.'

'What was she wearing?'

'A sort of long housecoat thing,' Midley replied with the faint embarrassment of a man unused to describing women's cloth-ing. 'And one of those net caps over her hair, like a turban.'

'And what did she say?'

'I couldn't catch all the words. She always speaks very softly but when Dr Jordan said we were going, she replied, "Very well, Howard." Then he half-closed the door and I couldn't hear the rest of it.'

Finch and Boyce exchanged brief glances. Midgley's account gave Jordan an alibi. It was now quite out of the question that he could be in any way directly implicated in his wife's disappearance.

'I'd like to turn now to later in the day,' Finch continued, 'after your return from London.'

Here, too, Midgley's account tallied closely to what Jordan had already told them – the discovery that Mrs Jordan was missing, the search of the house, Jordan's departure to the village to make inquiries, the subsequent search of the outbuild-ings and grounds of the clinic.

'Thorough, was it?' Finch asked.

'Oh, yes,' Midgley assured him. 'We'd been split up into two groups and told to search under any undergrowth although, with the leaves not yet out, there wasn't much cover apart from the evergreens. We looked under those individually.'

So that seemed, Finch thought, to dispose of the theory that Mrs Jordan could have been killed in the clinic woods and her body concealed close to where the attack took place. Unless her body had been moved somewhere else, which didn't seem very likely; not in broad daylight.

It was a point he made to Boyce when, having thanked Midgley and concluded the interview, they left the office.

7

'So what happens now?' Boyce asked. They were standing in the corridor that led to the kitchen, talking in low voices. A faint clatter of china and the sound of voices came from one of the rooms off the entrance hall where presumably the patients were still at dinner.

'We press on with the present inquiry,' Finch replied, 'and hope that by solving one, we come up with the answer to the other. We still can't interview Jordan or Mrs Hart and Marsh hasn't come back yet with Mrs Ingham, so we're a bit limited at the moment. There's Simmonds, of course. He returned Mrs Jordan's car to the house on Monday morning. It's possible he knows something. At the same time, he can show us round the yard where the attack took place. I assume Marsh and Kyle have already searched the area?'

'Yes, and found nothing.'

'We'll take a look ourselves all the same. I'd like also to check with Simmonds that the search of the woods was as thorough as Midgley says it was.'

They found Simmonds in the kitchen, eating his own supper at one end of a large, central table. It was a large room, high-ceilinged, the tiles on the floor and walls giving it a resonant quality. Three catering-sized cookers took up an entire wall and a pair of double stainless steel sinks occupied the space below the window.

While Simmonds finished his meal, Finch wandered about, checking the lay-out. It was through the window, he assumed, that Mrs Hart had seen her attacker. He peered out of it himself. It overlooked a small, cobblestoned yard, one side of which was bounded by low, slate-roofed outbuildings, the other by a high,

121

windowless wall, with an arched opening in it. In the bright light streaming out through the uncurtained window, it was just possible to see to the end of the yard although it would be impossible to make out anyone's features. A glazed door beside the sinks led directly out to the yard through which Finch assumed Mrs Hart had left the kitchen and returned.

Another door in the adjoining wall opened into a pantry which was larger than he had expected. It, too, was equipped with a double sink and working surfaces. It also appeared to be used as a food store for it contained deep-freeze cabinets and refrigerators. As Dr Kerr had said, the window was made of frosted glass so that anyone standing at the sink had no view of what was going on outside.

He returned to the kitchen where Simmonds, who had finished his meal, began putting on his jacket.

'Before we look at the yard,' Finch said, 'there's a couple of points I'd like to clear up first. I believe you returned Mrs Jordan's car on Monday morning?'

'That's right,' Simmonds replied. 'I drove it back to the house about nine o'clock. The garage was unlocked so I put it inside.'

'Did you go to the house?'

'No. Why should I?' Simmonds sounded faintly belligerent as if he had been accused of some dereliction of duty. 'I didn't see no need. Besides, I had to walk back and I'd wasted enough time already. I'd got work to do.'

'Did you see Mrs Jordan?'

'No. There was no sign of anyone about.'

'What did you do with the keys?'

'I left them on the ledge under the dashboard where she'd find them when she needed to use the car. It seemed safe enough. No one was to know they were there.'

Finch let that one pass. Simmonds was a tall, lugubrious man who, the Inspector judged, wouldn't put himself out more than he had to.

'Did you notice anyone hanging about the house?' he asked.

'No.'

'Or on your way back to the clinic?'

'I told you, there was no sign of anybody.'

'About the search of the woods,' Finch began.

'What about it?' Simmonds asked truculently.

'It was thorough?'

Simmonds took a deep breath. 'It was. I told the men, "You make bloody sure you look proper. We don't want the bloody job to do twice." Same with the search of the golf course.'

'You took part in that, too?' Finch asked quickly.

'Dr Jordan said, "Take the ground-staff and help out." Those were his orders. As if searching the woods wasn't enough, we was tramping about there half the bloody morning. Now, do you want to look at that yard or don't you? I'm supposed to be off duty, you know.'

Finch took the hint and, accompanied by Boyce, followed Simmonds out of the back door.

It was still raining, a fine, misty drizzle that coated the cobblestones with a thin layer of moisture, slippery underfoot. 'It's the service yard,' Simmonds explained as they picked their way over the damp, uneven surface. He had had the foresight to bring a powerful torch with him and in its beam, the stones glistened blackly.

'What's through there?' Finch asked as they passed the arched opening on their right.

'The stable-yard, or what used to be. All the loose boxes are turned into garages now. It's the back of them that forms the wall. Over here,' and he directed the torch to the left, 'there's various storehouses with the boiler house at the end. You'd better watch out where you're walking,' he added. 'It's muddy up here.'

The cobblestones ended in a rutted drive that swung away to the right behind the stable-block.

'It's where the vans and lorries come delivering stuff,' Simmonds said. 'Ought to be hard-surfaced, if you ask me. I've told Dr Jordan often enough. One of these days, a lorry's going to get stuck and it'll be a hell of a job shifting it. It's here Mrs Hart must have been set on,' he added, 'from what my wife told me.'

He shone the torch to the left where an area of rough grass extended into the darkness. 'According to her, he dodged round the end of the boiler house and then jumped out on her. She must

123

have fallen in them bushes. I'll get them cut back one of these days.'

The brambles formed a large, sprawling heap, growing against the end wall. An area to the front was flattened, the long sprays pulled awry as if something had fallen on them and struggled to escape.

'No chance of any footprints,' Boyce observed gloomily. 'The grass is too long.'

'How could the man have got here?' Finch asked.

Simmonds shrugged.

'From any direction. There's only a low iron fence round most of the grounds, not even that in places. He could have come through the woods or across there through the kitchen garden.'

'I've heard you had trouble last year with vegetables being stolen,' Finch said. 'Any idea who did it?'

'No, but I'd like to get my hands on him. Cheeky bugger! He even pinched stuff from the greenhouses. The local bobby came up but, like he said, there wasn't much he could do unless the bloke got caught red-handed.'

'So no one was suspected?'

'Not that I know of. But whoever it was must have been warned off. We've had no trouble since.'

'And you've heard of no one in the village who might have a grudge against the clinic?'

Simmonds looked surprised.

'Why should they? Quite a few of the locals work here. They'd be hard put to it to find other jobs in the area.'

It was a point, although it didn't necessarily follow that everyone in Hawton shared the same sanguine view.

At this moment, they were interrupted by the arrival of Marsh, a heavy-jawed young Detective Constable, who was picking his way up the yard towards them.

'One of the women said you'd be out here, sir,' he said to Finch.

'You've brought Mrs Ingham back with you?' Finch asked, preparing to turn back towards the house.

'No, sir. She wasn't at home. At least, the place was in darkness and her car wasn't in the garage. I had a look. I checked next door, too. The neighbours haven't seen her all evening, or heard anything of her either. So I came back.'

Finch exchanged a quick glance with Boyce and was glad that the darkness hid their expressions from the other two, especially Simmonds whom Finch asked as casually as he could, 'Where would Mrs Ingham keep her car at the clinic?'

'Through here,' Simmonds said, leading the way back towards the archway in the stable wall. It opened out into a larger yard, also cobblestoned, enclosed on three sides by loose boxes, the central block of which had a small clock tower erected on its roof. The yard was lit, although dimly, by electric lights under thick glass covers that were burning at sparse intervals along the three sides and casting a subdued glow in their immediate vicinities only. On their right, the end wall of the east wing of the clinic formed the fourth side of the square, its lighted windows casting more brightness. Alongside it, a wide gap gave access to the side of the building and presumably to the service drive which would follow round the whole block to the small adjoining yard.

'That's her garage,' Simmonds said, pointing to the left. 'The one at the far end.'

'Thank you,' Finch said firmly. 'I don't think we need bother you any more, Mr Simmonds.'

'Right you are,' Simmonds replied. He didn't appear at all put out by his dismissal. In fact he seemed relieved as he walked away and let himself into the clinic by a door, the upper part of which was glazed with opaque glass.

The end stable, like the others, had been converted into a garage by widening the original opening and substituting an up-and-over garage door in light aluminium which, as they approached, they could see was closed.

'Get it open,' Finch told Marsh, 'and for God's sake cover your hand, man. I don't want your dabs all over it.'

Marsh produced a handkerchief from his pocket and, grasping the handle gingerly, swung the door upwards.

'Wait here,' Finch told him and, as Marsh stepped back, he and Boyce entered.

A dark blue Renault stood inside, taking up most of the space so that they had to edge past it to get to the driver's door which was open. But even before they reached it, they could see the legs which were sticking out and, by the loose, pathetic way in which they hung down, they guessed that Janet Ingham was already dead.

Leaning across them, Finch peered into the interior, dimly lit by the light which was burning. She had fallen sideways across the passenger seat, her head resting against the window and turned so that the wound in her temple was terribly apparent. It had bled copiously and the blonde hair was black with blood.

Finch backed away. He had seen enough.

'Murder,' he said briefly over his shoulder to Boyce.

Part Six

1

Finch backed carefully out of the garage and, leaving Marsh to stand guard, he returned to the clinic with Boyce and alerted headquarters, using the telephone in the general office, before returning to Dr Kerr's consulting room. Boyce had already informed her of Janet Ingham's death and, as Finch entered her room, he found her sitting behind her desk as if she had not moved since the news had first been broken to her, her features wearing a mask-like rigidity, the face very white, the hair and eyes very black; devoid of all expression except fixed disbelief.

'I shall need somewhere to work from,' he told her. 'An office of some sort, with a telephone.'

It was several seconds before she replied. Shock had slowed her down, making her uncharacteristically subdued.

'Of course,' she said at last. 'You can use mine or Donald Midgley's.'

'I'd prefer not to disrupt the clinic,' he replied. 'I may need it for some considerable time.'

'There's the medical room. It's not used very often. You could take it over temporarily until another office can be prepared for you.'

She led the way down the corridor and showed him into a square, plain room. Finch looked round it briefly. It would do. It was well lit and there was a large table in it, standing under the window with a telephone on it and nothing to distract the eye on the white painted walls. The only disconcerting feature about it was the glass-fronted cupboards containing drugs and medicines that lined one side, which were hardly objectionable enough for him to ask for other accommodation. Besides, it had

127

one big advantage. It was situated off the passage leading to the kitchen area, well away from the main rooms, and therefore would not be under the direct gaze of the patients and senior members of the staff.

'You realise I shall need to interview everybody who was in the building,' he told her. 'And that includes the patients.'

At last she showed some reaction.

'Can't that wait until Dr Jordan's return?' she asked with some of her former brusqueness.

'I'm afraid it can't,' he retorted. 'This is a murder inquiry now. I'm not hanging about waiting for Dr Jordan's permission. Meanwhile, I'd rather you didn't try contacting him again. Leave that to us.'

Kyle should have arrived in London by now, he thought, and would be watching Jordan's flat. He didn't want Dr Kerr tipping him off first. He wanted to do that himself and see the man's reactions.

He moved behind the desk, taking possession of the swivel chair and indicating to Dr Kerr the upright one that stood on the further side for the patient's use.

'Sit down,' he said. 'While you're here, I'd like your account of this evening's events as they relate to Mrs Ingham.'

It was odd, he thought, how being seated on the far side of a desk gave one an immediate advantage. Dr Kerr, for all her authority, was now reduced to the position of interviewee, a role that she obviously found unfamiliar for she immediately assumed a belligerently defensive pose, crossing her legs briskly and sitting very upright; nice legs, he noticed, surprised into regarding her in a more feminine light; slim and shapely, and he wondered again about the nature of her relationship with Jordan.

'You've already been told much of what happened,' she replied, 'when you questioned me about Mrs Hart. As I said before, we were in the staff sitting-room having sherry before dinner. Janet was there but she seemed unwell. She normally stayed for dinner but she said she felt tired and preferred to go straight home. She left soon after Donald Midgley joined us. I assumed she'd collected her car and driven back to the village. We continued talking and then Eunice Hart left to supervise dinner. It was shortly after that that Mrs Simmonds came to tell us that Eunice had been attacked. The rest you know.'

'What do you know about Mrs Ingham's background?'

'Not a lot. She's been with the clinic longer than any of us. She worked for Dr Jordan in London as his secretary before this place was opened. She's divorced, I understand for several years now.'

'Any men friends?' Finch asked.

'I suggest you ask elsewhere,' Dr Kerr replied coldly. 'I don't inquire into other people's private lives. I consider it their business.'

It seemed to Finch an odd way of putting it but before he could press the point, Boyce stuck his head round the door.

'I've been looking for you everywhere,' he remarked in an aggrieved tone and added succinctly, 'They've arrived.'

Finch rose to his feet. Dr Kerr remained seated in her chair.

'I have your permission to inform the patients of what has happened,' she asked, 'and to warn them that they may be questioned?'

'Yes, although I'd prefer it if you tell them as little as possible at this stage,' Finch replied.

She raised her eyebrows at him ironically, as much as to say, Do you think I'm a fool? and left the room, giving Finch the distinct impression that, although she had said nothing, she had somehow managed to have the last word.

2

The cars which had brought in the experts, Pardoe, the police surgeon, McCullum, the photographer, and a small army of plain and uniformed men, were already parked in the stable-yard as Finch, accompanied by Boyce, let himself out of the back door of the clinic and, for the next hour, he was fully occupied in directing the investigation. Lights were set up, Stapleton and his men despatched to make a search of the area, and McCullum edged his way into the garage to photograph the scene. When he had finished, Pardoe would make his preliminary examination of the body.

When McCullum had gone, Finch took a second look himself. The initial shock and compassionate distaste had been replaced by an attitude of unemotional objectivity and, as he squatted down in the narrow space beside the car, he took in details that his first horrified glance had failed to absorb. She was dressed, he noticed, in an expensive-looking grey coat with a collar of matching fur, its soft pale texture stiff and dark with blood that had trickled down from the head wound. Underneath, where the coat had fallen open, he caught a glimpse of a navy blue skirt and white silk blouse. The expression on the face, as the head lolled back against the window, was one of stupefied surprise, the mouth hanging loose, the eyes gazing blankly at some point beyond his shoulder. But she had been attractive in life, Finch thought, remembering the too ready smile, the professional amiability. Certainly, Boyce had found her so. He himself regretted that he had been less impressed, now that death had reduced her to this pathetic, huddled bundle.

He retreated in his turn, leaving Pardoe to take over, and turned his attention to the other aspect of the inquiry, the interviewing of the staff and patients of the clinic. He chose two men for the job, Formby for the staff, and, as a sop to Dr Kerr, Bradshaw to question the patients. Bradshaw was one of the new breed of coppers, a University graduate with pleasant manners and an acceptable middle-class accent who would probably, Finch realised, with an awareness of younger talent treading on his heels, finish up as a Chief Superintendent.

'You know the drill,' he said as he briefed them. 'A list of names and addresses, where exactly they were between half past six and seven; whether they heard or saw anything suspicious or out of the ordinary. Report back to me when you've finished.'

Two rooms had been set aside for the interviewing, the writing-room for the patients, the small staff sitting-room for the employees.

As he returned to the medical room to begin his own inquiries, the first patient was being fetched from the main drawing-room where they had been told to assemble by Dr Kerr.

130

He sent for Midgley first who entered looking worried, his pleasant, earnest features crumpled up into an expression of concern that made him appear even more middle-aged than ever. His account, when he had got over the preliminary protestations of horror and surprise which Finch gave him time to voice, tallied exactly with Dr Kerr's. Janet Ingham had left early, pleading tiredness, although she normally stayed for dinner which was served in the adjoining staff dining-room, the same room, Finch learned, where the dinner-party had been held the previous Sunday. Janet Ingham had been distressed, Midgley added, by Mrs Jordan's disappearance, a piece of information that Dr Kerr had failed to mention.

'I'm afraid,' Midgley explained, 'that the conversation upset her.'

'Yes?' Finch said encouragingly.

Midgley looked embarrassed.

'It was suggested that she might not always have been as friendly to Mrs Jordan as she might have been,' Midgley confessed. 'Not openly, of course; Janet was never rude to her face but that she'd made her feel a bit well, *de trop* at times.'

He offered the phrase reluctantly as if its very foreignness suggested some hidden, salacious meaning.

And I bet I know who said it, Finch thought. It had the ring of Dr Kerr's acidity. It cast a new and interesting side-light, too, on the relationship between Janet Ingham and Mrs Jordan, an aspect of the case worth further examination once the more pressing issues had been cleared up.

'And then what happened?' Finch asked.

'Janet left. The rest of us talked for a little longer and then Mrs Hart went out to supervise dinner. She was rather upset, too. Of course, we were all rather on edge.'

It was said defensively and Finch guessed that something else had happened which was still causing Midgley acute embarrassment. It didn't take much to imagine either who had been behind it: Dr Kerr.

He cocked an interested eyebrow but Midgley wouldn't be drawn.

'Well,' he replied, fixing his eyes on a point beyond Finch's right shoulder, 'Dr Kerr said Claire would probably be found

131

dead somewhere and Eunice wouldn't believe it and walked out of the room. That was all.'

It probably wasn't but Finch decided to leave it there. It was clear that some other remark had been passed to distress Mrs Hart, almost certainly by Dr Kerr and probably of a malicious nature, the exact content of which Midgley preferred not to repeat, but at the moment it seemed a minor issue.

'What time was this?' he asked.

'About a quarter to seven, I think,' Midgley replied, sounding relieved at the change in the subject.

'Mrs Ingham would have left by the back door?'

'I suppose so.'

Finch had already checked the route. Just outside the staff sitting-room, the corridor made a right-angle turn where a green baize door shut off the rest of the passage with its kitchen and other domestic offices from the main part of the clinic. At the end of this passageway, the half-glazed door, by which he himself had left and entered the building, opened directly into the stable-yard. It seemed reasonable to assume that Janet Ingham too had left by this exit. After all, her car was garaged in the yard. She would hardly have left by the front door which would have necessitated her walking round the house to reach the back.

It also occurred to him that Midgley and Dr Kerr provided each other with alibis. They had both been present in the staff sitting-room when Mrs Simmonds had entered to tell them of the attack on Mrs Hart and it would appear that neither of them could be under any suspicion either of that incident or the murder of Janet Ingham although, with the exact time of her death not yet established, he couldn't eliminate either of them yet.

'And now,' Finch continued, 'I'd like to question Mrs Hart if she's well enough.'

Midgley left the room, returning shortly afterwards to announce that Mrs Hart was indeed a little better and, if the Chief Inspector would follow him, he'd show him the way to her room.

3

A back staircase, intended originally for the servants' use, led from the downstairs passage to a similar long landing on the upper floor. Mrs Hart's bedroom opened off it, and Finch took a look about him as Midgley, looking very serious and professional in a pair of horn-rimmed glasses, checked Mrs Hart's pulse before nodding to Finch that he could continue with the interview and leaving the room. Its general air was one of cosy, cluttered femininity in the number of small objects it contained: embroidered cushions, potted plants, ornaments and pictures; none of them valuable or particularly beautiful in themselves but, seen grouped together, they made the large, high-ceilinged room with its two long, severe sash windows appear homely and welcoming.

A divan bed occupied the wall opposite the fireplace, with a chintz cover to match the chairs and paired lamps at either end so that, by day, it would appear as a sofa. Mrs Hart was lying in it, propped up against pillows, her hands lying flaccidly on the cover. She was an attractive woman and would, normally, Finch guessed, be of a relaxed and cheerful disposition; sensible, too, and practical with an understanding of the basic good things of life: warmth, food, comfort. But it was evident that she was still suffering from shock and the effects of the tranquillisers. Her mouth trembled and her dark, handsome eyes still held a dazed, unfocused look.

The extent of her injuries were immediately apparent. There were gauze dressings on her hands and arms while a loose bandage encircled her throat.

Finch drew one of the armchairs round to face her and sat down. It was obvious that he couldn't be too rigorous in his questioning of her and he began quietly.

'If you're quite sure you feel up to it, Mrs Hart, there's a few inquiries I'd like to make.'

133

'Of course,' she replied in a low voice. 'Anything I can do, especially now that Janet...'

She broke off and seemed close to tears.

'Dr Midgley told you?' he asked. He would have preferred if this shock could have been kept from her until, at least, the morning.

'Yes, but you mustn't blame Donald. I heard all the cars arriving, you see, so I guessed something had happened.'

'You realise the two incidents might be connected?' he said. 'That's why it's so important that you tell me as much detail as you remember of the attack.'

Her account, which came haltingly and with many pauses as she stopped to regather her strength, tallied exactly with what he had already learnt. She had been in the staff sitting-room until nearly a quarter to seven, she said. She seemed more aware of the time than either Midgley or Dr Kerr, probably because of her own duties in the kitchen. Yes, she agreed, Janet Ingham had been upset but, like Midgley, she made the excuse that they were all tired and on edge. Janet left and she herself returned to the kitchen a few minutes later. No, she hadn't seen Mrs Ingham in the passage. She must have already left by the back door and gone across the yard to her garage. She herself had gone straight into the kitchen and begun work preparing the salads while the other two women were in the pantry preparing vegetables. Dinner was at eight o'clock and she liked to have everything ready in good time. She had heard and seen nothing of what had happened in the stable-yard which was understandable. The kitchen faced the service yard and the stable wall blocked her view.

She had been standing at the sink only a few moments when she noticed the man at the far end of the yard, near the boilerhouse, and had gone out to see what he was doing. By that time, he had disappeared from sight behind the outbuildings and she assumed he had made off. The attack took her completely by surprise. She had been seized from behind and then dragged into the brambles. At this point she had screamed and the man ran away; she thought in the direction of the kitchen garden although she couldn't be sure.

'Can you describe his appearance?' Finch asked.

'I only caught a glimpse of him at the end of the yard,' Mrs Hart explained. 'He was of medium height and rather thin. Youngish, I should say, but that's only an impression. I didn't see his face when he attacked me. He came out of the shadows behind the boilerhouse and it all happened so quickly, I didn't have time to register anything very much.'

'Was it anyone you knew?' Finch asked, thinking of Simon Boyd.

'No; at least, I don't think so.'

'Would you recognise him again if you saw him?'

Mrs Hart looked doubtful.

'I don't think so; not to make a positive identification. I wish I could. It's all been so dreadful, first Claire disappearing and then Janet being killed. God knows what effect it's going to have on Howard. Does he know yet?'

It seemed typical of her, Finch thought, that her first concern should be for others. He imagined she had probably spent her life looking after other people's needs with that selfless, practical, common-sense altruism of middle-aged, middle-class women that was so often channelled by the voluntary charitable organisations like the WVS or Meals on Wheels.

'No,' he replied, 'we haven't been able to contact him.'

It was unwise, he thought, to continue the cross-examination and he hastened to conclude it.

'Just one more question, Mrs Hart,' he said, 'and then I'll leave you in peace. Referring to Mrs Jordan's disappearance – I believe you were friendly with her? Has she at any time discussed the possibility of leaving her husband?'

'Oh, no!' Eunice Hart cried, sounding distressed. 'It wasn't an ideal marriage but I don't think Claire ever considered ending it. Or Howard come to that.'

'Or was there any possibility of her committing suicide?'

Her distress increased.

'I don't think so. I thought she might have lost her memory and wandered off somewhere. But I'm not sure now. She'd surely have been found? I wish I'd done more now to help her; persuaded her to confide in me. She was lonely, I know, poor woman. Perhaps it all got too much for her and she decided to end it, dreadful though it is even to think about.'

135

She began to cry awkwardly, like a woman unused to tears, turning her head away from him towards the wall. He got to his feet. It was possible she could be right, he thought, and that Claire Jordan had taken her own life, even though both Rose Vincent and Jordan, who after all must know her best, had been convinced that it was out of the question.

'Would you like me to send for Dr Midgley?' he asked.

She nodded, too distraught to speak, and Finch left the room, feeling guilty at the part he had played in adding to her distress, to find the doctor and hand her over to his professional care.

4

Simon Boyd accepted a cup of coffee from Mrs Simmonds and moved away from the trolley to stand by himself at the far end of the drawing-room. He preferred to be alone and, for that reason, was careful not to catch the eyes of any of the other patients who, like him, had been asked to remain in the room by Dr Kerr until sent for by the police.

There had been, she had explained, an accident involving Mrs Ingham and everyone would be questioned in the course of the official inquiry. The announcement, which had been made while they were at dinner, had been brief, almost curt. Having delivered it, she had merely turned on her heel and left the room before anyone could ask her any questions although it was surprising how quickly the rumours had spread.

'Murder!' Ransome had murmured briefly in Boyd's ear as they got up from the table and then he had moved on to repeat the remark to several others, his handsome, ruined face animated by this new excitement.

He feeds on sensation, Boyd had thought with a shiver of disgust. There seemed to him a quality of obscenity in Ransome's eagerness which reminded him of one of those flesh-eating plants which suck the life from its living victims, absorbing their essences in order to maintain its own corrupt and sinister beauty.

He was afraid, too, of how the implications of Ransome's remark, if it were true, might affect himself. Since his return to the clinic, he had tried to obliterate the shame of his confrontation with Finch and the subsequent questioning in the back of the police car. Nothing had been said then about murder and he had assumed they were interested only in Mrs Jordan's disappearance. But now he remembered Finch's curiosity about his movements and he was afraid.

Could Ransome be right? he thought. Were they in fact investigating a murder and if so, whose? Was it Janet Ingham's or Mrs Jordan's? Dr Kerr had spoken only of an accident and, as far as he knew, Mrs Jordan's case was an inquiry into a disappearance.

The lack of any information frightened him. He felt implicated in something that he didn't properly understand in which his own actions, such as his visits to the Jordans' house, could be misinterpreted.

He longed to seek Ransome out and question him further while, at the same time, he wanted nothing more to do with the man or his unhealthy fascination with sudden death.

As he hesitated, torn between the two desires, he saw Ransome enter the room, pausing in the threshold with that almost innate compulsion to make an entrance and, in the moment when Boyd might have turned away, their eyes met and Ransome, with a quick smile of recognition, came across the room towards him.

'Murder?' Simon Boyd heard himself repeating.

'Oh, it must be,' Ransome said with the air of pleased casualness of someone in the know. 'Didn't you see the cars? Masses of them parked round the back. And an ambulance. I went into the linen-room at the end of the upstairs corridor and had a grandstand view. They'd even set up lights. It was just like a scene from one of those Pinewood thriller movies – policemen in capes searching in the rain. Marvellous shadow effects and atmosphere. All that was missing were the cameras and the director although I suppose Finch must fill that role. I saw him standing about in that dreadful old mackintosh of his, hands in his pockets, looking like a farmer at a livestock sale. All part of his camouflage, of course.'

137

'Camouflage?' Simon Boyd asked.

'Oh, surely you realise he can't be the simple country copper everyone's been led to believe? If he's in charge of a murder investigation, he must be fairly high-ranking. I thought everyone knew that, although God knows how he got involved in the first place. After all, it was only a Missing Person's case. Jordan must have pulled a few strings.'

Simon Boyd opened his mouth to speak and then shut it again. Ransome was eager enough to gossip without his supplying him with the information that it was, in fact, Sutton who had used his influence. If he passed on the conversation which he had overheard in the entrance hall on the morning Mrs Jordan disappeared, he would only be giving Ransome more material. Ransome, in his eagerness to talk, had, thank God, noticed nothing.

'I wonder how she was killed?' he was saying. 'Stabbed, do you suppose? Or shot?' Catching sight of Boyd's expression, he added, 'Oh, for God's sake, don't look so shocked!'

'She may not be dead,' Boyd protested. 'Dr Kerr said an accident.'

'Accident? Balls! That's official eyewash. They'd hardly carry her out covered with a sheet if she was only injured. Didn't I mention that? Of course, I only caught a glimpse. They'd backed the ambulance right up to the garage door. I had to crane my neck to see. But I'm absolutely certain the sheet was right over her. Besides, you can always tell by other people's reactions. They assume that rather self-conscious pose, like spectators at an Armistice Day service; respect for the dead and all that.'

It was extraordinary how powerfully Ransome conveyed the scene, summoning it up as if it were actually taking place. As he was speaking, Simon Boyd seemed to see it: the body being carried away, the bystanders drawing themselves up as Ransome himself was doing, chin slightly tucked in, shoulders and spine rigid, eyes lowered in respectful reverence, and for the first time he was aware of the nature of the tragedy in relation to its victim, Janet Ingham. He tried to visualise her, too, but could remember nothing more about her except her back as she had left the room on the Sunday evening, shortly after Mrs Jordan had also disappeared through the same double doors, and he glanced at them now, their panels outlined in gilded beading, half-expecting to see her figure still retreating, her fair hair glistening under the lights, one hand holding up her long black skirt and revealing a glimpse of a satin heel. The shock of the memory, which he had not recalled before, blotted out some other recollection, quite trivial, which he couldn't bring into the conscious level of his mind. It was overlaid by Ransome's conjured image of the sheeted body, the rain and the shadows.

Ransome's voice also persisted in breaking into the memory.

'Jordan's going to find quite a scandal on his hands,' he was saying with a gratified air. 'One or two people are already talking about cutting short their treatment, Sutton among them. Personally, I think I'll stick it out. It'll be fascinating to be on the inside of a police investigation. The only other case I was involved in was a suicide; a young chap called Terence who hanged himself in his digs during a production of *Hamlet*. Actually, it did me a bit of good professionally. I was understudying his Horatio and so got taken straight out of the crowd into a speaking part. I had damned good reviews and a picture in the *Express*. You could say it was my first lucky break. Well, they seem to have started,' he remarked, as the double doors were opened and a young, fresh-faced, uniformed constable appeared, conferred briefly with those standing near the door and retreated again, accompanied by one of them, a businessman called Palmer. Ransome himself, to Simon Boyd's relief, drifted away to find out from those closest to the door exactly what was going on and Boyd heard someone explain to him, 'We're to go out one by one. They're interviewing us in the writing-room. If you ask me, it's a damned imposition. I'm not paying Jordan's fees for this kind of treatment.'

His own turn came about half an hour later. The constable who stationed himself unobtrusively by the door between each interview, nodded towards him pleasantly enough in the relaxed, informal manner in which the whole business seemed to be conducted and, as Boyd crossed the hall, remarked in a conversational voice, 'It shouldn't take long, sir. Just a few minutes. In here, if you please.'

He ushered Boyd inside the writing-room and then retreated,

leaving him face to face with a tall, wavy-haired, extremely clean-looking man in his late twenties who was seated at one of the desks which were scattered about the room and who, rising as he entered, held out a hand and said in an educated voice, 'I'm sorry you've been inconvenienced, sir. Do sit down. I'm Detective Sergeant Bradshaw. Would you mind telling me your name?'

It was done with such aplomb and social grace that, almost before he knew what he was doing, Boyd had taken the chair indicated and had given his name.

'And your occupation, Mr Boyd?'

He told that, too. Bradshaw himself took no notes but merely smiled at him across the table with the pleasantly respectful courtesy of a young man who, while in no way underestimating his own value, is willing to concede superiority and respect to his elders, expecting in return an equal measure of politeness. It was like talking to a charming nephew or godson and Simon Boyd wondered sardonically which of the public schools and universities had provided him with this disarmingly engaging manner.

At the same time, he was aware that another man, older and so ordinary and nondescript that Boyd had scarcely registered his presence in the room, had taken a seat just behind him and, turning his head quickly, he saw that the man had silently produced a pencil and notebook. The quiet, professional efficiency of it all struck him as ominous but there was no time to express any objection, even if he had considered it necessary or prudent. Bradshaw was recalling his attention with a graceful compliment about his performance at last season's Promenade Concerts.

'Yes, yes,' Boyd said distractedly. Oddly enough, now that the time had come, he found such small talk exasperating. He wanted the interview over and done with. The worst part, as he knew from experience, was always anticipation. He felt his hands go cold and the preliminary lurch of his stomach before the familiar sick churning sensation that inevitably followed and he said quickly, 'Can't we get on with it?'

He was aware that his voice was too tense and high-pitched

and he saw Bradshaw's face take on a look of fleeting surprise before resuming its bright-eyed, interested expression.

'Of course, Mr Boyd. There's only a few questions I want to ask which shouldn't take up too much of your time. Firstly, did you hear or see anything unusual during any part of the early evening?'

It sounded innocuous enough and he had no hesitation in answering.

'No, I didn't.'

Bradshaw smiled as if the answer gave him personal pleasure.

'May I then ask you what you yourself were doing, say, from about six o'clock?'

'I – I was in my room.'

His voice was still not under proper control and there was a hesitation, not quite a stammer, but a slight, breathy catch as he began to speak.

'Alone?' Bradshaw suggested gently.

'Yes, alone. I was reading.'

'Until what time, Mr Boyd?'

The sting's in the tail, Simon Boyd thought. Young as Bradshaw was, he'd already got the technique of cross-examination off pretty well and he wondered who had been his mentor. Finch, perhaps? Finch might lack his suave, public school manner but the low-key approach was typical of the Chief Inspector.

'About a quarter past seven.' He paused, wondering if Bradshaw would ask any further questions and then, without waiting, plunged into explanation. 'I went for a walk. I had intended going to the Jordans' house to see if Mrs Jordan had returned home but before I reached there, I was stopped by the police and questioned.'

If his hurried account surprised Bradshaw, he showed no sign of it. Nor did he remark, as Simon Boyd half-hoped he would, that this fact was already known to him, thus confirming his own fears that he had been asked by Finch to re-examine his original statement. He merely nodded, as if quite satisfied and remarked, 'I see, sir. Could anyone verify the time you left the clinic?'

'No,' Simon Boyd replied.

'No one was in the hall when you came down the stairs, for example?'

'No.' It seemed too bald a reply and he added, 'You have only my word for it.'

Bradshaw made no answer except to rise to his feet and, extending the polite hand once more, apologised for taking up his time.

'Mrs Ingham . . . ' Simon Boyd began.

'Yes, sir?' Bradshaw's face was bland, with that pleasant, official blankness that gives nothing away and yet manages to discourage further inquiries. But the question had to be asked. Simon Boyd knew he could not leave the room without posing it. Ridiculously, he felt suddenly young and inexperienced compared to this clean, good-looking young officer, at least fifteen years his junior, who nonetheless represented authority and the whole weight of English law. 'Is she dead? People have been saying...'

'There'll be an official statement made later,' Bradshaw replied.

And that was that. Boyd found himself walking out of the room, past the nondescript man who meanwhile had put his notebook and pencil discreetly away, and across the hall accompanied by the fresh-faced policeman who had first conducted him there.

'If you wouldn't mind not returning to the drawing-room, sir, for the time being,' he murmured.

'Of course,' Simon Boyd replied. For a moment he didn't understand the reason for the request and then he realised it was to prevent those who had been interviewed from conferring with those whose turn had yet to come. The police were clearly taking no chances on information being exchanged and yet so little, in fact, had been given that the precaution seemed unnecessary.

It was Ransome who made him see the point of it. He was waiting on the landing when Simon Boyd went up the stairs to his room.

'Now then, sir,' he asked in the tones of a comic policeman, 'hand what may Hi hask was you adoing between the howers of 'alf past six and seven?'

His light-heartedness angered Boyd who replied snappily, 'I was reading in my bedroom.'

'Oh, my God!' Ransome cried, holding up his hands in mock horror. 'No alibi!'

Simon Boyd stopped short. How stupid he had been, he thought. All his concern had been centred on the later time when he had left the building and had been walking in the grounds towards the Jordans' house. Those had been circumstances in which Finch had seemed most interested and for which he himself felt he had most to fear. In his anxiety, he had discounted the earlier part of the evening. Now Ransome's remark made him realise how doubly vulnerable he was.

Ransome had begun to laugh with genuine amusement that had nevertheless a ring of malice in it. He put an arm across Boyd's shoulder.

'Good Lord, Simon, don't look so stricken! Finch is hardly likely to suspect you of murder. You don't look the homicidal type.'

It was small comfort and, as Simon Boyd ducked away from the contact and entered his room, he wondered if that very suspicion hadn't been in Finch's mind from the moment he had seen him, silhouetted in the car's headlights, at the edge of the drive.

5

When Midgley had been despatched to Mrs Hart, Finch returned to the yard just as Pardoe, that other medical practitioner whose concern was with the dead rather than the living, emerged from the garage, carrying his bag.

'As usual, you'll want some sort of a report,' he said to Finch in his abrupt manner which in anyone else would have been downright rudeness. 'Well, I can tell you this – it was a blow from a metal weapon, about two inches wide and rusty; I've found particles of rust in the hair – and struck with sufficient force to kill her. It was aimed from above and slightly to one side; in other words while the victim was probably seated in the car and had leaned out of the door to look back towards the garage entrance. Whoever killed her was standing just behind her and brought the weapon down on the right temple. My guess is that he then bundled her back into the car in the position in which she was found. Otherwise the weight of the body and the angle at which it was leaning would have caused it to slump sideways out of the car and on to the floor.'

'So the killer might have blood on him?' Finch suggested.

'It's possible, although don't count on it. With a head wound like that, you don't get blood spurting out as you do when an artery's severed. As for handling the body, the murderer could have tipped the body backwards simply by raising the legs. That way, he needn't have touched the head at all.'

'And the time of death?'

Pardoe gave him a small, bleak smile.

'I guessed you'd ask me that and I can't, at this stage, be more precise but, from the body temperature and the degree of rigor mortis, I'd say she's been dead about two hours.' He glanced at his watch. 'In other words, between six and eight o'clock.'

Which tied in with the other evidence already given him by Midgley, Dr Kerr and Mrs Hart, Finch thought, and strongly suggested that Janet Ingham had been killed shortly after she left the clinic at about quarter to seven.

'And that's about all I can tell you,' Pardoe continued, buttoning up his coat briskly. 'It was difficult enough examining her as it was. I'll need to have her on the slab before I can give you a detailed report.'

He walked off to his car, leaving Finch to supervise the removal of Janet Ingham's body to the waiting ambulance which then also departed. The breakdown truck was next backed into position to tow the car away. Finch gave the job of organising this to Boyce and went to look for Stapleton, the tall, slow-speaking Inspector whose men were searching each individual garage in turn.

'You know what sort of weapon we're looking for?' Finch asked him.

144

'Yes; Pardoe passed the word on to me. Nothing like that's been found yet,' Stapleton replied.

'He must have got rid of it somewhere in the area, so go on looking,' Finch told him.

'What makes you so sure of that?'

'Because shortly after he killed Mrs Ingham, he attacked Mrs Hart; at least, all the evidence so far suggests that's what happened. He must have left the stable-yard by that archway over there which leads into a smaller yard behind the kitchen where Mrs Hart saw him. But he simply pulled her to the ground, which suggests to me he no longer had the weapon with him. So my guess is he'd already thrown it away.'

'We'll keep looking,' Stapleton assured him. 'Once the men have finished here, we'll move into the other yard and give that a going-over.'

'We may have to search the whole bloody grounds,' Finch said. He was overcome by sudden gloom in which the darkness, the fine rain that was still falling, surrounding the arc lamps with a nimbus of water vapour, the sharply etched shadows, even the stooped figures of the men in their glistening capes all played a part. There was something unreal and infernal about the scene. 'There could be another body.'

'Mrs Jordan's?' Stapleton asked. Finch had already given him a brief account of the three cases and their possible connection on his arrival.

'Yes. They've been searched by Jordan's staff but it's possible she could still be lying out there somewhere.'

'That'll have to be left until daylight. We could bring in tracker dogs but, if you want my opinion, it'll be a waste of time. The ground's too wet for them to pick up any scent.'

Finch's gloom seemed to be matched by Stapleton's.

They both looked up at the sky, quite black and seemingly empty above the bright, theatrical lighting in the yard, as if there were nothing there, a mere void.

Boyce joined them.

'Formby and Bradshaw have sent out word that they've finished the interviewing,' he told Finch. 'Where do you want them to report? Out here?'

'No; inside, in the medical room,' Finch replied.

He saw them separately, Formby first and then Bradshaw and their reports, summarised by Finch on two separate sheets of paper, amounted to this: of the six members of staff who had been present in the clinic at the crucial times, four had alibis; Mrs Simmonds and Mrs Brooks who had been together in the pantry; Simmonds himself who together with George, who acted as porter and handyman, had been mending one of the showers in the sauna. Those who had no alibis were Mrs Summers and Mrs Kitson, both of whom had been alone laying tables in readiness for dinner, one in the patients' dining-room, the other in the staff's. Both, however, had been seen emerging from the two rooms shortly after the attack on Mrs Hart had taken place, which didn't give them enough time, in Finch's estimation, for either of them to be seriously implicated. Of the professional staff, only Dr Kerr and Midgley remained and they provided alibis for each other.

The report on the patients was more detailed. For one thing, there were more of them, but out of the sixteen, nine had alibis; four had been playing bridge while the other five had been watching television or talking together. That left seven who had been alone in their bedrooms, Simon Boyd among them.

Finch questioned Bradshaw closely about the interview with Simon Boyd.

'He seemed nervous,' Bradshaw admitted, 'and very anxious to explain about the walk he took before dinner. Oddly enough, he didn't seem to be worried about the earlier part of the evening, between half past six and a quarter to seven, when the murder must have taken place. I don't think it had occurred to him that he had no alibi to cover those times. He mentioned, by the way, that he was stopped by the police and questioned on his way to the Jordans' house. I assumed it was you, sir?'

'Yes, you're right,' Finch replied. 'We picked him up on the way here, before we knew Janet Ingham had been murdered. What was your impression of him? Guilty, would you say?'

He still felt uneasy about Simon Boyd and was hoping that Bradshaw's opinion might help him settle his doubts one way or the other.

Bradshaw looked dubious.

'He's a very tense man and I got the impression that

something's worrying him. Whether or not it's murder, I wouldn't care to hazard a guess.'

A careful man, Bradshaw, Finch thought as he dismissed him; not the sort to jump to conclusions. He'd weigh up the evidence first before making up his mind. Perhaps lacking in imagination but, all the same, he ought to go far; not that this helped him much on the question of Simon Boyd's guilt or innocence.

When Bradshaw had left, Finch studied the list of names and occupations more carefully, looking for a clue to the identity of the man whose influence had first got him called in on the case of Mrs Jordan's disappearance, but none of them meant anything to him. Their various occupations weren't any help either. They were mostly listed as businessmen or civil servants although one, he noticed, was an actor, and Bradshaw had noted down Boyd's occupation as 'professional pianist'.

Well, the man's identity no longer mattered, Finch decided. The time for discretion had passed. It was now a case of murder and no one, not even the Chief Constable, could expect him to keep that under wraps.

He was still studying the list when Dr Kerr knocked and entered. She looked exhausted, he thought, as if the evening's events had taken all the vigour out of her.

'I've asked the kitchen staff to prepare something for the men,' she informed him. 'It won't be much, I'm afraid; just tea and biscuits. The women are short-staffed with Eunice still off-duty but Mrs Simmonds has offered to organise it. They'll get it ready when they've finished washing-up.' Hardly giving him time to thank her, she continued, 'I see you have a list of the patients. May I ask how many, if any, are under suspicion?'

'Seven have no alibis,' Finch replied, 'which doesn't necessarily mean they're considered as suspects. They may have to be questioned again, of course.'

'May I see the names?'

He passed it over to her, adding as he did so, 'I'd like your opinion of them.'

'As potential murderers?' she asked, raising sarcastic eyebrows. 'You can hardly expect me to supply you with that kind of information, Chief Inspector.'

'I wasn't asking for it,' Finch returned snappishly. He was too tired to wish to indulge in another verbal bout with her. 'But, under the circumstances, I think I'm entitled to know if any of them are potentially violent.'

She acknowledged the point with a brief nod of the head in his direction before reading the list and handing it back to him.

'Without divulging any details of their medical histories, my answer is none of them is dangerous. There are four cases of straightforward exhaustion; one of anxiety neurosis; one insomniac and one whom I suspect is using the firm's money to escape from his wife for a couple of weeks and lose some weight. None of which adds up to anything like a real psychosis.'

There was a dismissive air about her that was almost contemptuous, as if she despised some of the patients, and he wondered how far she found the work at the clinic really satisfying.

As if in answer to his unspoken query, she added, 'We're not in the business of treating seriously sick mental patients, Chief Inspector, although the people who come here have their problems. We occasionally take on a more difficult case, a drug addict or an alcoholic for example, but not often. They require specialised nursing and the expense and effort are often not worth it.'

'Are you treating any at the moment?'

'No, although Dr Jordan is considering admitting an addict next week. It's the reason he's gone to London, I believe.'

Finch was aware of an undercurrent of irony under her remarks, directed both at the clinic and its director, which was revealing, although he pretended not to notice it.

She continued, with a wry twist of the mouth, 'He's going to be faced with an unpleasant surprise when he returns, isn't he? Poor Howard!' And then, suddenly, she dropped the sarcasm and sounded genuinely sorry. 'He's worked damned hard to build this place up. Its reputation is bound to be affected.'

It gave Finch a lead into his next line of inquiry.

'It has a good reputation, has it?'

'Oh, yes indeed!'

'So no one, say an ex-patient, has any reason to bear a grudge against the place?'

148

'Not that I'm aware of. Howard and I discuss each case in some detail before a patient is discharged. If there had been any dissatisfaction, I'm sure it would have been mentioned at the time.'

'Or any patient who might have a personal animosity against women?'

She looked at him sharply with that direct, disconcertingly intelligent gaze.

'You're thinking, of course, that all the victims have been women? Do you include Mrs Jordan in that category?'

It was too damned perspicacious of her and he answered cagily, 'That still remains to be seen, Dr Kerr. But you haven't answered my question.'

'I wasn't trying to avoid it. The answer quite simply is: no. I know of no patient, either currently or in the past who has ever showed symptoms of psychosis to such a degree that I would expect violence to result from it.'

'What about the village? Has anyone voiced any strong objections to the clinic being here?'

'There was a public inquiry, of course, before it was opened and certainly some disquiet was expressed at having a place like this on their doorstep. I think they imagined lunatics on the loose. But Howard spoke at the meeting and assured them it would all be highly respectable and we wouldn't be treating certifiable patients, only tired businessmen. The protests died down and I've certainly heard nothing recently to suggest anyone bears a grudge against the place.'

'No threatening letters have been received then?'

'None at all. Is there anything else you want to know? If not, I'll tell Mrs Simmonds to start preparing the refreshments.'

'One more thing before you go. You've given me a little on Mrs Ingham's background. I'd like to know something of Mrs Hart's.'

'There's not much I can tell you. Eunice is widowed. Her husband died some years ago, I believe. There are no children, at least, I've never heard her mention any family. She joined the staff as soon as the clinic was opened. Before coming here, she was deputy matron and housekeeper at a boys' preparatory school in Dorset, so she's well qualified for the job.' Her voice had grown more staccato as if the questioning wearied and exasperated her. 'Is that all?'

'Not quite. I'd like to go back to the conversation between the four of you earlier this evening . . . .'

'I've told you all I know,' she interrupted him.

'I think not, Dr Kerr.'

Her face hardened.

'What has Donald Midgley been saying?'

'Very little. That's why I'm asking you.'

She seemed on the point of refusing to answer for she walked to the door where she paused, before turning back to face him.

'I said several things which I have since regretted, Chief Inspector; personal remarks I had no right to make. And that's all I'm prepared to say, except that if I could take any of them back, I would gladly do so.'

He let her go. There seemed no point in pushing her too far. After all, with Jordan absent, she had the whole responsibility of running the clinic on her shoulders, an onerous enough task in itself without the additional burden of a murder inquiry taking place at the same time, and he wished to hell Jordan could be contacted as much for her sake as his.

In the event, it was nearly one o'clock in the morning before any news of Jordan was heard. By that time, the main on-the-spot inquiry into Mrs Ingham's death had been concluded and the men had gone, including Stapleton who, before leaving, had reported to Finch that the murder weapon had not been found. The search would be resumed the following morning and widened to include the whole of the clinic grounds. Only Boyce, Finch and Bradshaw were left, the young sergeant remaining on duty to man the telephone in the medical room in case Boyce and the Chief Inspector were occupied elsewhere.

It was Bradshaw who brought the message: Kyle had phoned in to report Dr Jordan's return. Finch took the call in the medical room.

'He's just got back, sir,' Kyle informed him.

'Right!' Finch said. 'Simply tell him that he's needed back here urgently as there's been a serious development in the case. If he asks for details, you're to plead ignorance. Is that quite clear? I assume he's driving his own car?'

'Yes, sir; a Rolls.'

'Well, keep as close behind him as you can. I want to know if he stops anywhere, even for a few minutes.'

'Very good, sir,' Kyle replied and rang off.

6

Bradshaw, who had been posted at the main entrance of the clinic, escorted Dr Jordan to the medical room an hour and a half later and, as he was shown in, Finch noticed how much he had aged even in the short time since he had last seen him, his face gaunt, his shoulders rounded under the expensive camel-hair coat he was wearing.

'You've news of my wife? She's been found?' Jordan asked, immediately on entering the room. 'That damned policeman you sent to collect me wouldn't tell me anything.'

'I'm afraid there's still no news of Mrs Jordan,' Finch began.

'Then what the hell's going on? Why have I been dragged back from London? I was told there has been a serious development in the case.'

'There has,' Finch explained. 'Two attacks were made this evening, one on Mrs Hart, the other on Mrs Ingham . . .'

'Eunice!' Jordan interrupted. He seemed literally staggered by the news and lunged towards the table, grabbing at its edge for support and lowering his head as if about to faint.

Boyce got hastily to his feet and, fetching a chair, placed it close behind Jordan before helping the man to sit down.

'Brandy!' Finch ordered and, as the sergeant left the room, he continued, addressing Jordan, 'Mrs Hart fortunately wasn't seriously injured but I'm afraid Mrs Ingham is dead.'

Jordan made no response except to shake his head slowly from side to side as if refuting the information.

'Dr Jordan,' Finch said sharply, 'you must realise that we are now investigating a murder and an attempted murder, and that

151

the two attacks could possibly be linked with your wife's disappearance.'

'No!' Jordan replied with unexpected vehemence and, raising his head, glared into the Chief Inspector's face. Finch was aware for the first time of the man's eyes as separate features. Before, he had seen him as all of one piece in which his clothes, his hair, the smoothly-shaved contours of cheek and chin had presented a total image of well-dressed, carefully groomed and yet curiously anonymous completeness. Now, focusing on his eyes alone, grey, opaque, fixed, he was conscious of complexity reduced to something much more basic: fear and a desperate panic to escape. It was an expression he was familiar with, that split second as the adrenalin begins to spurt in which almost any reaction is possible, violence, rage, accusation, confession or tears.

Finch watched him warily as he might an animal he had backed into a corner. But Jordan showed none of these expected reactions. The focus of his eyes shifted and, at the same time, a shudder ran through his body, as if the muscles, tensed in readiness for some great feat of physical confrontation, had suddenly relaxed.

'It is not possible,' he added in a low voice.

Finch could only marvel at his incredible self-control while, at the same time, bitterly regretting it. He had lost Jordan. Whatever the man had been about to say would never now be spoken.

As if to emphasise the changed atmosphere, Boyce chose this moment to bustle in with an important air, bearing the brandy in a large, cut-glass goblet which he handed to Jordan, bending solicitously from the waist so that, seen from the back, he looked like a butler in mufti. Finch turned away in disgust.

When Jordan had finished the drink, he resumed the questioning.

'We were speaking of a possible connection between your wife's disappearance and the two attacks this evening,' he began. Jordan interrupted him. He had recovered some of his former presence and assurance and was now sitting upright in the chair although he was still ashen-faced.

'I can only repeat, Chief Inspector, that the idea is ridiculous.'

'Three women, all middle-aged, all associated with the clinic?' Finch deliberately left the sentence dangling in mid-air, inviting Jordan to pick it up and complete it, but Jordan was not going to be drawn. He merely recrossed his legs.

'No connection?' Finch persisted. 'No one from the village or an ex-employee who might want revenge?'

Jordan pressed his thumb and forefinger against the bridge of his nose in a weary gesture and shook his head.

'No patient or former patient who might bear a grudge whether against the clinic or against women in general?'

This time he got a more positive reaction. Jordan looked at him sharply.

'No, no one. All my patients are most carefully vetted. I have never treated anyone who showed such behaviour patterns.'

It was in substance the same as Dr Kerr had already told him and Finch decided to abandon this line of inquiry and move on to another. He nodded to Boyce who, picking up the cue, shifted his buttocks into a more comfortable position on the hard chair and took up the questioning.

'What were your own movements this evening, Dr Jordan?'

Jordan appeared to find the query impertinent for, having looked at the sergeant with distaste, he turned in appeal to Finch.

'Is this necessary, Chief Inspector?'

'Everyone has been questioned,' Finch replied peaceably. He had apparently retired from the interview and was sitting, elbows on the table, drawing little boxes on a sheet of paper and carefully shading them in.

'Including my patients?'

'Yes, indeed. And your staff.'

'I fail to see the necessity,' Jordan began.

Finch laid down the pencil before replying.

'May I remind you that your secretary has been murdered,' he pointed out and then, lowering his head, returned to his sketching.

'Your movements this evening,' Boyce repeated.

'I was in my flat,' Jordan replied. There was a defiant, take-it-or-leave-it air about him.

'All evening?

'No. I went out.'

'At what time?'

'I'm not sure exactly. Does it matter?'

'It would help our inquiries if you could remember,' Boyce said with massive patience which contrasted with Jordan's rising irritability.

'Very well.' He shrugged as if the question were trivial and time-consuming. 'I'd arranged an interview for four o'clock. It took about an hour, I suppose, and I left shortly after it was completed. So the time must have been about quarter past five.'

'And then?'

'I drove about London.' Jordan paused fractionally before continuing at a faster rate. 'I was restless. The whole business of my wife was preying on my mind. I wanted to be alone and, strange though it may seem, I find driving relaxing.'

Finch laid down his pencil again. There was a watchful air about the two men which Jordan was aware of, for he glanced rapidly from one to the other.

'There is nothing against that, is there? I may go out for a drive without having to account for every moment of my time? I consider the whole business a damned imposition!'

There was a silence before Boyce resumed the questioning in the same impassive tone.

'How long were you driving for, sir?'

'I don't know. I can't remember.'

But he had gone too far. He was being merely petulant and Boyce responded with a slight shake of the head like a Nanny deprecating rude and silly behaviour on the part of a charge.

It was Finch who replied. His stance and expression had subtly altered. There was an alert and yet curiously impersonal quality about his face and voice as he spoke.

'I think I should warn you, Dr Jordan, that any statement you make will be checked. Would you care to begin again? We require an exact account of your movements. You left the flat at approximately a quarter past five. You went for a drive.

Where did you go? And how long were you alone in the car without witnesses?'

Jordan sat silent and motionless, staring straight ahead of him with an odd peering intensity as if he were trying to focus on something in the far distance. In the silence, the faint hum of the strip-lighting was clearly audible.

'I went to visit a friend,' Jordan said at last.

'Name and address?' Boyce asked, his pen poised over his notebook.

Jordan appealed once more to the Chief Inspector.

'Do I have to answer?'

'It would be in your interest if you did, sir,' Finch replied in his official voice. The balance of power had shifted and the control was now in his hands although he did not seem to find any personal satisfaction in the situation. The interview had settled down into the routine question and answer session with which he was familiar and he seemed prepared to stay there, all night if necessary, until the last query had been completed. Even the room had taken on the atmosphere of a police station. The blind had been drawn down over the window and the strip-lighting glared back from the shiny walls and glass fronts of the drug cupboards.

'Very well.' Jordan turned to look directly at Boyce and began speaking in a flat, colourless voice. 'I went to see a woman. Professionally she is known as Sylvia Austin although I doubt very much if that is her real name. She is a call-girl.' Boyce's pen faltered momentarily and then scribbled on. 'I have been visiting her at regular intervals over the past eighteen months and our relationship is merely sexual. I pay for her services. I had telephoned her earlier to make arrangements to pick her up at her house. She lives in Hanover Grove, off Regents Park, a respectable address.' He smiled briefly; perhaps with self-mockery. Finch wasn't sure. Until that moment, Jordan's expression had been tight, the muscles round his nose and mouth particularly taut, hiding, Finch guessed, a deep sense of shame. 'I arrived there at about half past five, stayed until seven and then took her out to dinner. I suppose you'll want the name and address of the restaurant? I thought so. It's Bellini's in Tite Street. When you make your inquiries there, ask on behalf of Mr

Howard. The table was booked in that name. We left together at approximately nine o'clock and went back to her place. I finally returned to my own flat at about one o'clock. No doubt your own constable will be able to verify the time. He approached me just as I was unlocking the front door.'

7

It was almost half past three in the morning before the police finally left. Howard Jordan escorted them personally to the front door, an act of courtesy which, in the absence of any other member of staff, seemed only fitting for him to perform. And prudent. He wanted to make sure they actually left the premises. Not that there was anybody left for them to talk to. Everyone else had gone to bed and only the minimum of lights were left burning, those in the downstairs passages and at the head of the stairs. The rest of the house was in darkness and possessed that deserted, vaguely sinister air that all houses assume in the early hours, with that added quality of resentment as if the empty rooms and corridors were holding themselves aloof from the intrusion.

There was another reason why he wished to see them to the door. He felt that, in his absence, Finch had taken too much on himself. His commandeering of the medical room was one instance of this. So, too, was his questioning of the staff and patients. Of course, Jordan could see the necessity for it but, all the same, it was time, he felt, to re-establish his own authority and to show Finch that the final command still rested in his own hands.

Standing at the top of the steps, he watched them walk away to their car; the Chief Inspector with his disconcertingly shabby appearance and faint local accent which, like a fool, he had taken to mean limited intelligence and saw now, too late, was merely a useful cover from behind which a very watchful and perceptive mind was quietly observing him; the sergeant, too, whom he had also mentally dismissed, with his ridiculous suit and patterned tie. What he hadn't seen until this evening was that together they formed a team which was quite formidable.

But not formidable enough, he thought, as the car backed and turned and finally headed off down the drive. It was unlikely they would ever find the answers to the questions they were asking because it hadn't occurred to them that the questions themselves were the wrong ones.

It was all mad, of course; a walking nightmare in which very little made sense – Janet dead, Eunice attacked. Claire, too, of course. And yet that was, crazily enough, the only comfort he could find in it all: the very fact of its terrifying madness. If he himself could understand only part of it, then Finch would certainly be unable to unravel the tangle of lies and hidden motives and desires which lay behind the events of the past two days.

As for the participants, he could not bring himself to think of them. They loomed briefly into his consciousness as figures in a nightmare, mere presences which seemed to stand just behind his shoulder as they do sometimes in dreams, while all that remained in focus were certain objects and images connected, in some strange, surrealistic manner, with the people they represented. So, while he could not envisage Claire's face, he could see the bowl toppling by degrees from the dressing-table, as if photographed in slow motion, releasing the cloud of pale powder which floated up lazily around his feet. As for Janet, he saw only her shoes; black, patent-leather pumps with small silver buckles. He couldn't even remember when he had noticed them but it must have been on one specific occasion for he could picture them quite clearly, the right shoe turned inwards, the left facing him and on a slightly higher plane so that he realised she must have been sitting with her legs crossed.

He could not recall Eunice's features at all. If someone had spoken her name in one of those word-association exercises which he sometimes used on his patients, he would have replied with the one word: firelight. It was all he could summon up and even that was overlaid by other images. He saw, for example, not the wood fires that burned in the main rooms of the clinic – surely the most obvious and immediate connection – but

157

another fire the memory of which, he realised, went back many years to his childhood: a Guy Fawkes bonfire burning in a small, suburban back garden, its leaping flames reflected in the windows of the house so that, for one terrible moment, he had thought that it, too, was ablaze.

It formed, also, part of the sensation of dislocation that went with nightmares; that sense of impending chaos, as if everything were poised on a brink ready to slide downwards into annihilation.

The clinic was behind him. He was aware of its bulk, the great doorway in which he was standing with its solid pillars; the façade stretching away on both sides, massive, settled; the chimney stacks clustered like bulwarks. And yet that, too, seemed to be on the point of dissolution and, unable to turn back and face it, he walked on down the steps towards the lawn.

It was here that Simon Boyd found him a little later. He had been unable to sleep and, from his bedroom overlooking the front of the house, he had heard Jordan's voice bidding goodnight to Finch and his sergeant and then the sound of their car driving away.

What he had not heard, although he had lain awake listening for it, finding even an attempt at sleep impossible until it came, was the noise of the heavy front door closing and Jordan re-entering the house.

When one listens at night, expectant of hearing certain noises, other sounds in their turn become magnified and, after what seemed a long time, he was aware of footsteps descending the steps and crossing the gravel.

Something in the sound of them, as melancholy as a train heard in the distance, sharpened his curiosity and, putting on his dressing-gown and slippers, he went to the head of the stairs.

The hall, huge and deserted, extended beneath him, lit only by the wall lamps so that the shadows enlarged it and gave it the appearance of a vast tank filled with massed clumps of darkness, like black weed.

The front door was open, the terrace beyond it empty, as he discovered when, descending the stairs and crossing the hall, he emerged on to the flagstones.

On the other side of the drive, barely visible, was the figure of Jordan, standing on the lawn with his back to the clinic, his shoulders bowed.

There was something intensely private about the man's attitude, as if he were indulging in some secret grief, and, unwilling to intrude into such a moment, Simon Boyd was about to retreat into the clinic when Jordan turned and called out, 'Who's there?'

There was nothing he could do except walk forward and identify himself.

'Ah, Boyd,' Jordan said abstractedly, as if the name meant very little to him, and then, with an effort to pull himself together, he added more briskly, although with the same remote air, 'You're on Dr Kerr's list, aren't you? How's the treatment progressing?'

'Satisfactorily,' Boyd replied. He felt impelled to continue. 'Are you all right, Dr Jordan?'

'All right? All right?' Jordan repeated. The phrase seemed to puzzle him.

'I wondered if you were ill.'

'No, I'm not ill.' There was a pause. 'You've heard what happened this evening?'

The question was asked abruptly, almost peremptorily.

'To Mrs Ingham and Mrs Hart? Yes, I have. I'm dreadfully sorry.'

'I can't believe she's really dead,' Jordan said, almost to himself.

It was impossible to see his face. The night was quite dark and the subdued light from the hall did not reach that far across the drive. All that was discernible was his hunched shape, particularly the heavy head and shoulders which appeared larger than normal, dwarfing the rest of his body and making it seem curiously misshapen and disproportionate. His voice came out of the shadows and that, too, seemed magnified as if the enlarged upper portion of his trunk was acting as a sounding box. Even though he was speaking in little more than a whisper, it had a harsh yet muffled resonance that reminded Boyd of someone speaking from behind a wooden mask. Its effect was

159

disturbing and he was about to withdraw when Jordan asked another question.

'There's been talk, of course?'

It seemed useless to deny it and Boyd replied, 'Yes, I'm afraid there has.'

'People don't like it. Scandal, I mean. They'll leave.'

Boyd was silent.

'Sutton's already asked for his account. There'll be others. It's just the beginning.' Again he paused before continuing in the same jerky, disjointed manner. 'It took me twenty years to get this far. Twenty years. And it could all be ruined in a matter of days. Odd, isn't it? Time, I mean? When you're young there seems to be so much of it. And then, suddenly, you realise it's too late.'

'I know the feeling,' Boyd replied and was surprised when Jordan seized eagerly on the remark.

'Do you? Do you really? What do you regret?'

'Regret?' Boyd repeated. It seemed significant that, while he had made no mention of the word, Jordan should choose to interpret it in this way. 'A lot of things, I suppose. Relationships mainly. People I should have been kinder to, spent more time with, listened to with greater care. You say to yourself: Tomorrow I'll make the effort. But you never do.'

'And then you feel overwhelmed with guilt?' Jordan put in with the same eagerness. It was posed as a question rather than a statement, as if Jordan were trying to assess Boyd's own reactions. At the same time, Boyd was aware that, while he himself had been referring to his own experience, particularly his relationship with his parents, Jordan had taken the comments personally and was attempting to understand, through Boyd's explanation, something about his own nature as if he were, for the first time, facing certain truths about himself which he had never properly examined before or put into words. 'But don't you find it a negative emotion?'

'I don't believe any emotion is entirely wasted, not even fear.'

''Who taught you that?' Jordan's voice, coming out of the darkness, had an ironic sharpness. 'Dr Kerr?'

'She made me understand that the energy in the emotion can

be misdirected. But I've always believed myself that it is better to have negative feelings rather than none at all.'

'"I feel therefore I am"?'

The sarcasm deepened.

'Something like that,' Boyd replied lamely.

He did not like the turn the conversation had taken. The situation, too, had developed a bizarre quality. It was nearly four o'clock in the morning and he was standing on the lawn in his dressing-gown and slippers, exchanging remarks on the nature of guilt with the director of the clinic.

'Or "I suffer therefore I am"?'

There was an unpleasantly probing insistence in Jordan's question and Simon Boyd remained silent.

'Don't believe it!' Jordan continued, raising his voice. 'There is nothing noble in suffering, either mental or physical. That's one of the greatest confidence tricks played on mankind in the name of religion. It is merely degrading!'

He stopped abruptly, stood completely motionless for a moment and then, with a muttered remark which Boyd could not hear, pushed past him and walked rapidly back towards the clinic.

Part Seven

1

The following morning, Bentley, the liaison officer at the Yard, telephoned. Finch took the call. He had arrived late himself after a sleepless night going over the case in his mind, to find the office empty and no sign of Boyce whose absence added to his irritability.

The call, however, went some way to restoring his good humour.

'We've traced the taxi driver,' Bentley announced sounding jubilant and it occurred to Finch again, as it had done many times in the past, how the excitement of a murder investigation brushed off on to those not immediately concerned in the inquiry. 'It was a bit of luck, mind you, that she dropped her gloves. The man wasn't able to make an ID on the photo. Do you want his name and address?'

Finch took it down although he was eager to ask the next question. 'Where did he drop her?'

'Hampstead. Right outside the tube station.'

'Damn!' Finch said softly.

'Sorry about that.' Bentley sounded defensive as if it was all his fault. 'She never gave an address. She simply said Hampstead and when he got to the top of Heath Street she tapped on the window and told him to stop. "This'll do," she said. "I'll walk from here." At least, that's the driver's version of the conversation.'

'Did he notice which way she went after she'd got out of the taxi?'

'No, he didn't. Someone else hailed him and he was more interested in his next fare.'

Boyce entered the office as Bentley was speaking and Finch

went through a pantomime of pointing significantly to his watch and pulling a face at the sergeant over the top of the receiver to which Boyce responded by lifting his shoulders until they covered his ears and holding out both hands in a gesture of abject apology. He looked, Finch thought with amusement, like a ham actor playing Shylock.

He also looked exhausted, a fact that the Chief Inspector was only aware of as Boyce walked heavily across the office to hang up his coat.

'Alarm didn't go off,' Boyce explained succinctly as Finch, having thanked Bentley, rang off.

It was almost certainly a lie, although one that Finch was prepared to ignore on that occasion. Instead he said, 'I've got a job for you.'

'Oh, yes?' Boyce sounded wary.

'A nice, simple, sitting-down, office job where you can drink as much tea as you like.'

Boyce's expression of mistrust deepened as Finch continued cheerfully,

'Get hold of a London telephone directory L-R and look up a name for me.'

'What name?'

'Ah, there's the rub. We don't know. All we do know is it begins with the letter R and the address must be somewhere in the Hampstead area.'

Boyce was silent for a moment until the truth of it finally dawned.

'But there must be bloody thousands!' he protested.

'Oh, only hundreds, surely,' Finch corrected him. 'And we know the first name begins with M so it narrows the field a little. All the same, you'll need help. Rustle up Kyle and Marsh and anybody else who's standing about doing nothing. A quick raid on the canteen might be a good idea. What I want is a list of everybody with those initials; names, addresses, telephone numbers. Put a star by anybody who seems likely; doctors, for example. We know Mrs Jordan had an appointment. We'll start with those and, if necessary, go through the whole damn lot.'

As it turned out, it was to prove necessary. When Boyce finally produced the list, and Finch ran his eye over it, he saw that it contained more than eighty names, beginning with Raban, Michael and ending with Rzysko, M.K. Only eleven were starred; three doctors, an accountant, a hairdresser, a masseur, a dressmaker and optician, two dentists and a taxidermist. He was inclined to dismiss the last three. It was unlikely that Mrs Jordan had travelled across London to visit a dentist when she had already had a dental appointment in the morning. Nor could he see any reason for her wanting to consult a taxidermist.

All the same, he put a couple of WPC's to the task of ringing all the numbers and, by giving the date of Mrs Jordan's appointment, to inquire, in her name, about a bunch of keys that had been lost on February 19th.

In all eleven instances, they drew a blank. On each inquiry, they received the same answer. Sorry, there must be some mistake. No one called Mrs Jordan had made an appointment for that particular afternoon and no bunch of keys had been found.

It was possible, Finch thought, that, in view of the secrecy surrounding the second appointment, she might have given a false name and, in that case, the three doctors ought to remain on the list. He saw no reason for her wishing to hide her identity from the others.

There was still the other list of over sixty unstarred names and numbers.

'Right,' Finch told the two women. 'Start at the top and work your way down. All I want you to do this time is to ask for an appointment in the name of Mrs Jordan for tomorrow morning. If anyone responds, try to find out what business they're running but do it discreetly. Let me have their names and addresses even if you can't make an appointment.'

He left them to it and returned to his own office to start work on the reports which were already beginning to arrive on his desk; mostly routine stuff; Kyle's on his surveillance outside Jordan's London address; Formby and Bradshaw on the questioning of the staff and patients at the clinic, including the more detailed word-for-word report on Simon Boyd which Finch read through with the same uneasy feeling he had experienced the previous evening that there was something not quite right about it. Even dismissing the fact that Boyd had no alibi, which in itself needn't necessarily be suspicious – quite innocent people often find themselves unable to account for their movements at a crucial time – there still remained the question of why he had visited the Jordans' house, which was still not satisfactorily explained. He had, on his own admission, only met Mrs Jordan on the Sunday evening. His concern for the whereabouts of a mere acquaintance of a few hours' standing seemed, therefore, excessive.

Boyd, Finch decided, as he put the typewritten sheets to one side, would have to be questioned again.

Last of all came Stapleton's report on the search of the stable-yard and the garages which had produced nothing in the way of evidence. Stapleton and his men should be extending that search at that very moment, Finch realised, consulting his watch, to include the whole of the clinic grounds. If they drew a blank there, either on the weapon that had killed Janet Ingham or Mrs Jordan's body, the area would have to be extended even further.

The prospect filled him with gloom. God knows where it might finish up. Turning over the whole village? Or the surrounding woods and farmland? And that would mean a hell of a lot of earth, not to mention undergrowth and ditches, in which a body, let alone an iron bar, could be hidden.

There was nothing yet from Pardoe nor from the forensic lab where Janet Ingham's clothing had been sent for expert examination. Nothing either on the car. Not that he was expecting any reports on these. It was too soon. All the same, until they arrived, with, he hoped, crucial evidence to prove the murderer's identity, there was nothing he could do except carry on with his own side of the investigation. A fingerprint or two would be hitting the jackpot. He'd be willing to settle for much less.

It was mid-morning before one of the WPC's tapped on his office door, bringing the results of the telephone inquiries. There were only three new numbers to add to the list; all the others had been private householders. They consisted of a corset-fitter, unlisted as such in the book, Finch suspected, for tax purposes;

a lady offering colonic irrigation in the privacy of her own home and a third whose occupation was unknown.

'Why in God's name didn't you ask?' Finch snapped. The sight of the reports lying on his desk and the prospect of more to come had soured his good-humour. However, he immediately regretted his outburst of ill temper. The WPC was a plain girl whose plump figure was unappealingly exaggerated by the bulky uniform. He tried to avoid looking at her hips, remembering the sobriquet he had once overheard in the canteen – Bottlebum.

'I'm sorry, sir.' The girl looked unhappy and flustered. 'I made an appointment but the woman rang off before I could ask any more questions. I thought it might look suspicious if I rang back.'

'All right,' Finch conceded. 'When's the appointment for?'

'Tomorrow morning at a quarter past eleven.'

'And you say a woman answered the phone?'

'Yes, sir, but the number's listed under a man's name.'

Finch consulted the list.

The name, he saw, was Maurice Royston and the address was Number 17, Fox Grove, Hampstead.

2

Walking down Fox Grove the following morning, he might have imagined himself in a side street of a small, well-preserved country town. It was a narrow cul-de-sac, ending in a row of iron bollards where three steps led down to a lower level, and was lined on both sides with eighteenth century terrace cottages, each with a long, carefully-tended front garden, full of early spring flowers and blossoming trees so that the total effect was of the calm, leafy abundance of some Cathedral close. The roar of Hampstead where the traffic went grinding up Heath Street, past the boutiques and antique shops and expensive restaurants, seemed miles away.

Number 17 had a bright blue front door and white and purple hyacinths in window-boxes. Finch went up the path and banged on the dolphin-shaped brass knocker. The door was opened by a quiet-spoken, middle-aged woman who asked him his name.

'Finch,' he replied.

'Have you an appointment?' she asked doubtfully.

'In the name of Jordan.'

Oddly enough, it seemed to satisfy her for she showed him into the front room, small and furnished with spindly antiques, inlaid with mother-of-pearl and marquetry in delicate garlands of leaves and flowers so that the room seemed to echo the shapes and patterns of the garden. Behind the net curtains, the stiff, upright heads of the hyacinths seemed artificial in comparison.

Presently, the woman returned and showed him into a back room where a man rose from behind a small table set in front of a pair of French windows and indicated a chair opposite. Finch sat down, taking his time and glancing about him as he did so. This room was also furnished in the same delicate manner and was flooded with green light from the garden where trees and bushes were so closely planted together that there was no view of the surrounding houses except for an occasional chimney. A stone Pan stood under an arch of ivy, playing on his pipes; his head, with its two little horns, tipped to one side, as if he were listening to his own silent music.

Maurice Royston seemed, at first sight, ill-suited to his surroundings. He was a small, plump man with neatly cut grey hair and gold-rimmed glasses and possessed the unhurried, judicious air of a family solicitor or the bank manager of a provincial branch. It was only his clothes that suggested otherwise: a pink shirt worn under a pearl-grey cashmere cardigan and a silk tie that was a little too large and flowing. And his hands. They rested on the inlaid table top, as white and manicured as a woman's, a ring with a dark red stone in it on his little finger. Beside them lay a pack of cards.

'Mr Finch?' Maurice Royston inquired gently.

'Detective Chief Inspector,' Finch explained, producing his official identification.

'I see.'

Maurice Royston pursed his lips in faint disapproval and his hands reclasped themselves but otherwise he showed no reaction. He might be about to turn down, after careful consideration, a request for a small overdraft.

'Are you here on official business?' he asked.

'I've called to inquire about a woman who I believe is one of your clients; a Mrs Jordan who had an appointment with you for 3 p.m. on February 19th.'

Without replying, Maurice Royston opened a drawer in the table and took out a leather covered book which he leafed through slowly, a plump, white finger finally coming to rest against a name.

'I think you are mistaken,' he said, looking at Finch over the top of his glasses. 'I had no client of that name on that particular day.'

'She may have used a false identity,' Finch replied and, taking Mrs Jordan's photograph from his pocket, he handed it to Royston who studied it carefully for a few moments before handing it back.

'Yes, that is the woman you mentioned,' Royston replied. 'But she made the appointment in the name of Mrs Vincent.'

It followed, Finch thought, that she should have chosen her sister's name.

'It does happen,' Royston continued. 'Some clients prefer to use another identity when they come for a consultation.'

'From the cards?' Finch suggested. He was aware that he sounded critical and faintly derisive although it was unintentional.

Royston smiled primly and, picking up the pack of cards, spread them fanwise across the table with the dexterity of a cardsharper.

'The Tarot, Chief Inspector; one of the oldest forms of divination. On what particular problem did you want an answer? Or have you come for a general reading?'

'I'm sorry,' Finch apologised. 'Although I admit I'm a sceptic, I'm genuinely interested in any information you can give me about Mrs Jordan.'

Royston made a small, gracious inclination of the head, accepting the apology.

'In whatever way I can. In fact, you know, your visit isn't entirely a surprise. At her last consultation, the cards indicated she was in some danger; quite close, in fact. I assume something has happened to her. Is she dead?'

The question startled Finch and recalled his own feelings when he had stood under the trees in the clinic grounds and knew with absolute certainty that Mrs Jordan was no longer alive. Royston's query gave him the small, jolting sensation of *déjà vu*. It also surprised him into frankness.

'We're not sure. At the moment, she is simply missing.'

'I see. The cards are not always specific but, if I remember correctly, these were among Mrs Jordan's spread on the day she came to see me.' He took three from the pack and laid them on the table in front of the Chief Inspector. 'The Queen of Cups, the King of Batons reversed and the Four of Swords, also reversed.'

'Meaning?' Finch asked, fascinated despite himself.

'The Queen of Cups would signify Mrs Jordan herself, imaginative, intuitive, inclined to be dreamy and impractical. That is what the card would indicate. Of course, observing her, I noticed other qualities which helped me to interpret it in more detail. She was a woman who found it difficult to assert herself and was too easily influenced by others; who longed for affection and reassurance but hadn't found it, and whose own natural gifts had been suppressed. In close association with her was the King of Batons reversed.'

He placed the card so that it overlapped the first, covering the gentle profile of the woman with the hard, full-faced image of the king who sat, knees belligerently apart, flourishing a sword in both hands.

'An autocratic man, intolerant of weakness, strong-minded and capable but someone who could be ruthless in attaining his own ends. Her husband, possibly, or her father?'

He looked directly into Finch's face who kept his expression deliberately bland, giving nothing away although he was surprised by the accuracy of the remarks which could apply to Jordan or, equally correctly, from what Rose Vincent had told him, to Claire Jordan's father.

'And then there was the Four of Swords reversed,' Maurice Royston continued in the same conversational voice, laying the card with the others. 'Briefly interpreted it means exile or banishment, a severance of some kind.'

'A broken marriage?' suggested Finch.

'That's perceptive of you, Chief Inspector. Yes, it could indeed be given that meaning but in Mrs Jordan's case I sensed something more than this – great danger to her personally, a strong feeling of threat.'

'Possibly suicide?'

'No, I don't think so. The danger came from an outside agency.'

'Did you tell her this?'

'Not in so many words. My clients come to me for reassurance and, although I do warn them of possible future events that could have unpleasant consequences, I take care not to be too specific unless I feel the client is capable of hearing the truth. I might, for example, see bankruptcy in the cards but I will simply warn of financial dangers ahead and advise great caution in business transactions. In Mrs Jordan's case, I simply told her that she could expect problems in some close personal relationship and that she was not to be too trusting of those near to her.'

'What were her reactions?' Finch asked curiously.

'She nodded her head as if it confirmed something she already knew.'

'Was it her first visit?'

'No. She had been to consult me several times; not often but I believe on three or four occasions over the past seven years.'

So Mrs Jordan had been consulting him while she was still living in London, Finch thought.

'Looking for reassurance?' he asked out loud, picking up Royston's remark.

'Yes, and the hope for future happiness. Most of my clients come with these motives. Why else would they consult me? I'm afraid I saw nothing in her cards to suggest this possibility. In fact, there was only isolation and loneliness. There was a marked deterioration, too, in her psychic energy, an emotional exhaustion which grew increasingly apparent.' He paused and looked again directly into Finch's face, fixing it with his pale eyes. 'You were aware, of course, that she was becoming more and more dependent on alcohol?'

The information was quite new to Finch and he asked sharply, 'Are you sure about that?'

'Oh, yes, quite sure. I didn't need the cards to tell me that. I could see the physical symptoms for myself. Had she continued, she would undoubtedly have become an alcoholic. I've seen many in my career and I've learnt to recognise the signs.'

Royston began to gather up the cards, leaving only the Queen of Cups on the table, and Finch regarded it in silence for a few seconds. If what Royston had told him was true, it cast an entirely new light on Mrs Jordan's disappearance although what exactly its significance might be he wasn't himself certain. Jordan had said nothing to him about his wife's drinking habits, an omission that wasn't in itself necessarily suspicious. He might well have preferred to keep it a secret. Who else might be aware of them was another matter entirely.

He started to button up his overcoat in preparation to leave when Royston placed the finger that bore the red-stoned ring across the face of the Queen of Cups. The action was oddly disturbing. So, too, was his parting remark.

'If you want to find Mrs Jordan, Chief Inspector, I advise you to look where there is freshly-dug earth.'

3

'You mean a grave?' Boyce asked incredulously. He had listened with increasing restlessness to Finch's account of his interview with Maurice Royston, his face expressing disbelief. 'But you're not telling me you were taken in by that mumbo-jumbo?'

'No, I wasn't,' Finch replied, feeling on the defensive. 'On the other hand, Royston must have met hundreds of people of all different types over the years and, like us, has developed an intuitive response to them.' As Boyce still seemed unwilling to concede even this point, he added, 'Come off it, Tom! Even you go by instinct sometimes.'

171

'I don't know about that,' Boyce replied. He sounded as if the Chief Inspector had accused him of some unnatural and antisocial behaviour. 'I can usually tell when a man's lying.'

'Exactly! And I think Royston works on the same principle. He picks up small gestures or changes of expression, only with him it's more highly-developed. Some of it's nothing more than inspired guesswork. That card, for example, that was supposed to symbolise Jordan himself, or Mrs Jordan's father. I've no doubt it turned up in her reading but he interpreted it the way he did because of what he knew of Mrs Jordan – someone shy and timid, easily bullied by the men around her. What I'm not sure about is how he came by the idea she might be dead. I said nothing to suggest she might be in any danger.'

'He probably picked that up from you,' Boyce pointed out. 'After all, a Chief Inspector's not likely to turn up inquiring after one of his clients unless it's something serious.'

'I could have been investigating a robbery or blackmail.'

'Fair enough,' Boyce admitted. 'I still think it was a lucky shot in the dark. The fact that she may have drunk is interesting, though. Jordan's never mentioned it, has he?'

'No, neither did her sister, Mrs Vincent, although at one point during the interview she hesitated as if she was about to tell me something and then changed her mind. It's possible she was going to refer to it. Jordan must know, though. He can't have lived with her all those years and not be aware of it. The wine merchant's bills alone would give it away. How far it affects her disappearance remains to be seen.'

'I'd've thought it would add to the suicide theory,' Boyce replied. 'She's unhappy; she starts drinking; then on Monday morning she decides she can't stand it any more so she walks out of the house and jumps into the nearest river. Don't forget there's one only a mile from the house. We could have it dragged, I suppose,' he added, without much enthusiasm.

'No, not yet,' Finch said. He couldn't explain why the decision seemed the right one. Had Boyce pressed him for an explanation, he would have given as his reasons the absence of a suicide note and the strongly-held belief of both Rose Vincent and Jordan that Mrs Jordan had not killed herself, a conviction that even Royston had held. He could see equally clearly the arguments that Boyce would bring to refute his reasoning: that not all suicides are accompanied by a letter and that Rose Vincent, Royston and Jordan himself could be wrong.

No, his decision was based on more nebulous premises and he realised that, like Maurice Royston, he was relying on some intuitive process that defied any rational interpretation.

Mrs Jordan was dead. He felt this more strongly than ever. And she had not died by her own hand. Some outside agency, to use Royston's words, was responsible.

He could express the idea to Boyce only as a hypothesis.

'Look,' he said. 'We've got one murder, one attempted murder and Mrs Jordan's disappearance to bear in mind. Let's suppose for a moment that Mrs Jordan has also been murdered. It's possible, as I've said before, that all three cases could be linked. All the women were middle-aged; all were connected with the clinic; all had some close personal or professional relationship with Jordan which ought to make him our prime suspect. But Jordan has an alibi both for the morning his wife disappeared and for Tuesday evening when the attacks took place. So we've got to look elsewhere. Of the others who were close to the three women, Hannah Kerr and Donald Midgley can also be crossed off the list. They give each other alibis for Tuesday evening. So who are we left with? Simon Boyd or some unknown outsider.

'Simon Boyd's a possibility. He's been hanging about the Jordan's house; he has no alibi for the time of the attacks and he could fit Mrs Hart's description of the man who struck her. It's not a very good description, I admit, and eye-witnesses are notoriously unreliable but Simon Boyd could be that man. One point in his favour is lack of motive. I can't see any reason why he should want to attack any of the three women involved.

'As for the outsider, the crank who has a grudge against the clinic or the homicidal maniac who kills merely for pleasure – well, frankly I don't believe it. If there's a pattern, which I'm sure there is, there's got to be a motive, however obscure. I'm convinced those women weren't chosen at random. And I'm equally convinced Mrs Jordan's body will turn up somewhere. By the way, has Stapleton phoned in yet? Do you know how the search went?'

'Oh God!' Boyce exclaimed, looking contrite. 'I meant to pass

173

the message on and all that talk about fortune telling put it clean out of my mind. Stapleton rang through about an hour ago. They've completed the search and found nothing. But they're going back to the clinic in the morning. They didn't have time to examine the drains. Stapleton's planning to make a start on those about nine o'clock tomorrow.'

4

'And you found nothing?' Finch asked. It was the following morning, fresh, clean, after the previous day's rain, the sky, which had lifted and soared away, an immense fragile blue, lightly brushed with pale cloud.

'Nothing that would interest you,' Stapleton replied.

They were standing in the service yard, together with Boyce and some of Stapleton's men, watching a young constable who, with his jacket off and his sleeves rolled up, was attempting to lift an iron grating over the central drain, cemented into place over the years by the accumulation of dirt. Their conversation was almost desultory, their attention centred on the man's exertions, the tightened cords and muscles in his arms, the angle of his body as he strained against the long iron crow-bar, with the fascination of bystanders observing someone else at work. The covers in the stable-yard had already been lifted and the drains searched with no result.

'And no signs of recently dug earth?' Finch added, remembering Royston's parting remark.

Stapleton turned his attention momentarily from the constable to give Finch an amused, sideways glance.

'My men would recognise a grave if they saw one,' he replied.

His humour, Finch thought, was like the man himself, inclined to be slow and heavy.

'Well,' he said, shifting about restlessly from foot to foot, 'I'll wander off for a bit. I want to look in daylight at the place where Mrs Hart was attacked. I only saw it after dark.'

The site was more open than he had first thought. Where the drive swung round behind the outbuildings, its deep ruts still containing rainwater which reflected the blue of the sky, quite a large area of rough grass extended back, before the trees of the surrounding woods began. Over to his right were the kitchen gardens. He could see the peaked roof of a greenhouse, its glass glittering wickedly in the sun, and a line of runner-bean poles, leaning together like tent frames.

The blackberry bush, further disturbed by yesterday's search, sprawled more untidily than before, its long brambles turned back to expose the whitish undersides of the leaves.

He glanced back toward the yard, seeing in more detail the route Mrs Hart had taken. The rear façade of the clinic now faced him, with its rows of windows, smaller and more humble than those on the front, and its complex festoons of down-pipes running across the brickwork. The kitchen door and window were clearly visible; so, too, was the frosted glass of the pantry window. On one side, the outbuildings stretched out towards him, their slate roofs gleaming dully; on the other, the blank, back wall of the stables with its one arched opening, decorated, as he saw for the first time, with a large key-stone carved in the shape of a horse's head. Just above it, he caught a glimpse of the white-painted, octagonal wooden clock-tower which crowned the central block in the adjoining stable-yard. A little further back from the archway, the cluster of men still stood round the constable who, even at that relatively short distance, seemed curiously remote and silent, like a figure on a stage miming human endeavour.

As he watched, the grouping broke up. The constable staggered backwards, the watching men moved eagerly forward. There were derisive cries of approval and admiration. The drain cover had finally been lifted from its bed. Stapleton stepped in front to peer down into the oblong hole and then, turning to Finch, raised an arm.

'I think we've found it!'

Finch set off down the yard at a loping run, the skirts of his mackintosh flapping against his knees.

It was odd, he thought, how often men on a murder investigation behaved like schoolkids at a treasure hunt. Any

175

piece of crucial evidence, a discarded shoe, a fragment of blood-stained clothing, could arouse in them this thrill of discovery. There was something else that was odd about the situation which he couldn't for the moment quite place.

In this instance, the treasure was an old iron bar, leaning at an angle against the side of a brick-lined sump-hole, at the bottom of which lay a pool of dark, stagnant, evil-smelling water. As Boyce, his hand covered with a plastic glove, retrieved the bar, stirring up the water, the stench rose strongly. He held the bar out at arm's length for Finch to examine it.

It was roughly three feet in length, two inches wide and half an inch thick, the right dimensions, according to Pardoe, for it to be responsible for the head injuries inflicted on Janet Ingham, and was heavily pitted with rust, so there was little chance of finding any fingerprints on it although, on the end near where Boyce was holding it, the surface flakes had been rubbed off as if in contact with a hand. The other end, which had presumably struck the blows, was covered in black slime and Finch doubted if forensic would be able to raise much from that either in the way of blood or hairs, although there was a chance that some fragments of skin might still be embedded in the metal.

He had no doubt that it was the murder weapon and, as Boyce carefully wrapped it in plastic, in readiness for it to be sent to the lab, he glanced about him to fix in his mind the route which the murderer must have taken when, after killing Janet Ingham, he had moved into the service yard, discarding the bar on the way, before attacking Mrs Hart.

It was then he realised what was odd about the situation.

5

Simmonds heard the car before he saw it. It came roaring up the drive and, swinging round in front of the clinic, drew up at the door in an abrupt halt that sent gravel showering across the lawn.

'Bloody fool!' Simmonds said out loud and, still clutching the rake with which he had been smoothing the surface of the drive, he began to walk towards the small, bright-red Morgan, prepared to give the driver, whom he expected to be some young tearaway with more money than sense, a piece of his mind. There was a 5 m.p.h. speed limit in the clinic grounds and no one, patient or visitor, was going to get away with breaking it or mucking up his lawn into the bargain. It was bad enough having the police trampling about the place, making a second search, as if his own hadn't been properly done, an interference on their part which still rankled and which put him in the mood for a row with someone.

He hesitated, however, when he saw the driver get out. It was a woman, middle-aged and smartly dressed in a mink jacket and a pair of red trousers that matched the car and obviously very angry from the way she slammed the door and set off up the steps, her high heels clicking purposefully on the stone.

Drawing back, he watched Miss Ogilvie, Jordan's temporary replacement for Janet Ingham, let her in, wondering who the woman was and what scene was about to take place because it was quite obvious, from the set of her shoulders and the violent way in which she had rung the bell, that some quarrel was brewing.

'I want to speak to Dr Jordan,' Rose Vincent said imperiously as soon as she was shown into the hall.

'Have you an appointment?' Miss Ogilvie asked.

'No, I haven't,' Rose snapped, 'but I intend seeing him at once. Tell him Mrs Vincent is here.'

'I'll see if he's available,' Miss Ogilvie replied nervously. Like Simmonds, she was aware of the woman's anger and, moreover, had the unpleasant task of facing it at close quarters. Being new to the clinic, she wasn't sure how to deal with the situation. Dr Jordan was in his consulting room but had given orders that he wasn't to be disturbed.

She returned to the general office, aware that Mrs Vincent was following close behind her, and did not even have time to press the intercom switch to announce her arrival before Mrs Vincent, taking matters into her own hands, had crossed the room and, flinging open the communicating door, marched in without any preliminaries.

177

'Rose!' Jordan exclaimed, getting hastily to his feet. He was both startled and dismayed to see her. The events of the past few days had left him emotionally exhausted and it was as much as he could do to cope with the routine running of the clinic. A confrontation with his sister-in-law was the last thing he wanted. 'Won't you sit down?' he added, drawing forward one of the armchairs.

But Rose refused it. She had no intention of letting Howard resume his own seat behind the desk and take over control. Having worked herself up to a first-class, stand-up row, she wasn't going to be cheated out of it. All through the long drive down from London she had been rehearsing what to say but, now that she was face to face with Howard, the sentences refused to shape themselves into a coherent expression and remained a confused clamour in her mind so that, for a moment, she was at a loss to know how to begin and could only glare at him speechlessly.

She noticed how much he had changed. There was a furtive, uncertain air about him that she had never seen before although he still retained his prosperous appearance. His hands, the fingers of which were pressed down on the surface of the desk as if for support, were white and well-tended, and the broad, plain gold wedding band he wore was caught in the sunlight that came pouring in through the long windows and seemed to flash directly at her.

The sight of it finally released her rage.

'What in the hell have you done with Claire?' she shouted. He made a conciliatory movement with the ringed hand but she overbore him. 'I don't want any of your damned excuses. You can be so plausible, Howard, when it suits you. But you're not going to get round me, or bully me into keeping quiet as you used to with Claire. I'm not afraid of you. And I don't intend leaving until I know the truth.'

'For God's sake, keep your voice down,' he implored her.

'Afraid of scandal?' she retorted, speaking even more loudly and turning towards the door. 'Afraid some of your precious reputation might suffer! Well, let them all hear! I'd like them to know the truth about you! Howard Jordan, the famous Harley Street psychiatrist, with the soothing bedside manner, who'll guarantee you happiness and peace of mind! That's how they see you, isn't it? God, it makes me sick, you bloody, smooth-faced hypocrite! You turned my sister's life into a hell for all these years and then you killed her!'

'That is a monstrous suggestion!' Jordan cried, raising his voice above hers. He was trembling with rage. For him, it was a sudden release of tension. All the emotional stress of the past few days burst inside him and he jumped to his feet, thrusting his face towards her across the desk.

'Is it?' she replied. There was an odd note of triumph in her voice. She was glad she had roused him. It gave her a sense of power, as it had done all those years before when she had succeeded in breaking through Father's calm urbanity, reducing him to the same state of trembling, impotent male fury.

'I was in London when Claire disappeared . . .'

'Oh, I've no doubt you were, Howard,' she interrupted. 'You're quite intelligent enough to arrange a simple matter like an alibi.'

'The police are satisfied,' he countered.

He's too anxious to explain, she thought. An innocent man would have chucked me out long ago.

'Then all I can say is, they aren't as clever as you. But sooner or later they'll work out how you arranged it. Finch isn't as stupid as he looks.'

On the other side of the communicating door, which Rose in her eagerness to burst in unannounced on Jordan, had left ajar, Finch smiled quietly to himself. He had returned to the clinic from the service yard, shortly after her arrival, intending to interview Jordan again and, as he now had the run of the place, he had let himself in by the back door and gone straight to the general office in order to arrange the interview with Miss Ogilvie whom he found standing by her desk, looking alarmed at the quarrel which was clearly audible, uncertain what to do. Finch had recognised Rose Vincent's voice at once. The abrupt, direct manner of speech, raised now in anger, was quite distinctive.

He, too, hesitated to break in on them but for other reasons than Miss Ogilvie. Had he been alone, he would have eavesdropped unashamedly. However, now that his name had been

179

mentioned, it seemed his responsibility to act and he was about to step forward towards the door when Dr Kerr forestalled him.

She had entered unheard behind him and, in a few seconds, had taken in the situation and dealt with it, despatching Miss Ogilvie, standing as motionless as a mesmerised rabbit, to collect some files from her office, a mere pretext, Finch felt, to get the woman out of the room, before turning to Finch, her dark eyes bright with an amused, almost malicious, irony.

'You may know the quotation, "Heaven has no rage, like love to hatred turned",' she remarked to him in a low voice.

'"Nor Hell a fury, like a woman spurned".' Finch completed the couplet.

'"A woman *scorned*",' she corrected him with a smile and, walking to the door, flung it wide open.

Jordan and Rose Vincent were facing each other across the desk, Rose flushed and triumphant, Jordan pale and dishevelled. Anger suited her better than him, Finch thought, as he entered at Dr Kerr's heels. It enhanced her, giving her handsome features an added brilliance. He merely looked diminished, as if rage had undermined the carefully-constructed persona he presented to the world.

Oddly enough, both of them seemed relieved at the interruption and while Jordan's reasons were understandable, Rose Vincent's were less obvious.

'Ah, Dr Kerr!' Jordan exclaimed. 'And Finch!'

'There's a patient I'd like your opinion on,' Dr Kerr said crisply, nodding pleasantly to Rose Vincent as if she had heard nothing of the quarrel and, as Jordan turned towards his assistant, Finch took Rose Vincent gently by the elbow and led her out of Jordan's office and along the corridor to the medical room where he found her a chair. He waited quietly while she scrabbled about in her handbag for her cigarettes and lighter and, as she lit one and raised her eyes to his, he understood the reason for her relief. She was on the point of tears. They spilled over as she took her first deep intake of smoke, pouring down her face soundlessly and without any apparent effort.

He, in his turn, was relieved that she coped with them with so little fuss. Women in tears always embarrassed him. He never knew whether to keep silent or offer sympathy. Besides, they usually looked so grotesque that he was ashamed for their sakes.

Rose Vincent simply placed her cigarette carefully in the ashtray and, producing a handkerchief, wiped her face in the same brisk, no-nonsense manner in which a mother might wield a wet flannel on a child's dirty face and, picking up her cigarette again, crossed her legs.

'You heard?' she asked.

'Some of it,' he replied.

'Is it true Howard has an alibi?'

'It would appear so.'

'Then you've got to break it,' she told him.

'You're quite convinced Dr Jordan is guilty?' he countered.

'Of course.' She said it with total conviction and he wondered if Dr Kerr could be right. Was it possible that Rose Vincent's hatred of her brother-in-law covered a love of which she herself might not be aware?

'And what about Janet Ingham's murder?' he asked. He assumed Jordan had told her but it was clear from the expression on her face that she knew nothing about it.

'Janet?' she asked sharply.

It was too late to withdraw. Besides, there was no reason why she shouldn't be told. It would be interesting to see her reaction.

She listened in silence while he gave her a brief account of the attack on Eunice Hart and the murder of Janet Ingham.

'And you say Howard has an alibi for that, too?' she asked when he had finished.

'He was in London at the time,' he replied, 'and there are witnesses.'

'Reliable witnesses?'

'A restaurant full of people.'

There seemed no point in telling her about Jordan's mistress although her next remark seemed strangely relevant.

'You realise Howard could have had a motive for killing Janet? They were lovers, you know.'

'No, I didn't know,' he replied, matching her brusqueness with his own. 'When was this? Recently?'

181

'No, several years ago in London, before Howard opened the clinic. Perhaps I should have told you when you came to see me the other afternoon. Would it have made any difference?'

There was a note of appeal in her voice, asking him to deny that she had any responsibility and he nodded acquiescence, covering up his exasperation.

Damn the woman! She might have told him; not that he could see how the knowledge might have saved Janet Ingham's life. But all information was useful and she had deliberately withheld a piece vital to his understanding of the relationship between Jordan and his secretary.

'I told you Claire used to do all his office work when they were first married,' Rose Vincent continued. 'Then, after a few years, when he had set up his private practice with Claire's money, he took on Janet Ingham, partly to get his own back, in my opinion. Claire was a perfectly competent secretary but he hated to be under any kind of obligation to her. He was ambitious and determined to get to the top but it was to be all his own effort. So he took Janet on. Funnily enough, she looked a bit like Claire; at least, as Claire used to look when she was younger; pretty, with the same fair hair and similar shaped faces. Had you noticed?'

He hadn't although, now that she had pointed it out to him, he could see a likeness between the gentle, pointed features of Mrs Jordan's photograph and Janet Ingham's more obviously glamorous good looks. It was perceptive of her to see the resemblance. He would never have noticed it himself.

'She was a cow, of course; Janet, I mean. Very sweet on the surface and as hard as nails underneath. I saw at once what was going on. I used to visit them in their flat over Howard's office and quite often Janet would be there, staying on late to type up reports and being very kind to Claire but, at the same time, making it clear just where she stood with Howard. She hadn't long been divorced and was living in a flat not far away; a perfect set-up.'

'Did Claire know?' Finch asked. It seemed perfectly natural to use her Christian name.

'She must have done. She wasn't stupid. But she was in love

with him and preferred to close her eyes to what was happening. In the end, it was I who forced the issue.'

'How?'

'I had him followed,' she replied and laughed suddenly. 'It was so easy. I knew the evenings he was supposed to be making house visits and I paid a private detective to tail him. When I'd got the evidence, I gave it to Claire but, like a fool, she wouldn't make use of it. It led to a first-class row with Howard, of course. He refused to have me in the house after that. Claire used to have to sneak out to meet me. So he won out in the end, as men like him always do. God knows how they manage always to be in the right, however outrageously they've behaved. And the extraordinary thing is, their women take it. They've been so conditioned over the years that they've lost the will-power to stand up for themselves.'

She was talking, he realised, not just about Jordan but some other man, probably her father, and he wondered if, in trying to punish her brother-in-law, she wasn't also attempting to pay off an old score that went deep into her childhood experience, although her admission that she had wanted to break up her sister's marriage might give credence to Dr Kerr's theory.

'He was more discreet about his affairs after that,' she continued. 'There were other women but he was damned careful not to choose them quite so near to home. And he kept Janet on. It was the price Claire had to pay for not divorcing him. "Howard feels we ought to be civilised about it," she told me. Civilised! My God, I'd've kicked the bloody woman straight out of the door! But Claire had to go on facing her day after day; another turn of the screw; another of Howard's subtle little ploys to keep Claire in her place.'

'Did the affair continue?' Finch asked. He would have liked to tell her that her action had had some effect: Jordan had been reduced to the degrading position of buying sex in temporary, joyless relationships, which must have damaged his self-esteem.

'God knows. It's possible, of course. Claire stopped confiding in me after the row with Howard and anyway, when they moved down here, I only saw her two or three times a year. I was never allowed to visit her at the clinic. Howard vetoed that.

But when I heard Claire had disappeared, I was damned if I was going to sit back and do nothing. I made up my mind to confront him with the truth.'

'That he killed your sister? But that doesn't fit the facts,' Finch reminded her.

'Then look at them again,' she told him, getting to her feet.

He escorted her to her car and it was only after she had got into it that he mentioned the other piece of information she had withheld.

'How long had your sister been drinking?' he asked.

She looked up at him from the low-slung driver's seat, her face suddenly sad.

'Several years. But she wasn't an alcoholic. You must believe that. She just needed the stimulus if things were going badly or if she had to meet people. She was desperately shy. Sometimes she wouldn't touch the stuff for weeks. How did you find out about it?'

'Someone told me,' he replied with deliberate vagueness.

She pulled a wry face.

'One of her so-called friends I suppose. Howard would never admit to it. That's something else he's guilty of. But if there's any justice, he'll pay in the end. What's the sentence for murder these days? Fifteen years? Well, it's not bloody long enough!'

With that parting remark, she slammed the car door and, turning the car rapidly, she accelerated off down the drive.

Finch walked slowly back to the medical room, deep in thought. Rose Vincent's utter confidence in Jordan's guilt had impressed him, in spite of himself. Could she be right and had he, in some unforeseen way, managed to contrive his wife's death in his absence? It didn't seem possible and yet, as he had said to Boyce, Jordan would appear the prime suspect. In his position, he could easily find the means and there was no need to look far for a motive. Only the opportunity was missing. Once again, he came back to the question of Jordan's alibi which appeared unshakeable.

And yet he couldn't forget Rose Vincent's remark, flung at him like a challenge, that he should look again at the facts.

Well, he'd take her up on it; go back to square one and bloody well start all over again, re-examining the evidence he'd

184

collected so far and seeing if the pieces couldn't be shuffled around to form a new pattern.

Reaching his office, he sat down at the table and, taking out a clean sheet of paper, began to write.

Fact number one: Jordan was in London when his wife disappeared. Witness: Donald Midgley.

After he had written the sentence down, he looked at it for a moment and then drew a large question mark after it, forming it carefully with an elaborate curl to its top and a perfectly round dot under the downward stroke.

Above suspicion. The phrase that Rose Vincent had used during his first interview with her in London came into his mind. She had applied it to Claire Jordan but it could be as applicable to Jordan himself. All the same, the question mark seemed to stare back at him from the page with the same defiant directness which had been in Rose Vincent's eyes when she had told him to look again at the facts.

Midgley held the key, of course. Midgley was Jordan's witness and Midgley, too, was above suspicion. Finch had no doubt that he had been speaking the truth when he said that he had seen Mrs Jordan alive on the Monday morning before he and Jordan left for London. He hadn't lied about that. Finch knew enough of human nature to back his own judgement on this particular issue. Midgley might admire Jordan and wish to protect him but his naïve, transparent honesty makes a poor liar. His evidence could be relied on. It was another fact and yet, leaning forward and picking up his pen again, Finch traced over the question mark, adding another small curlicue to its top so that the curve now joined the main stem, forming a certain shape which, in its dark, heavy roundness, reminded him of something else: a pair of spectacles.

And suddenly it all made sense and, throwing down the pen, he went in search of Boyce.

6

'What the hell put you on to it?' Boyce asked when, a few minutes later, he and Finch returned to the medical room where they were closeted together with the door firmly closed.

'You're not going to believe this,' Finch replied. 'It was a doodle, a little squiggle I drew on a piece of paper.' He pushed it across the desk towards the sergeant. 'See?'

Boyce examined it critically. 'No, I'm damned if I do,' he admitted after several moments' careful scrutiny.

Finch produced his pen and added another small, rounded shape to the one already decorating the top of the question mark.

'Now do you get it?'

Boyce nodded.

'Obvious, isn't it?' Finch said. 'So damned obvious that I overlooked it and yet I ought to have tumbled to it earlier. After all, I was there when he examined Mrs Hart.'

'You'll question Midgley again, of course?'

'Of course. But we're not home and dry quite yet. Before I see him, there's a few more details to be cleared up first. The question of the coat cupboard for a start, and for that I think I'll have a chat with Miss Ogilvie. She's new to the clinic so she's less likely to put two and two together.'

Miss Ogilvie listened to Finch's request without showing any surprise and seemed only grateful that Finch made no reference to the quarrel which he had witnessed, the memory of which still caused her acute embarrassment.

'Where do I hang my outdoor things?' she asked. 'I'll show you.'

She conducted them across the hall and down the corridor leading to the east wing where, at the point at which the passageway made a right-angled turn, she opened a door in the side of the stairs, revealing a cupboard. Finch stuck his head inside. It was a large space, tall enough for someone to enter with bent head and fitted with a rail on which several coats were hanging.

'I'm sure you could leave your own overcoats here,' she added. 'I don't suppose anyone would mind.'

Finch thanked her gravely and watched her depart before looking up and down the passage as if seeing it for the first time although this area of the clinic was familiar to him. He even pushed open the green baize door which shut the domestic offices off from the main building. Beyond it, the kitchen door was ajar and from inside came the sound of women's voices and the clatter of washing-up.

Satisfied, he nodded to Boyce and together they returned to the medical room.

'We'll see Simon Boyd first, I think,' he said. 'And then Dr Kerr.'

7

Simon Boyd entered the medical room reluctantly. It was the mid-morning break between treatments and he had been in the drawing-room, drinking coffee and reading the *Guardian*, when the message came that the police wanted to see him and, as he got to his feet, he had been aware of the curious glances of the other patients, Ransome's particularly who had given him an ironic thumbs-up sign as he passed his chair.

Finch and Boyce, however, appeared relaxed and cheerful. As Boyd searched their faces, he could see nothing inquisitorial about either of them.

'I hope I shan't have to keep you too long, Mr Boyd. There's a few further details I'd like you to help us with,' Finch explained.

'Yes?' Boyd said cautiously, taking his seat on one of the hard metal and plastic chairs.

'I'd like to go back to Sunday evening and the dinner party which was held here in the clinic.'

Boyd was surprised and relieved. He had been expecting

another cross-examination about his movements on Tuesday evening, the night Janet Ingham was murdered, and was holding himself tense in readiness for it.

'I'd like you,' Finch continued, 'to think very carefully back to that evening and tell me if you noticed anything at all unusual about Mrs Jordan; her behaviour or appearance; anything at all that struck you as odd.'

Boyd had the feeling that Finch was looking for some particular response which he did not want to evince by direct questioning and he searched his memory, wondering what it was that the Chief Inspector wished him to recall. Finally he shook his head.

'I'm sorry but I can't think of anything,' he replied. 'She was distressed but I've already mentioned that to you before.'

Finch went on probing.

'Go back to the earlier part of the evening, Mr Boyd, to the dinner party itself. How did Mrs Jordan seem when she first arrived?'

'Well, she was late,' Boyd replied. He pictured the scene again: Mrs Jordan hurriedly drinking her sherry while Jordan stood impatiently at her side and then the long table with the silver and glasses catching the light, and the bowls of spring flowers, jasmine and freesias, set at intervals along the white linen. He seemed to catch their fragrance again. He remembered suddenly another scent and the surprise of recollection must have shown in his face for Finch asked eagerly, 'Yes?'

'It's something so small,' he began.

'Never mind that. What was it?'

'She smelt of cloves.'

It was Finch's turn to look surprised. He exchanged a puzzled look with Boyce who lifted his shoulders in perplexity and then his expression cleared and he made a quick gesture with one hand which Boyd saw too late to grasp its significance. But Finch seemed to understand it, for he nodded at the sergeant before turning back to Boyd with an air of satisfaction, as if the problem had been solved.

'I'd like you now to think of the later part of the evening, when coffee was being served in the drawing-room. You saw Mrs Jordan leave the room and you also noticed she had come back shortly after Dr Kerr and Dr Jordan returned. Did you see anyone else leave the room at about the same time?'

That was easier to answer. Simon Boyd had ready in his mind the memory of Janet Ingham walking out through the doors which he had recollected when Ransome had been talking to him.

'Yes,' he said quickly. 'I've remembered since that I saw Mrs Ingham leave the room.'

Finch seemed also gratified by this piece of information.

'Good! Can you say exactly when this was in relation to the others leaving?'

'I think I've already told you I didn't see either Dr Kerr or Dr Jordan going out. I only saw them come back. But Mrs Ingham left shortly after Mrs Jordan; about five minutes later, I think, although it could have been sooner. I didn't see her return but I noticed her talking to some of the patients when the others came back, so she must have re-entered the room before them.'

Finch smiled as if he found the statement to his liking.

'Now, Mr Boyd,' he continued, 'I want you to think very carefully about this. Take your time. Go over the whole of that part of the evening in your mind if you have to. The question is very important. Did anybody else leave the room during that same period?'

It was quite clear the inquiry was vital. Finch was leaning forward across the table, his eyes fixed on Boyd's face, and he took the Chief Inspector at his word, remaining silent as he tried to return to that Sunday evening in the drawing-room. Oddly enough, the scene was very similar to the one he had just left, except on the former occasion the curtains had been drawn over the windows and his fellow patients had been standing instead of sitting as they drank their coffee. Others, too, had been present: Mrs Jordan, Dr Kerr and Dr Jordan, Midgley and Janet Ingham. He tried to place them about the room.

As for the rest, the log fire burning in the huge marble fireplace, the bowls of flowers, the heated coffee trolley standing just inside the door – these were the same props that had been there on the Sunday evening. The cups, too; small coffee cans of fine white porcelain with a broad gold band round the rim. He realised he was trying to pin down the other recollection which had been at the back of his mind when Ransome had spoken of Janet Ingham's murder and he had seen so clearly her figure retreating through the double doors, holding up her skirt with one hand. Then Ransome's voice had broken in and the memory had never fully developed except as a faint, out-of-focus image.

Now, as he struggled to bring it into total recall, he could advance no further than the cup which he held in one hand and the sensation of warmth on his back from the fire where the flames from the logs went leaping up into the dark mouth of the chimney.

And, suddenly, as he saw the cup and the flames, the memory finally fell into place.

'Yes,' he said. 'Someone else must have left the room.'

8

'Almost there,' Finch remarked a few minutes later after Simon Boyd had left. They were waiting for Dr Kerr and were standing by the desk as if in readiness for her arrival. 'That business of the cloves didn't strike me until you pointed it out.'

Boyce repeated the gesture he had made which Boyd had only glimpsed, a quick flicking movement of the wrist, tipping the hand rapidly up and down.

'An old tippler's trick, that,' Boyce replied. He sounded pleased with himself. 'Covers up the smell of booze on the breath.'

Finch didn't have time to reply. The door was flung open and Dr Kerr entered, looking annoyed.

'I have just five minutes,' she informed him. 'I'm due to see my next patient at half past eleven so I hope it's not going to take too long.'

'It shouldn't,' Finch assured her blandly. He moved across to stand in front of the locked cupboards. 'There are a few questions I want to ask you and one small job I want you to do. Firstly, did you know that Mrs Jordan drank heavily at times?'

She met his eyes with cool directness.

'Yes, of course.'

'How many other people knew?'

'Most of the professional staff I should imagine, with the exception of Donald Midgley. I don't think he'd quite tumbled to the truth. But certainly anyone who'd been here any length of time and had any close contact with Claire must have guessed. They'd be fools if they didn't. We didn't talk about it, of course.'

'Why not?'

She shrugged.

'It was one of those small, degrading secrets that families prefer to cover up.'

'Families?' he repeated, surprised at her use of the word.

'Oh, yes, Chief Inspector; in many ways, we were a family with Howard as the father figure. At least, he liked to imagine himself in that role: paternalistic, benign when it suited him, but nevertheless wielding quite a lot of authority. God knows who was mother; Eunice, perhaps; certainly not Claire. Claire was the pathetic little skeleton in our cupboard. That's why we didn't talk about her drinking problem.'

Finch could now see the aptness of the comparison. They might squabble amongst themselves on occasions but, when threatened, they would close ranks and present a united front against outsiders like himself.

'And the other family secret?' he asked. 'How many of you knew Janet Ingham was Dr Jordan's mistress?'

The question shocked her as he intended it should. She stood for a moment in silence and then made a strange gesture with one hand, turning the wrist abruptly as if thrusting aside something distasteful.

'How many?' he repeated.

She walked away from him deliberately, going to stand at the window, her back towards him. His immediate reaction was one of fury. He'd get the truth from her if he had to bloody break her arm. Then he saw that she was holding herself rigid in an effort to contain the emotion which she did not want him to witness.

'I told the others on the evening Janet was murdered,' she said in a low voice. 'I was angry at what I thought was their complacency and I wanted to shock them out of it. It was meant as a kind of therapy, for them as well as for me. But I had no right; no right at all!' She swung round suddenly to face him. 'How did you find out? Did Howard tell you?'

There was a note of appeal in the question which he did not understand.

'No,' he replied. 'I found out from someone else, not connected with the clinic.'

She gave a small, lopsided smile.

'I didn't really imagine it was him. Should I have told you myself? Would it have made any difference; to Janet being killed, I mean?'

'I don't know,' Finch said. 'I doubt it.'

What was the point in telling her the truth? he asked himself. Besides, he was not even sure himself that, had he been in possession of that fact at the beginning of the inquiry when Mrs Jordan first disappeared, it would have made any difference. If he were to be totally honest with himself, the answer was probably no, he wouldn't have made the connection. He would simply have taken it as further evidence for Claire Jordan's possible suicide.

And, despite his anger and dislike, he could understand, even sympathise with, Dr Kerr's reasons for withholding the information. She was a hard, intelligent, self-contained woman, much more intelligent than Jordan although she shared with him a quality of ruthlessness. Jordan's, however, sprang from insensitivity and vanity; hers from an aloof detachment from any emotional involvement. She had viewed Jordan's affair with Janet Ingham from the point of view of the amused, ironic observer, to be used merely as a weapon when it suited her in order to gain the upper hand within the family-grouping of which she herself had spoken. To sum her up, she was a bitch with one saving grace: she was aware of it and ashamed of it, too.

It was this shame which had prevented her from admitting to

that malicious remark, made probably on the spur of the moment in a desire to score off the others and which she now bitterly regretted.

There was nothing Finch could do about it except to make damned sure he used to his own advantage the moral ascendancy it gave him.

'To go back to Sunday evening, Dr Kerr, when Mrs Jordan came into the office and found you and Dr Jordan together: you said she was distressed. What exactly had upset her?'

He already knew the answer but he was determined to hear the truth from her. To give her credit, she made no attempt to evade the question.

'I think she misinterpreted the situation. I believe she thought Howard and I were lovers.'

'And were you?'

'No.'

A bitch but an honest one, he thought. The simple denial was enough to convince him.

'Did Mrs Jordan say anything to give you this impression?'

'As she was leaving, she said she felt she was in the way.'

'Was that all?'

'I think so.'

'But I don't, Dr Kerr. She said something else. She must have done.'

Otherwise the whole bloody case he'd built up didn't make sense.

She accepted his judgement without comment, frowning slightly in the effort of recall.

'Yes, you're right. She did say something else. It didn't strike me at the time as being important. Howard started to say, "For God's sake," when she interrupted him. I can't remember her exact words but the remark was something like, "I don't believe in God any more. I should have listened to Rose. She knew the answers." It seemed a trivial, meaningless comment, the sort a neurotic woman like Claire would make.'

It was said quite unemotionally and yet Finch realised it was offered as a challenge.

You see, I make no allowances, not even for the dead, she was telling him. You can judge me as you wish. It makes no difference to me as I do not seek either your disapproval or your good will.

In response, Finch kept his face expressionless as he moved on to the last part of his inquiry. Turning to indicate the drugs cupboards, he asked, 'These are always kept locked?'

'Yes, of course.'

'Who has the keys to them?'

'All the full-time professional staff. I believe Simmonds also keeps a spare set of all the clinic keys in case of emergencies.'

'Did Mrs Jordan have any?'

'No, certainly not.'

'Could she get access to them?'

He saw her expression sharpen and, having now got her measure, he knew how her mind was working. Did his question imply that Claire Jordan had committed suicide? she was asking herself.

'Well?' he asked, pressing her for an answer.

'I suppose she could have done. Anyone of us might have left our keys lying about for short periods in the staff sitting-room or in our bedrooms.'

'What about the patients?'

'That's even less likely.'

'But possible.'

She conceded the point reluctantly. 'Yes, if they were really determined, but all of us are much more careful to keep our keys in our possession when we're on duty. If you're implying,' she added quickly, before he had time to pose the question, 'that some of the drugs are missing, I can set your mind at rest straight away, Chief Inspector. The contents of all the bottles are checked very carefully each week, the number of tablets counted and verified against the entries in the register.' As she spoke, she unlocked a drawer beneath one of the cupboards and took out a large, black book, resembling a ledger. 'Each dose is entered in here, together with the date and the patient's name and is initialled by the doctor who prescribed it. The two are then compared. If there were any discrepancy between the number of tablets issued and the number remaining in the bottles, it would be noticed at once.'

It was a factor he hadn't bargained for and some of his

discomfort must have shown in his face for she continued with that look of ironic triumph which so infuriated him, 'If you are interested in when the last check was made and by whom, I can tell you quite easily. It was made by myself on Monday morning at nine o'clock and there were no tablets missing.'

Hell and damnation! he thought furiously. If she were right, and he had no reason to doubt the truth of what she had told him, it meant that his nice, neat theory could be discounted almost before he had the opportunity to test it out.

And yet it had to make sense. Claire Jordan had been at the clinic on Sunday evening. On Monday morning, she had disappeared. Those two pieces of evidence were indisputable and there bloody well had to be a link.

He rapped on one of the glass doors with his knuckles.

'Are all the drugs in here entered on the register?' he persisted.

'Yes, all the potentially dangerous ones. The milder forms of pain-killers, such as aspirin, are not normally checked weekly although a regular prescription issued to a patient would be entered on that patient's medical card and cross-registered in the drugs book. These would be added up at the end of the treatment.'

She knew damned well it wasn't aspirin he was interested in and, on a sudden impulse, he said in a voice as brusque as her own could be on occasions, 'I want you to open these cupboards, Dr Kerr, and check every damn bottle if you have to. Something is missing; not aspirin; not even the milder forms of tranquil-lisers or sleeping tablets but a drug strong enough to kill if taken by a woman who was a heavy drinker and wasn't used to narcotics.'

He saw a startled expression come into her face when he mentioned the word 'narcotics' and, unlocking the doors, she began searching the shelves. Her movements were quick and efficient and yet there was an element of urgency in those briskly moving hands and the faint clatter of glass as the containers were struck against each other.

When she turned back towards him, her face was ashen.

'What's missing?' he asked.

'Some Diconal tablets. They were found in a patient's pocket

195

some time ago; a drug addict. They weren't entered on the register because they weren't part of the normal stock but they were locked up in here . . . .'

'And now they've gone?'

'Yes. I didn't notice on Monday when I checked but I wasn't particularly looking for them. The last time I noticed them, they were on the top shelf, behind some other bottles. Of course, they might have been destroyed. Dr Jordan mentioned to me after Eunice found them, that there wasn't much point in keeping them, although, as a patient's property . . . .'

No one had liked to get rid of them, Finch silently completed the sentence for her. It was the kind of procrastination that was typical of any organisation. At headquarters, there were cupboards full of objects and no one would assume the responsibility of emptying them.

'Diconal,' he repeated. 'What drug is it?'

'It's a proprietary name given to dipipanone hydrochloride, an analgesic related to methadone. It's quite often taken by addicts.'

'And the dosage?'

'For an addict . . .?'

'No, Dr Kerr, I'm not speaking about addicts.'

He stared her full in the face and was gratified to see her glance down at her hands.

'The normal dose would be one tablet to be repeated every six hours. It would start to take effect, if taken by mouth, after about an hour,' she said in a low voice.

'How many tablets were in the bottle?'

'I'm not sure; about ten, I think.'

'And the symptoms of an overdose?'

'A small amount would cause dizziness, nausea and faintness. A large overdose would paralyse the respiratory system.'

'Leading to . . ?'

She met his eyes.

'Death, Chief Inspector.'

Which was what he had wanted confirmed.

'Thank you,' he said quietly and, as she locked up the cupboards, he added, 'I believe I can trust you not to speak to anyone of this conversation?'

'Of course.'

She said it in the same clipped, unemotional voice she had used when speaking of Claire Jordan.

Walking to the door, he thought that it was a pity he found it so difficult to like her. There was much in her to admire.

He was about to leave, when she called him back.

'Chief Inspector, I think there is something else I ought to tell you. Early on Tuesday morning after Claire had disappeared, I found Howard in here, very distressed. I thought at the time he was simply suffering from normal reaction to the situation which is why I haven't mentioned it before.'

'But you now think he may have realised the Diconal tablets were missing?'

'It is not my job to draw inferences,' she told him coldly. 'That's yours. I simply offer you the piece of information. You can make of it what you will.'

'Oh, I shall, Dr Kerr, I shall,' he assured her and left the room with Boyce gratified that, on this occasion at least, he had managed to have the final word.

9

Shortly afterwards, the car containing Finch and Boyd drew up outside the Jordan's house and remained there for a short time while the Chief Inspector and his sergeant conferred briefly.

'Have you got the timing clear in your mind?' Finch asked. 'I don't want a cock-up. All right? You're sure? Well, let's get going. Mrs Leighton will be leaving in about quarter of an hour and the excuse for us calling is that we want her written statement.'

Boyce nodded impatiently, although he could understand Finch's concern, and the two of them got out of the car and, approaching the front door, banged on the knocker.

Mrs Leighton let them in and seemed to accept Finch's request quite naturally. Finch presented her with some sheets of official paper and settled her down in the dining-room to write her statement.

'And don't forget the bit about the shoes,' he reminded her.

'What shoes?' she asked. She had clearly forgotten them.

'The ones that were in the kitchen cupboard,' Finch reminded her.

Leaving her to complete it, Finch and Boyce retired to the small breakfast-room where they conferred in low voices.

'When are you sending for Midgley?' Boyce asked.

'When Mrs Leighton's finished her statement and left,' Finch replied. 'Meanwhile we can get set up in here. It shouldn't take long; a few minutes at most. That's all the time it took originally.'

He opened the door and listened carefully, before jerking his head to Boyce to follow. Stepping softly on the carpeted treads, they went upstairs where they were busy for a short time, although by the time Mrs Leighton finished her statement and came in search of them, they were waiting for her in the hall.

'I hope it's all right,' she said to Finch, handing over the sheets of paper. 'I've put in all I could think of, including the bit about the shoes and the clothes that were missing.'

Finch read it through and smiled his appreciation.

'That's fine, Mrs Leighton. I see you've remembered about the breakfast things not being cleared and her night clothes left lying on the bed.'

'I wasn't sure how important they were and then I thought: Well, it shows she left in a hurry so I'd better not leave them out.'

'I'm glad you didn't,' Finch said. 'Now, if you wouldn't mind signing each page, you can go. I don't want to make you late at the clinic.'

'You're not coming?' she asked, as Finch folded the completed sheets and put them in his pocket.

'No, there's one or two things we want to check on here, but don't worry,' he assured her cheerfully. 'If you lock the back door before you go, I'll make sure the front is properly closed.'

They watched her depart on her bike that had been leaning against the garage wall, the bag containing her working shoes and overall in the basket on the front and, as soon as she had disappeared up the drive, Finch turned to Boyce.

'Right! I'll phone the clinic and get Midgley down here straight away. All you've got to do is put your coat on and hang about so he gets a good look at you.'

Midgley arrived shortly after the call was made, parking his Renault behind their car before coming up the path, putting his glasses away into their case as he came. Finch and Boyce watched him from behind the net curtain that covered the hall window and Finch heard the sergeant give a small grunt of satisfaction.

'You wanted to see me?' Midgley asked as Finch let him in.

'Just a small point I'd like cleared up,' Finch replied. 'I believe you've met my sergeant? He's only just got here himself.'

Midgley seemed to accept the explanation for he showed no surprise at the fact that Boyce was wearing his tweed overcoat and a green pork-pie hat. Nodding briefly to him, Midgley turned back to Finch.

'Will it take long? I've had to interrupt an interview with a patient. Dr Jordan won't be pleased if he finds out.'

'You didn't mention this interview to Dr Jordan?' Finch asked sharply.

'No. I came immediately. You said it was urgent.'

'If you'll excuse me,' Boyce interrupted heavily. 'I'll just go and check those items.'

He walked away from them and entered the breakfast-room with a self-conscious air.

He'd make a lousy actor, Finch thought, the kind who'd trip over the scenery and wouldn't know what to do with his hands. Thank God Midgley was more concerned with the reason why he'd been called to the house than with Boyce's exit.

'Yes?' he asked Finch a little impatiently.

'I wanted to check on the morning you called here to meet Dr Jordan,' Finch said. 'Can you show me exactly where you stood when you saw Mrs Jordan in the breakfast room?'

'I was standing about here,' Midgley replied. He moved over towards the telephone table. 'As a matter of fact, I'd been looking at the water-colour hanging on the wall.'

'Here?' Finch asked with what to Midgley seemed a maddening attention to detail.

At that moment, they were interrupted by Boyce's voice calling out from behind the closed breakfast-room door.

'Could you spare a moment, sir? There's something here I'd like you to see.'

'I'm sorry,' Finch apologised to Midgley. 'I shouldn't be long.'

He disappeared inside the breakfast-room, leaving the door deliberately ajar so that Midgley had a clear view of the Chief Inspector and his sergeant standing in conversation at the window. The sergeant's deep-toned voice was also audible.

'Take a look at this, sir.'

At that moment, two things happened which Midgley was only able to co-ordinate coherently in his mind much later. The front door was flung open and Jordan entered at a rush, only to come to an abrupt halt in the hall, his face suddenly haggard as if the bones under the flesh had collapsed, leaving only sagging skin in which his eyes stared with terrible fixity at the scene being enacted in the breakfast-room. Almost on his heels came Boyce, no longer wearing his overcoat and hat, who banged the door shut and leaned against it, panting for breath.

Midgley, utterly bewildered, glanced from him back to the room where the sergeant's figure was still standing in front of the window.

The next instant, Finch emerged from the room, closing the door carefully behind him.

'Thank you, Dr Midgley,' Finch said quietly. 'I don't think we'll be needing you any more.'

'But,' Midgley began. He looked from Finch to Jordan and Boyce and then back to the Chief Inspector.

'That will be all,' Finch's voice was firm and steady, allowing for no further protest and Midgley walked towards the front door which Boyce held open for him.

'And Dr Midgley,' Finch added, 'I don't want this discussed at the clinic with anybody. Anybody, at all. You understand?'

'Yes, of course,' Midgley replied in a subdued voice.

They waited in silence until they heard the sound of his car driving away before Finch addressed Jordan.

'How did you know we were here?' he asked.

'I met Mrs Leighton coming into the clinic,' Jordan replied. 'She was worried about leaving you in the house to lock up. She felt she ought to mention it to me.' He laughed suddenly. 'Odd, isn't it? She wasn't certain how reliable you'd be.' His tone changed abruptly. 'I didn't kill my wife. I don't know if you'll be able to believe this but I swear it's the truth. She was dead when I found her.'

'Go on,' said Finch, his voice and expression showing no sign of any reaction.

'I came back late on Sunday evening. I assumed Claire was already asleep and, as I didn't want to disturb her, I went straight to bed.'

'In the small dressing-room?' Finch asked. Where you've been sleeping for the past year, he added silently to himself.

'Yes.' In his eagerness to clear himself, Jordan seemed unsurprised that Finch should be in possession of this piece of information. 'I'd set the alarm to go off at half past six. I wanted to be up in good time as I was going to London the following morning and there were some papers I had to check through before I set off. I made coffee for myself and then, about seven o'clock, I took tea up to Claire. I knew she'd been unwell the previous evening and I wanted to make sure she was feeling better before I left. Despite what people say,' and his mouth twisted wryly, 'I was concerned about her. I found her dead in bed and crumpled up on the bedside table was one of the little white envelopes we use at the clinic for individual doses of drugs, especially sleeping tablets. I don't like my patients when they're in my care being prescribed too many at once. The inference seemed obvious. Somehow Claire had got hold of drugs from the medical room, had taken them that night and had died as a result, I assumed accidentally. She didn't know about dosages or even the names of the different brands. She could have picked out a bottle, thinking it was a mild form of tranquilliser or sleeping tablet, taken too many and died of an overdose. She was unused to drugs; her system would have absorbed them quickly . . . .'

'And mixed with the alcohol she had drunk that evening would have been fatal,' Finch concluded. 'Oh, come on, Dr Jordan,' he added, as the man hesitated, 'you knew about your wife's drinking habits. That's why you wouldn't prescribe anything for her yourself, not even for the migraines she suffered from. I wondered why I found nothing in your bathroom cabinet, not even aspirin. You daren't risk it, knowing she drank heavily at times. In fact, she'd had quite a lot to drink Sunday evening, hadn't she, before she arrived at the clinic?'

'Yes,' Jordan confessed. 'There was a quarrel before we left; nothing much, but I admit I was impatient with her.'

'So she'd've needed something to steady her nerves before the dinner-party. What was her preference?'

'Whisky,' Jordan replied in a low voice. 'She began on sherry but lately she needed something stronger.'

'There was sherry for the guests at the clinic,' Finch continued, 'and wine with the meal; and afterwards, when she returned home, she probably had a couple of whiskies as well, because something else happened that evening to distress her; quite a large alcohol intake, in fact when it's all added up. Yes, I know about the scene in your office, Dr Jordan. Dr Kerr told me about it.'

'It was all such nonsense!' Jordan protested. 'Hannah and I were simply discussing a patient, that was all. If Claire chose to put some other interpretation on it . . . .'

'I don't think she *chose*. Given the circumstances, her reaction was perfectly natural. You'd already had an affair with Janet Ingham which your wife knew about. In fact, her sister had given her the evidence for a divorce which she refused to make use of. You had continued to employ your mistress and the affair itself had been maintained, only more discreetly. I'm not sure if Mrs Jordan was aware of this; most probably not, otherwise she wouldn't have accused you of being too intimate with your deputy director. But Hannah Kerr, a very intelligent and perceptive woman, knew. Of course, you were being unwise . . . .'

'Janet wanted it!' Jordan interrupted. 'My God! Do you think I wished to run that sort of risk? I'd've finished with her years ago, when Rose first had us followed by that damned private detective.'

Finch let it go. There was no point in stripping Jordan of the last rags of his self-esteem. There was a quality of tragic irony in the man's situation which was justice enough. In order to punish his wife, Jordan had insisted on keeping on Janet Ingham and Janet, in turn, knowing his weakness and susceptibility, had persuaded him to continue the relationship. The man must have felt hag-ridden at times. It was not surprising that, in seeking other extra-marital affairs, he had been forced to find sexual satisfaction in casual, mercenary relationships with whores. That, too, must have wounded his pride.

The final ironic twist to the situation had come when Claire, pushed too far, had at last turned and accused him of having an affair with Hannah Kerr whose relationship with Jordan had been strictly professional.

'But on Sunday evening when your wife found you and Dr Kerr together,' Finch continued, 'she assumed you were lovers and threatened you with divorce. Dr Kerr has just told me the exact words your wife used on that occasion which, at the time, she didn't realise were significant. Mrs Jordan said, among other things, that next time she would take her sister's advice and that advice, of course, was to start divorce proceedings against you. It must have worried you deeply. If Claire had carried out her threat, it could have finished you. Not only would you have to defend yourself against an accusation of adultery with your assistant but the whole business of your affair with Janet Ingham would have been dragged into the open. The popular press would have had a field day. Your reputation might have been ruined and with it the clinic which, of course, gave you a motive for murdering your wife and that, I suggest, Dr Jordan, is what went through your mind when you found her dead in bed. You couldn't go to the police; you daren't. There was no suicide note; nor was there any guarantee that the police would accept the theory that your wife died accidentally. The only way out of the situation, it seemed to you, was to get rid of your wife's body and pretend you knew nothing about her disappearance. That was bad enough but infinitely better than appearing in the dock on a murder charge. You'd have been wiser, though, to have got rid of some of your wife's clothing and a suitcase at the same time. That way, people would have thought she'd left you. After all, hundreds of women leave home every year and no one suspects foul play.

'But you couldn't do it, could you, Dr Jordan? It struck at your self-esteem. So instead you made it appear that she had walked out of the house on Monday morning and disappeared. Inquiries would be made, of course, but, under normal circumstances, the local police would have been called in. Instead of which, someone pulled a few strings and headquarters got involved. I'm curious, by the way, to know how. Who used their influence?'

'One of the patients,' Jordan replied. 'I'm not prepared to give his name. He's someone high up in the Home Office.'

'Ah!' said Finch. 'That explains it.' He seemed pleased to have this small point cleared up. 'Of course, you hadn't bargained for that but by keeping quiet and pleading ignorance, you hoped to get away with it. After all, you had an alibi to cover the time your wife disappeared and a witness, Dr Midgley, who would be prepared to swear that Mrs Jordan was alive when you left the house together on Monday morning. We know now that the alibi was faked; very cleverly faked, I'll give you credit for that. Considering the short time you had to work it out, it was intelligent and ingenious.

'Let's go back to that Monday morning. You have just found your wife dead in bed at seven o'clock in the morning and you have decided to get rid of the body. I think we can reconstruct what happened next. You stripped off your wife's night things, dressed her in clothes you found in the wardrobe and carried her body down to the garage where you placed it in the boot of the car, together with a spade which you would need later. You then returned to the house to fake the evidence, dirtying two sets of breakfast things so that when Mrs Leighton arrived later that morning, she would think that Mrs Jordan had eaten before leaving. That was simple, though, compared to setting up your alibi. You had all the materials for constructing it to hand, of course: the dressmaker's dummy in the sewing-room, your wife's housecoat and shower-cap, and the collection of tapes in your study upstairs on which Janet Ingham had recorded all the telephone calls coming into the clinic. Among them, as I've since discovered, were two made by your wife, both asking if you were going to be home for dinner on two different occasions. All you had to do was re-record one of them at low volume; it didn't matter which. Midgley wasn't meant to hear the words except for the final remark, "Very well, Howard," which was taped at a higher volume. You then set up the dummy, dressed in your wife's housecoat and shower-cap, in the window of the breakfast-room and waited for Midgley to arrive.

'When he did so, you pretended to say good-bye to your wife, deliberately leaving the door ajar so that Midgley could overhear what you said and your wife answering you. He also saw Mrs Jordan, or so he thought, standing by the window. And in order to create that illusion, you depended on two very important psychological factors. Firstly, you knew Donald Midgley was short-sighted but never wore his spectacles unless it was absolutely necessary, such as when he drove a car; a small, understandable vanity on his part. Knowing this, you counted on the fact that he wouldn't be wearing them when he arrived and was shown into the house. And secondly, most people will believe their eyes, especially if someone assures them of the truth of what they have seen. It's an old trick; most stage magicians rely on it and it invariably works. It certainly was effective as far as Midgley was concerned. He would have been prepared to swear on oath that he had seen your wife alive on Monday morning at 8.15 when, in fact, as you and I know, she had already been dead for several hours and was, at that time, lying in the boot of your car. The same trick worked again this morning.'

Crossing to the breakfast-room door, Finch flung it open to reveal the dressmaker's dummy standing by the window dressed in Boyce's checked overcoat and porkpie hat. Beside it on the table was a small tape-recorder, hidden behind a bowl of flowers. Having run the tape back, Finch pressed down the play button and Boyce's voice was heard, first calling out, 'Can you spare a moment, sir?' which was followed, after a pause, by the words, 'Take a look at this!'

'My sergeant,' Finch continued, 'had already left the room by the window. But Midgley accepted this as my colleague as he accepted the same dummy, dressed in your wife's clothes, as Mrs Jordan.'

As he was speaking, he began to dismantle the lay figure, stripping off the overcoat and the hat which had been propped up on top by means of a short cane.

'The last part was relatively straightforward. You had to be alone, of course, to get rid of the evidence so you needed some pretext to return to the house. What excuse did you use, Dr Jordan? I was going to check with Midgley but your arrival put paid to that.'

'I said I'd forgotten some letters that had to be posted,' Jordan said.

'Oh, indeed? And Midgley swallowed it, naturally. After all, you were only gone a couple of minutes, time enough to return the dressmaker's dummy to the sewing-room, throw your wife's dressing-gown across the bed and hang the shower-cap back in the bathroom; time enough, too, to return the tape-recorder to your study. We timed it ourselves, incidentally, when we set it up. It took Boyce exactly three minutes. Then, having disposed of the evidence, you drove Midgley to London, with your wife's body still in the boot of the car. Later that evening, when you returned to Hawton, you pretended your wife had disappeared some time during your absence, went through the pantomime of searching the house and finally, and I like this touch myself – it shows nerve and intelligence – you drove off in the car, telling Midgley you were going to search for her which gave you the perfect opportunity to dispose of her body. It was dark; if you came back covered with mud, your excuse was ready: you'd been tramping about the golf course in the rain, searching for her. Everyone accepted your story. You acted the part of the distraught husband, as no doubt you were. It couldn't have been a pleasant experience, burying her after carrying her body round with you all day.

'We come now to the early hours of Tuesday morning. By this time, you had returned to the clinic where Dr Kerr found you in a distressed state in the medical room. She put it down to natural strain following your wife's disappearance. But I believe you had found the Diconal tablets were missing and you were beginning to suspect that your wife's death was not accidental but murder. After all, why should she choose that particular bottle of tablets? They were placed, as Dr Kerr informed me, on the top shelf behind some other containers. It seemed more likely that someone had chosen them deliberately to give to your wife; someone who knew of their existence and who might wish your wife dead. To give you the full benefit of the doubt, I don't think you tumbled to the truth until Janet Ingham was murdered and Eunice Hart attacked. It was only then that you were quite sure. In fact, you gave it away when you returned from London, Dr Jordan. It was only one word but if I'd been quicker off the mark, I would have picked it up at once. As it was, it took me quite a lot longer to work it out. Means, motive, opportunity.' Finch ticked them off on his fingers as he spoke. 'It was the motive that was the main stumbling block. Why? I asked myself. It wasn't until this morning that I discovered the answer to that question.'

A look of deep distaste passed over Jordan's face.

'It was crazy!' he burst out. 'I would never have contemplated....'

'Of course not,' Finch agreed. He did not see the need to add that Jordan himself had unwittingly supplied that motive out of his own vanity and weakness.

'And because it was so crazy, you still hoped you might get away with it,' he continued, 'although it must have come as a shock when I started my inquiries and found that quite a few pieces of evidence didn't quite add up and began to get curious; the fact that none of your wife's clothes were missing, for example, except for those she was presumably wearing at the time she disappeared; that she hadn't cleared away the breakfast things as she normally did, or tidied up her nightclothes. And there was the small matter of her shoes.'

'Shoes?' Jordan asked. He appeared genuinely bewildered.

'The old walking shoes she normally wore when she went out. Of course, you didn't know she kept them in the kitchen cupboard. You found her macintosh hanging in the downstairs closet but you had to put another pair of shoes on her feet when you carried her out to the car; a small detail, Dr Jordan, but enough to make me suspicious about the exact circumstances surrounding your wife's disappearance. Which brings us to the last fact that needs to be established and that is: where exactly did you bury her?'

10

Jordan was silent during the drive except to give directions to Boyce who was at the wheel, Finch at his side. One of Stapleton's uniformed men sat in the back seat with Jordan who had already been cautioned by Boyce and had made a statement.

From time to time, Finch glanced at him curiously in the rear mirror as if checking on the other cars in the small convoy which followed them, the occupants of which – Stapleton and more of his men, Pardoe and McCullum – were bringing up the rear in an assortment of cars and a van. The departure had been delayed until their arrival.

Jordan seemed unaware of Finch's scrutiny. He sat with his face turned towards the window, the handsome profile immobile although occasionally he put up one hand to touch the side of his face, a small, nervous gesture that was curiously revealing, as if he were reassuring himself of his physical existence.

They turned off the main road on the far side of the village into a narrow by-road which was unfamiliar to Finch. Hedges enclosed it, sprinkled with hawthorn blossom. A wild apple tree bloomed spectacularly. Everywhere there were signs of spring: in the shrill green of the leaves; in the new grass pushing up through last year's dead litter; in the brilliant, glossy yellow of the celandines starring the hedge-bottom.

Suddenly Jordan leaned forward, grasping the back of Finch's seat so that he could feel the strain in the man's hands.

'The next gateway on the left,' he said.

They bumped gently into the opening, driving well forward into the field in order to give the other vehicles room to park and, while the uniformed sergeant got out and went round to

Jordan's side of the car, Finch remained in his place, staring out through the windscreen at the scene which lay before him.

It had once been a small wood. The strewn debris of broken branches and torn twigs bore witness to this; so did the scattered tree stumps which lay on their sides, their roots exposed. Here and there, a clump of bluebells or primroses clung on desperately among the devastation but most of the site was merely mud and excavated earth against which the blackened ground, where fires had been lit to burn off the smaller timber that was not worth logging, stood out in huge, dark, sacrificial circles.

Across the whole area, a long line of heaped, yellowish clay ran like a wide scratch where an excavator had clawed out a trench, presumably for a land-drain, judging by the broken pieces that lay beside it.

Look for freshly-dug earth, Royston had said. Well, there was enough of it here. The whole place looked as if a bloody bomb had hit it, Finch thought savagely.

He got out of the car and, slamming the door, stumped across to join the others.

'It was dark,' Jordan was saying. 'I'm not sure of the exact place but I think it's here.'

He was pointing to a section of the filled-in trench about four yards in from the edge of the field.

Stapleton gave orders to his men who moved forward with their spades.

'Do I have to watch?' Jordan was frantically addressing anyone who would listen and Finch nodded to Boyce who led him off to Stapleton's car.

He himself had no desire either to witness Mrs Jordan's exhumation and he wandered off, kicking moodily at the scattered debris.

Silver birch, he noticed, turning over a piece of thin, pale bark with the toe of his shoe. And chestnut, just coming into leaf. A little further on, he found a clump of young bracken, their heads as compact in their whorled formation as ears, crushed into the mud.

And Jordan had chosen this place as a burial ground for his wife.

The earth above her was loose and was soon removed. Finch

walked back and glimpsed the body briefly as McCullum took his photographs before it was lifted into the plastic coffin shell and put into the back of the waiting van. He could not have described it although later, when his rage had died down and he was able to examine the photographs objectively, he saw confirmed in black and white his first impression of the quiet, clay-stained face and the fine, bedraggled, greying hair.

'I didn't kill her,' Jordan repeated as Finch got into the car beside him. 'I've told you I found her dead.'

'Yes, sir,' Finch replied woodenly.

'How long will I get?'

'I don't know. That is for the court to decide.'

'Four years? Five?'

Finch was silent. It wasn't his job to inform Jordan that he might be charged with the more serious offence of being accessory after the fact of his wife's murder. That was up to the DPP.

Jordan continued, 'I shall plead guilty, of course; to the charge of burying her. Not to murder. I never touched her. There'll be remission, too, won't there, for good conduct? I could be out in a few years. And I'll be allowed to see a lawyer?'

'Yes, you'll be able to see your solicitor,' Finch replied.

The outpouring of questions told him, if nothing else, that Jordan had already faced up to the possibility of arrest and was planning, however incoherently, some future for himself, a fact that only added to his own anger and deep sense of injustice.

'Then I could arrange to have the legal papers drawn up and make Dr Kerr a partner. The clinic could continue under her directorship. She's quite competent to run it until I'm free to take over again.'

Finch got out of the car and waved it away, watching in silence as it bumped over the ruts in the gate opening, Jordan seated in the back, his face turned towards the Chief Inspector in a last look of haggard appeal which Finch pretended not to see.

11

'Not far to go now,' Finch remarked. He meant it metaphorically but Boyce, whose literal-mindedness could at times be almost inspired, replied in a matter of fact voice, 'About a mile, I reckon.'

His obtuseness dissuaded Finch from making his next comment which was to have been to the effect that he wasn't much looking forward to the next and final stage in the investigation, and he remained in silence during the drive back to the clinic.

As they turned in at the gates, another police car which had been tucked away unobtrusively a little distance off in a lay-by, started up its engine as Boyce flicked his lights in the agreed signal and the two cars moved in procession up the drive. Their slow, dignified progress, keeping to the 5 m.p.h. speed limit, reminded Finch of a funeral cortège and he thought sourly how apt the comparison was: they were about to take part in a final ritual which, in its solemn, formalised language, could be likened to the burial service.

The two cars drew up outside the clinic and Finch entered first, Boyce at his heels, followed in turn by a uniformed woman Inspector and a WPC from the second car. As they crossed the entrance hall, Miss Ogilvie emerged from the general office, in a flutter of anxiety, and seemed about to question their presence but Finch waved her back and began climbing the stairs slowly like a man tired after a long day's work.

At the top, he walked along the upper landing to where it made a sharp, right-angled turn into the east wing and where he paused outside a door. Having knocked and waited for a voice to invite him to enter, he turned the knob and stepped inside the room.

Eunice Hart was sitting by the side of the electric fire, one bar of which had been turned on against the morning chill, a book which she had been reading lying open in her lap.

God knows whom she had been expecting; certainly not them

for, at the sight of their presence, the smile on her face faded and she scrambled to her feet with the awkward, clumsy movement of a middle-aged woman trying to rise hurriedly from a low chair, the book sliding from her knees to crash into the hearth.

Finch signalled to Boyce who, stepping forward, began to repeat the words of the official caution.

As he spoke them, Finch remained in silence, watching Eunice Hart's face with an aloof, distanced attention. Afterwards, he could not describe it, any more than he could Claire Jordan's, but he could have itemised in detail the collection of small objects behind her on the mantelpiece: a photograph of a man in the centre, some china animals, one of those tubes of coloured sands from the Isle of Wight, a vase in the shape of a horse and cart, the container full of primroses picked probably in the woods surrounding the clinic.

To his left and slightly behind him, he was aware of the woman Inspector who had assumed the stand-easy position, hands clasped behind her back, feet the regulation distance apart, like a minor cleric at a graveside. Behind her but out of his range of vision, the WPC would also be standing, fulfilling an even more minor role. As Boyce finished speaking and moved back to take his place on Finch's right, the Chief Inspector stepped forward to enact his own part in the ritual.

'You realise, Mrs Hart, that you have been charged with the murder of Claire Jordan and Janet Ingham?' he asked. He felt obliged to put the question to her. She looked stupid with shock, her mouth slightly open, the loose bandage that still encircled her throat giving her a grotesque appearance.

For the first time since their entrance, she spoke.

'Claire's death was a mistake,' she began. 'I didn't mean to kill her...'

'I think you intended it to appear accidental,' Finch put in. Much of the deep anger he had felt when Claire Jordan's body had been uncovered had faded but enough remained burning like a dull fire to prevent him from remaining totally silent. 'That was to be your excuse, wasn't it, Mrs Hart? It was all a terrible mistake. I believe otherwise. I think an opportunity to murder her presented itself at the clinic on Sunday evening and you took it. The means were at hand – the Diconal tablets which were locked up in the drugs cupboard in the medical room. You knew of their existence. In fact, you were the person who found them in a patient's pocket and you knew also they were dangerous if taken by someone who was unused to drugs and who drank heavily on occasions, as Mrs Jordan did. Your training as a school matron and your experience here at the clinic would have given you sufficient medical knowledge to be aware of that. The symptoms of an overdose, too, tied in neatly with the effects of a migraine which Mrs Jordan complained of that evening – nausea, dizziness, faintness. You also possessed the keys to the cupboards in your capacity as housekeeper.

'On Sunday evening, Mrs Jordan left the drawing-room. She had already had quite a lot to drink before her arrival, a fact I think you were aware of; more before and during dinner, and it was likely she'd need two or three more whiskies after she returned home to calm her nerves; her only means, incidentally, as Dr Jordan had refused her any tranquillisers or sleeping tablets, knowing the risk. And she was very wrought up that evening, wasn't she? Because while she was out of the room, she witnessed a scene between her husband and Dr Kerr which distressed her. She ran away and hid somewhere; at least, I assumed that's what she did because it was some time before she returned to the drawing-room. Where was she, Mrs Hart?'

'She was in the coat cupboard under the stairs,' Eunice Hart replied. During Finch's account, she had slowly resumed her seat by the fire and sat perched on its edge, leaning forward tensely, her eyes fixed on his face. He sat down opposite her, also leaning forward, so that the interview took on the air of an absorbing *tête-à-tête*, in which the two of them were so fully involved that the presence of the others appeared to have been forgotten.

'Where you found her when you left the drawing-room to fetch the fresh coffee?'

There was no need to add that Simon Boyd had given him this particular piece of information, essential evidence in the case the Chief Inspector had been building up against her. It was a pity he hadn't remembered before that Mrs Hart had been making the rounds of the room, offering fresh coffee to the guests which must have necessitated her leaving the room in order to fetch it, but an understandable omission. Unlike the postman in G.K. Chesterton's short story, whose presence in the street had not been noted simply because he was expected to be there, it was her absence which had been disregarded; it had been accepted that she would come and go as she waited on Dr Jordan's patients.

'I heard her crying when I went past the cupboard on the way to the kitchen,' Eunice Hart was explaining. 'She had shut herself in there. She was trembling and wasn't very coherent. I took her into the staff sitting-room where it was quiet and asked her what was the matter.'

'What did she say?'

'She told me Howard had upset her and she was tired of everything. She wanted to end it all. "I can't go on like this, Eunice," she said to me. I thought at first she meant she might kill herself.'

A remark which, Finch thought grimly, had probably first put the idea of murder into Eunice Hart's mind.

'I said to her, "Don't do anything stupid, Claire," and she said, "If I can get the evidence, I'll divorce him".'

'On what grounds?' Finch asked quickly. 'Did she say?'

'No. I thought she meant mental cruelty. I didn't know then about Janet.'

Nor presumably that Claire Jordan suspected her husband of adultery with Hannah Kerr.

'You knew, of course, the marriage was unhappy?'

Eunice Hart gave him a strange look of pitying contempt as if, as a mere male, he couldn't be expected to understand these matters.

'Oh, yes; everyone knew that, even the domestic staff, but no one believed she'd be the one to end it. She wasn't the sort of person to take any initiative. I thought Howard might eventually force a separation. He sometimes hinted to me that he wished the marriage was over and he was rid of her. But it wasn't easy, you see; not in his position. Any breath of scandal and the clinic might suffer. So when Claire mentioned divorce, I was worried for his sake.' She seemed eager to talk now as if to explain and, in doing so, perhaps to excuse what had happened.

'I knew if she brought a mental cruelty case against him it could be unpleasant. All sorts of little things might come out in evidence which might ruin his reputation as a psychiatrist. The staff could even get involved and gossip would be repeated which the newspapers might pick up; it didn't bear thinking about. I went to get her some tranquillisers from the medical room. I had to calm her down somehow. She couldn't have returned to the drawing-room in the state she was in.'

She faltered and Finch took up the account again, his voice expressionless, merely stating what had happened.

'And you remembered the Diconal tablets on the shelf. It occurred to you then that if you gave those to her instead, she would probably die and there'd be no divorce and no scandal. How many did you give her?'

'Four. I told her they were very mild and it wouldn't harm her to take several. She was already complaining of a migraine and I said they'd do it good. I put the other four in one of the little white envelopes we use for the patients' doses and she put them in her handbag to take later. I said to her, "Don't tell anyone I've given them to you. I'm not supposed to hand out tablets." And she said, "Of course I won't, Eunice. I wouldn't want to get you into trouble".'

She began to cry, turning her face away as she had done when he had interviewed her after the supposed attack, ashamed of her tears.

'I did it for him! I only wanted to protect him! He wished to be rid of her and, after all the work he'd put into this place, it didn't seem fair that she might ruin everything for him. I knew him, you see, better than she did. He used to talk to me quite often in the evenings. I understood his problems, the worries he faced . . . I thought . . .'

'Yes?' Finch said gently as she broke off. She turned towards him, wiping her face with a handkerchief, encouraged by his voice. But even then she couldn't put into words the unspoken hope that had lain at the back of her mind for so long.

'We got on so well together, you see. He was always more relaxed in my company. "I like it here," he'd say when we sat together in the staff room. "It's so peaceful." He didn't want to go home to her. And then sometimes he'd put his hand on my shoulder . . .'

Finch nodded agreement as if he perfectly understood. In some ways, he did. He could see how Eunice Hart, desperate for love and security, would have misinterpreted those late evening conversations, those small gestures of intimacy, as expressing far more than Jordan ever intended. He was a man of limited insight, despite his profession; perhaps, ironically, because of it. He had been trained to treat the obviously disturbed patient and his main interest was centred in the male psychology, probably because he could relate to it more easily. Women, especially those closest to him, his wife, his sister-in-law, his female staff, were not worthy of close examination. They were mere appendages whose chief function was to serve him. Finch could see, too, how Jordan with his habit of making gestures, his own need to be liked and admired, might have touched Eunice Hart's hand or shoulder to indicate benevolence as a man might pat a dog.

But he could never tell her this nor could he repeat the remark that Jordan had made, with that look of deep distaste on his face, which had made it quite clear that he had never contemplated marrying her. It would have been too cruel.

'So Mrs Jordan took the Diconal tablets,' Finch continued. 'What happened then?'

'I went back to the drawing-room with the fresh coffee percolators. I told her to wait a little to let them start working and then follow me. When she entered the room, I saw one of the patients go over to speak to her; Simon Boyd, I think it was. He called Howard and I suggested she went home. Donald Midgley took her in his car.'

Knowing she'd take the other four later that evening, Finch added to himself.

'Howard didn't go home until much later,' Eunice Hart continued. 'He never left the clinic before midnight. I thought she'd probably be dead by the time he got home.'

'And you assumed he'd call a doctor?'

'Of course. That's what I expected would happen. I knew there'd be an inquest but that didn't seem as bad as a divorce. It would be treated as an accidental death I thought. Claire could have picked up someone's keys, mine even – I'd left my handbag in the kitchen while I was serving coffee – and taken the tablets herself, thinking they were pain-killers for her migraine. No one would have been blamed and Howard . . . .'

Might have eventually married her, Finch silently completed the sentence for her.

'Instead of which,' he continued out loud, 'Dr Jordan panicked and got rid of the body.'

'Yes! I still don't know why. It could have all been so simple.'

'He had his reasons,' Finch said shortly. He had no intention of explaining to her at this stage exactly what those reasons were. 'But it placed you in a dilemma, didn't it, Mrs Hart? You didn't know how to proceed now that the inquiry had turned unexpectedly into an investigation for a Missing Person. Should you, for example, admit to me or my sergeant that you'd spoken to Claire Jordan on Sunday night or should you keep quiet about it? You decided to keep quiet. After all, we were inquiring into what had happened at the Jordans' house on Monday, not the events that had taken place at the clinic on Sunday evening, so you still hoped you might get away with it. Then, as far as you were concerned, the circumstances took a very unpleasant turn late on Tuesday afternoon. You were talking with the others in the staff sitting-room when Dr Kerr made the comment that Claire must be dead and the police would widen their inquiries into her relationships with the clinic staff. It distressed Janet Ingham whose attitude to Mrs Jordan hadn't been all that sympathetic. It also frightened you because I believe when Janet Ingham left the drawing-room on Sunday evening she may have witnessed you talking to Mrs Jordan and you couldn't risk that coming out in the inquiry.'

'No,' Eunice Hart broke in. 'She didn't see Claire and me together. That wasn't it at all! She was crossing the hall just as I came out of the medical room. I wasn't sure if she'd seen me or not.'

It frequently happened, as Finch had noticed before, that those under arrest on the more serious charges would show deep anxiety to have all the facts, even the most trivial, correctly established as if this somehow lessened their guilt. He remembered in particular one man on a multiple murder charge, his wife and two children, arguing quite passionately that he hadn't stopped at a pub on the way home to buy a whisky as the landlord had testified, but a lager and lime and a packet of cheese-flavoured crisps.

'But the point was,' Finch insisted, pursuing the maïn line of the argument, 'she had seen you and that made her a potentially dangerous witness against you. Then later on that same occasion, after Janet had left the room, Dr Kerr passed on the information that Janet and Dr Jordan were lovers, a fact you were unaware of until that moment. It finally decided you that Janet had to die. After all, you'd killed once; you had no intention of letting Janet Ingham live to testify against you and then, as a last insult, marry Howard Jordan. So you followed her out of the room; not immediately; that would have looked too suspicious. You allowed two or three minutes to elapse, knowing that Janet would have to collect her coat from the cupboard, put it on and cross the yard to the garage. As you followed her out, you took the precaution of checking where the kitchen staff were by opening the door as you passed. Luckily for you, both women were in the pantry so there was no one to witness your movements. You crossed the yard, leaving by the door at the end of the passage just as Janet Ingham was ready to back her car out of the garage. There's only one detail I'm not sure of, Mrs Hart, and that is this: were you already carrying the iron bar which you used to kill her or did you find it later?'

'It was lying in a corner of the garage,' she said, in a low voice. 'I saw it in the rear lights . . . .'

'I see,' Finch commented blandly. He supposed that, had she not found it, Eunice Hart would have used some other method to murder Janet Ingham; strangulation, possibly. She was, after all, a strong, capable woman. Her hands, as they lay in her lap, looked broad and firm. As his glance rested on them, she lifted them to her face and began to rock herself backwards and forwards, as if trying to blot out the memory of what had happened in the darkness of the garage as Janet Ingham leaned out of the driving-seat to see who had entered.

Finch rose to his feet, nodding to the woman Inspector and the

WPC who stepped forward, the Inspector laying a hand on Eunice Hart's shoulder.

'We're taking you to the station,' she explained. 'You'll need to pack a few things to take with you. We'll help you get them ready.'

Finch jerked his head at Boyce and they left the room.

'No point in pushing her too far at this stage,' he commented as they stood in the corridor. 'She can give us the rest when she makes her official statement.'

'You mean the fake attack?' Boyce asked.

'Yes. It wouldn't have taken her long. Once she was sure Janet Ingham was dead, she only had to slip through the archway into the adjoining yard, throw herself down in the brambles at the far end and then return to the clinic by the kitchen door, dropping the iron bar through the grating over the drain as she passed it. It struck me as odd at the time why the murderer should have decided to hide it there. Why not sling it away into the bushes? The drain was nearer to the clinic than the archway which meant he must have doubled back on himself to get rid of it. It made sense, of course, once I realised Eunice Hart was the murderer. She'd pass it on her way back to the kitchen.'

'She almost got away with it, too,' Boyce pointed out. 'If Boyd hadn't remembered she'd left the room on Sunday evening, we could still be fumbling about in the dark.'

'Above suspicion,' Finch said, half to himself.

'What's that?'

'I said: above suspicion. Mrs Hart, I mean; the one person in the clinic who treated Claire Jordan with a little kindness and whom she trusted. The last person, in fact, who'd be suspected of her murder. Jordan tumbled to her, though.'

'I was going to ask you about that,' Boyce interrupted. 'You told Jordan he'd said one word which could have given the game away. I can't think what the hell it was.'

'If you remember, when he returned from London early Wednesday morning and we informed him of Janet Ingham's death and the attack on Eunice Hart, it was her name he spoke, not Janet's which was surprising, given the fact that it was Janet who was dead. I didn't pay all that much attention to it at the time; the man was shocked. I believe now the news must have been more shattering than either of us imagined. He thought Eunice was guilty of his wife's death and suddenly he was confronted with evidence which seemed to prove that he was wrong. He must have wondered what the hell was happening.'

He broke off as the WPC opened the door and announced, 'We're ready, sir.'

They re-entered the room.

Eunice Hart was now standing by the chair, dressed in a coat and shoes instead of the slippers she had been wearing, the woman Inspector holding her by one arm, a small suitcase at her feet.

'Come along, dear,' she was saying brightly, like an infant teacher addressing a five-year-old. 'It's time to go now.'

As they passed Finch and Boyce on their way to the door, Eunice Hart stopped.

'I'll see him again, won't I?' she asked.

By 'him' they both knew she meant Jordan.

'It's possible,' Finch replied. He didn't like to tell her that the next time she would be face to face with Jordan, she would be in the dock and he would be in the witness box, giving evidence against her.

Her mouth trembled then, at a touch on the arm from the Inspector, she moved on and the door closed behind her.

Finch bent down to turn off the electric fire, a task which no one else had remembered to do. Behind him, he heard Boyce remark, 'Well, we got there in the end.'

There seemed no appropriate reply that he could make. It was over and done with. Two people were dead and two were under arrest. On paper, the case had been satisfactorily cleared up. It was futile to feel such a sense of loss; not for Janet Ingham, oddly enough, although he still felt her death keenly, but for a woman whom he had never met and for whom his sense of mourning was based on no closer acquaintance than a photograph and a blurred image in his memory of a mud-spattered face.

As he straightened up, he took a last look at the objects on the mantelpiece: the memento from the Isle of Wight, the little china cart full of primroses.

From somewhere unseen outside the window, possibly the

clock tower in the stable-yard, a bell rang out with three slow, heavy chimes.

'Time to go home, Tom,' he said. He meant headquarters.

12

Simon Boyd watched them leave, the short, dumpy, round-shouldered figure of the Chief Inspector first, followed by the taller, broader sergeant. Finch, in particular, seemed exhausted, climbing into the front passenger seat with a weary air that seemed, even at that distance, expressive of something more than just physical tiredness.

Behind him, Ransome's voice broke into his thoughts.

'You've heard, of course, what's happened? Imagine, Eunice Hart! And Jordan! They say he'll get at least four years, if not more, although it'll be life for her, I'd imagine. My God, the excitement! Will you stay on? I shan't. But you're one of Dr Kerr's patients, aren't you? She'll be running the place from now on, or so the rumour goes. I can't say I fancy being under her treatment. Far too hard-faced for me. If I have to put myself in the hands of a woman, and it's quite frankly never exactly been my scene, it would have to be someone with much more feminine appeal.'

The car was moving off. Boyd caught a last glimpse of Finch as it passed in front of the drawing-room windows, his profile closed and inscrutable.

Turning to Ransome, he said quite clearly and calmly, raising his voice only slightly above normal, 'Why, in God's name, don't you piss off?'

An undercurrent of murder . . .

THE DARK STREAM

June Thomson

The small, peaceful Essex village of Wynford was the sort of place featured on postcards of genteel rural England. So when Stella Reeve was found drowned in the stream which skirted the little community, everyone was sure it was just a tragic accident.

But to Inspector Finch, there was a taint of violence about the scene. He couldn't rationalise it but he could sense it almost as if it were an odour in the air. But even if his intuition was sound he'd need a very clear head to follow the swirling, shifting eddies of motive, intrigue and guile which lay behind this extraordinary case . . .

'Neatly plotted and trimly told' *Punch*

Also by June Thomson in Sphere Books:
SHADOW OF A DOUBT
SOUND EVIDENCE
TO MAKE A KILLING
A DYING FALL

0 7221 8441 7   CRIME   £2.75

THE MAN WHO STOLE THE Mona Lisa

MARTIN PAGE

'I imagine you want me to steal the *Mona Lisa* from the Louvre.'

Morgan felt a pimple above his left nostril about to burst.

'Otherwise, John Pierpont Morgan would hardly go to such inconvenience, and risk such potential embarrassment, to meet the man with the reputation as the world's most skilled thief. Why else would you do that, except to have me steal the world's most valuable object?'

Paris, 1911: somehow, someone achieves the impossible. Only one man could be so audacious, so ingenious, so meticulous a subversive, such a master of disguise and strategy, so silver-tongued to pull off the crime of the century . . .

'Outrageous . . . marvellously plotted, line by line it's fascinating' Los Angeles Times

0 7474 0031 8   CRIME   £2.75

A selection of bestsellers from Sphere

FICTION

THE LEGACY OF HEOROT	Niven/Pournelle/Barnes	£3.50 ☐
THE PHYSICIAN	Noah Gordon	£3.99 ☐
INFIDELITIES	Freda Bright	£3.99 ☐
THE GREAT ALONE	Janet Dailey	£3.99 ☐
THE PANIC OF '89	Paul Erdman	£3.50 ☐

FILM AND TV TIE-IN

BLACK FOREST CLINIC	Peter Heim	£2.99 ☐
INTIMATE CONTACT	Jacqueline Osborne	£2.50 ☐
BEST OF BRITISH	Maurice Sellar	£8.95 ☐
SEX WITH PAULA YATES	Paula Yates	£2.95 ☐
RAW DEAL	Walter Wager	£2.50 ☐

NON-FICTION

FISH	Robyn Wilson	£2.50 ☐
THE SACRED VIRGIN AND THE HOLY WHORE	Anthony Harris	£3.50 ☐
THE DARKNESS IS LIGHT ENOUGH	Chris Ferris	£4.50 ☐
TREVOR HOWARD: A GENTLEMAN AND A PLAYER	Vivienne Knight	£3.50 ☐
INVISIBLE ARMIES	Stephen Segaller	£4.99 ☐

All Sphere books are available at your local bookshop or newsagent, or can be ordered direct from the publisher. Just tick the titles you want and fill in the form below.

Name _____

Address _____

_____

Write to Sphere Books, Cash Sales Department, P.O. Box 11, Falmouth, Cornwall TR10 9EN

Please enclose a cheque or postal order to the value of the cover price plus:

UK: 60p for the first book, 25p for the second book and 15p for each additional book ordered to a maximum charge of £1.90.

OVERSEAS & EIRE: £1.25 for the first book, 75p for the second book and 28p for each subsequent title ordered.

BFPO: 60p for the first book, 25p for the second book plus 15p per copy for the next 7 books, thereafter 9p per book.

Sphere Books reserve the right to show new retail prices on covers which may differ from those previously advertised in the text elsewhere, and to increase postal rates in accordance with the P.O.